Margaret James

H

c

pl

seve at her schoo 2019, inspired by a positive experience and encouraging feedback from the Introduction to Writing Crime Fiction course run by UEA, she carved out space in her diary and wrote *Secret Places*, the first in her series featuring DCI Greg Geldard.

The space between the play and the book has been filled by a busy career mainly in agriculture. She has been a senior civil servant in the Ministry of Agriculture / Defra (her farmer husband was described as 'sleeping with the enemy') and has bred both sheep and alpacas commercially. Since then Heather has pursued her passion for animal welfare and served on a number of Boards as Chairman or Director. She is currently Chair of Lantra UK, a Trustee of Norfolk Citizens Advice and a volunteer both in the Witness Service and as a Covid vaccinator. She lives in Norfolk with her husband, two springer spaniels and four hens. www.heatherpeckauthor.com

GLASS ARROWS

Heather Peck

SilverWood

Published in 2021 by SilverWood Books

SilverWood Books Ltd
14 Small Street, Bristol, BS1 1DE, United Kingdom
www.silverwoodbooks.co.uk

ISBN 978-1-80042-085-4 (paperback)
ISBN 978-1-80042-086-1 (ebook)

British Library Cataloguing in Publication Data
A CIP catalogue record for this book is available from the British Library

Page design and typesetting by SilverWood Books

Acknowledgements

My thanks again to Geoff Dodgson for his meticulous and encouraging comments on the first draft of this novel, to Rob Barker for his advice regarding the work of a First Responder (and indeed for providing the initial inspiration for the career of Ben Asheton) and to various banking experts who tried to help on bank procedures without giving too much away. You know who you are! And of course to my husband Adrian for his support and encouragement.

1

Cambridgeshire, Sunday 1 April 2018

The call came Sunday evening. Emma and her husband Sam had been halfway through the traditional BBC 'bodices and bonks' drama, when the phone rang. Sam hit the pause button and picked up the receiver.

'It's for you,' he said, and de-reclined his side of the sofa in order to fetch a fresh glass of wine from the kitchen while Emma took the call. On the big screen were two maidens with bosoms frozen in mid heave and a generously hirsute horseman leaning down from the saddle.

'Hi, it's Emma.'

'And this is Kate, with the call you didn't want to get.'

'Oh Lord. Tell me it's not foot and mouth. Or pheasants again.'

'No, not foot and mouth nor Newcastle disease in pheasants again.'

'Swine fever? Equine flu in Newmarket?'

'How about I tell you what it is, rather than we go through the list of what it's not? It's bird flu in turkeys and possibly ducks. In Norfolk. We'll be managing it from the Vet Office in Bury St Edmunds. Can you get yourself there by 8am tomorrow? The Regional Chief Vet will be expecting you and I'll let your Director General know you've been taken off your usual beat.'

'I was due to see the Minister of State about genetically modified maize on Tuesday. The DG'll need to deputise someone to do that.'

'I'll let him know when we speak. Don't you worry about that. It's not your problem now. We'll speak tomorrow when you get to Bury. There's a bird table meeting scheduled for 11am. Do you know the vets at Bury?'

'Not well. Anything I need to be aware of?'

'No. Easy chaps to get on with. Speak tomorrow. Thanks, Emma,' and Kate rang off.

Sam came back with his brimming glass of red and sat down again.

'I assume you'd better not be drinking any more this evening if you're off early tomorrow.'

'At least I'll be able to stay home for this emergency. It's bird flu and I'm to be based in Bury. I will need to be off early though, so let's watch the rest of this and then I'll go and get everything sorted for the morning.'

'Ok. Although I must say I'm beginning to lose interest. It's all a bit predictable, isn't it? There'll be more heaving of bosoms that would fall out altogether if they weren't fastened in with gaffer tape, followed by a nude male torso doing something energetic with bales of straw, and we'll both sit here wondering how they're going to cover the ensuing rash with make-up. Then all parties will run gaily through a field, ruining someone's hay crop, before a lot of rumpy pumpy that flattens more grass than a band of rampaging badgers.'

'You're right,' said Emma. 'Working in agriculture does tend to ruin period drama, especially when you sit there pointing out the tramlines in fields supposedly sown by hand. Perhaps I'll just go and look out my things for tomorrow.'

An early start was not Emma Knight's idea of heaven, but they did happen often enough that the morning routine was well established. Sam got up early anyway, so an alarm was rarely necessary – just the determination to get up and get moving rather than roll over for another nap. She shook her short hair dry and fluffed it out with her fingers before adding the usual lick of mascara. A quick slide into smart dark trousers, white shirt and tweed jacket, and 6am saw Emma speeding (in every sense of the word) through the morning heavy goods vehicles en route to Felixstowe. The A14 to Bury St Edmunds was no more than normally busy but as her red BMW Z4 got its wheels in the HGV ruts and performed a wild wiggle across the carriageway, she reflected ruefully on the fact that responding to a bird flu emergency did not warrant blue lights, no matter how great the urgency, and sharpened her lookout for traffic cops.

Norfolk, same morning

In the kitchen of Riverside Hens, bijou smallholding by the River Ant, the proprietors were having their regular morning argument. Tina, making coffee, banged the kettle on the Aga with considerably more force than called for.

'Did he cross our fields?' she snapped.

Her husband, Nick, wished yet again that he'd never mentioned his evening encounter with their awkward neighbour.

'Yes,' he mumbled, and added, 'I can't see a way to stop him. He takes a shortcut from his shed to where he leaves his van. Short of raising our fences and electrifying them, there's nothing we can do.'

'You could ask him not to. You could point out that we are under animal health restrictions.'

'Yes. And we know how well that went last time. All we got was a mouthful of foul language and a not very hidden threat.'

'Well if you don't, I will.' Tina was still making coffee with unnecessary force and water sizzled on the hotplate as she poured it rather randomly from the kettle to the cafetière. 'And if he threatens me, I'll film him on my phone.'

Wondering if the insurance policy covered a phone tossed in the river, Nick forbore to comment further. He knew Tina's fears for their hens were real, but he had a visceral fear for Tina herself, if their neighbour turned nasty.

When the disastrous 2001 foot and mouth outbreak exposed more than a few shortcomings in contingency planning for animal health emergencies, the manual had undergone a major rewrite. One change was Emma's role – the Regional Operations Director. The ROD was plucked from their day job and dropped in at short notice to take overall responsibility locally for the emergency response. Emma had now carried out the role more times than anyone else, and had developed a methodology for quickly picking up the reins. First, get there early. Second, don't piss off the lead vets; they have enough to deal with without a self-important administrator making waves. To Emma's mind, the ROD was there to help and take up some of the burden, not to throw their weight around. Third, don't dither.

The mobile rang just as she turned the corner by the sugar factory. It was Bill McNee, Chief Regional Vet.

'Emma, I gather you're our ROD for this one? I'm clearing my office for you.'

'No, don't do that,' she interrupted. 'Any spare office will be fine. I don't need to disturb you. I'm only five minutes away, so you can bring me up to speed then. Just two things to be going on with. All I know is, it's bird flu in turkeys. Do we know which strain yet? And which company?'

'Strain not absolutely confirmed, but looks like it's the nasty one. H5N1. And it's Stalham Poultry. So, the route of infection is a bit of a mystery. They're not admitting to any recent imports of live birds or fresh meat and there are no pools of infection on the near continent. We'll catch up when you get here.'

Forty miles further north, Lukas was picking up dead birds in Shed Two and trying to hide his tears. No one expected a rough tough poultry farm worker to have a soft side and Lukas took good care to conceal it. But he'd been rearing these birds from poults and it broke his heart to find limp white bodies where yesterday there had been an energetic, greedy gabble. The armful of corpses went into the lidded skip, and Lukas went through to biosecurity to shower and change into his outdoor clothes. He hung the contaminated clothes on the dirty side of the changing room, then he sat for a moment, head in hands, breathing hot, dust-laden air and wondering where the disease had come from. He knew *he* had stuck to the rules. But had everyone? Who had brought the virus in?

He listed the regular workers and visitors to the farm in his mind. The management team? He hesitated, feeling that he should be able to exonerate them out of hand, but aware that he was uneasy about some of their attitudes. His fellow workers? He didn't know any of them well, given they lived in company accommodation and he lived with his wife, but he did know their conditions were not good. Perhaps there was a lack of hygiene there? But on the other hand, none of them had travelled anywhere recently – were not allowed to travel anywhere. The conversation with his wife came back to mind, when he had voiced his concern about his fellow workers and she advised avoiding trouble. He sighed heavily, staring across at the bench with the white wellies beneath, not really noticing the blue box in the corner shadows that shouldn't have been there.

The bang of the outer door being flung open disturbed his thoughts and he looked up as his assistant for the day came in.

'Jonas,' he said in Lithuanian. 'All finished in Shed One? How was it in there today? Many dead?'

'A few,' Jonas replied. 'Twenty, maybe thirty. I didn't bother to count. I put them in the skip like you said.' He looked at Lukas slightly contemptuously. 'I don't see why you care. It makes no difference to us whether they're alive or dead. Maybe if they shut this place down, we can move somewhere better. There can't be anywhere worse.'

Lukas looked at the floor. Guilt that he had taken no action about the conditions of the men around him bothered him. Especially as his inaction was driven by fear. Fear of losing the opportunity he had. Fear of threats to his wife. And also, an atavistic fear of authority, even here in England where they were supposed to be different. The worm of fear in his gut had coiled and hissed when he suggested to his wife that they report what he had seen to the police. It had only lain quiescent when he had concurred with her advice he keep his head down.

'I know I'm lucky,' said Lukas. 'Lucky that I came here independently, and lucky that I have a different contract to you.'

'Contract, what contract?' sneered Jonas. 'Oh, you mean the one that promised us work and a place to live, charged us a fortune to bring us here and said nothing about having to do what we're told, when we're told, or expect our families back home to pay the price? The one that keeps us in conditions worse than your precious turkeys, and provides bully boys from Vilnius to make sure we stay put? The one that confiscated our papers so we can't go home even if we could afford to? The one…' He fell silent as another door banged somewhere and voices were heard in the distance.

The two men waited in silence, then as Lukas started to speak, Jonas interrupted him.

'Don't worry. I've found a way out and a way to get my own back.'

*

The Defra disease management team swung into practised action within the day. The movement ban was in place by lunchtime. Police supervised access to the farm as the gassing chambers were brought on site and set up for action. Catching teams began the work of rounding up the remaining turkeys and discovered, as ever, that slim teenage turkeys were a lot more agile than oven-ready fat ones. Watching, with the welfare of his remaining birds in mind, even Lukas couldn't avoid a grin. The catchers were rather more oven-ready than their prey, and increasingly mad grabs after fleet-of-foot, long-legged gabblers left several catchers face down in the sawdust. Lukas decided to stick around, in case bad temper spilled over into bad handling. Amid a lot of cursing the cull began.

The following morning began with an early briefing. Pete Willis, nominally Stalham site manager, was grinding his teeth over a pile of spreadsheets, the immaculate and imperturbable Mrs Pritchard at his elbow. If there was one thing calculated to rub his face in the fact that he was, as ever, just doing as he was told, it was the presence of the faultless factotum to his left. He rubbed coarse fingers through the hair he no longer had and sighed heavily. He was not normally visible at 6am, but he had his instructions from on high. Given the PR and financial disaster that resulted from a notifiable disease outbreak and a compulsory cull, the company didn't want the already bad news to be worsened by stories of problems with the officials. Company Director Austen Collier was on standby to liaise with the Government Regional Operations Director, one Emma Knight. Pete had been given firm instructions that the company was to cooperate fully with the cull, hence his unusually early start and the even more unusual procedure of a staff briefing.

A man with large hands and large features, he stood at the front of his motley crew and sighed heavily again. His company overalls had the crispness that occasional wear permitted, while the workers in front of him were clad in rather scruffier and worn versions, clean but with logos wearing off or missing altogether, and with collars and cuffs fraying at the edges. It was a tight squeeze getting everyone into the site office and there was overspill into the corridor. He ran his eyes over the crowd, doing a quick head count. The six burly men in the catching team were tending to lurk towards the back in the fond belief they could hide their cigarettes from his view. The farm workers who would normally at this time of day be checking feed levels and monitoring environmental factors were perching on desks in the office. There should be three of those, but at the moment he could see only two. Then, of course, Mrs Pritchard, site office manager, brown hair in a tight French pleat, sensibly but smartly dressed in a trouser suit, taking this invasion in her stride but looking slightly daggers at anyone disturbing her immaculate piles of paper. The other two men were from head office. James Metcalfe was the health and safety man, currently glowering over folders of hazard assessments and accident reports. Stan Innes was biosecurity across the whole company, and in consequence his already long face, rendered yet longer by a straggly beard, was looking more than a little glum.

'Right, let's get started. We've two tasks in front of us. First, to make sure this blasted cull gets done and dusted as fast as possible. We don't want any suggestion from Defra that we held things up. Then the sooner our sheds are empty, the sooner we can start the clean and disinfection and get ourselves up and running again.'

'Once we have Defra sign off for that,' interrupted Stan.

'Yes I know. But the first step is speeding the cull up.' Pete looked over at the catching teams, ill-shaven and many hiding half-smoked cigarettes in their fists. 'I understand yesterday's hold-up was with catching. We need to make sure that the gassing containers are used to capacity. What was the problem?'

The team leader Andrey spoke up. 'Young birds,' he said succinctly. 'Young birds fast. Much fast than old birds. Take long to catch.'

'Will more men help?'

'Maybe two more. More than that just get in the way.' His team members nodded. 'Better help,' he added. 'Some fences.' He was interrupted by one of the others and corrected himself. 'Some hurdles, to help pen birds.'

'Mrs Pritchard, will you see what you can source at short notice please? Liaise with Andrey. Lukas, do we have enough help on hand to empty the gassing containers after the birds are processed.'

'Should do, once we have go-ahead from vets. But Jonas not here this morning. We're one man down.'

'Mrs Pritchard, get on the phone to the gangmaster and get them to send another man immediately. If Jonas shows up late I'll deal with him, but we can't afford to be short-handed today.

'Ok, the Defra team will be on site shortly. The lorry to take the dead birds to the incinerator is only a few minutes away, so we can get going. Get them loaded as soon as they give the all-clear to enter the containers. Andrey, you should start catching and crating. James and Stan, we need a word before we meet up with the vets.'

Lukas' team made the discovery. Turkeys weren't the only things that had been culled.

2

0615, 4 April 2018

It was Lukas who raised the alarm. He'd been helping the gassing unit supervisor Joe check that the container was safe to enter and was the first to spot the human arm visible between crates full of dead turkeys. For a moment he froze in disbelief. Then he shouted for help in Lithuanian and while the words were obviously obscure, the need for assistance was not. Jim, the Defra vet, took one glance to see what the problem was, then reached for his phone and dialled 999. Lukas started hauling crates to one side to get at the body.

'Police and ambulance please,' he said, once through to the emergency services controller. 'We've found a casualty in one of the gassing containers being used for the turkey cull at Stalham Poultry.

'I'm through to the ambulance service. They want to know, is the casualty breathing?' he called across.

Lukas was still struggling with crates, but he managed

to get a hand on the casualty's neck. 'Don't know. Don't think so,' he called back. 'No beat.' Then he added, 'It's Jonas,' as Jim cut the connection.

'They say start resuscitation as soon as we can and they have a paramedic on the way. They've notified the police on the gate, so they'll be round shortly too. Is there a defibrillator?'

'In the office.' And while Joe ran for the office, Jim and Lukas pulled the body free from the crates and into the yard. Lukas noticed that Jonas was stiff and cold, his face dead white and his eyes closed. As they laid him down on the dirty concrete of the yard in his scruffy, stained overalls, Lukas placed his hand behind Jonas' head to avoid it banging down. When he pulled his hand away, there was blood on it.

'What about spine?' asked Lukas with some anxiety.

'I think we worry about that after we get a pulse and some respiration,' said Jim shortly. 'You blow and I'll pump,' he said to Lukas, and started pumping, with 'Staying Alive' playing in his head, as rehearsed in his first aid courses.

Pete Willis had barely begun his discussions with James and Stan when Joe burst into the office.

'Casualty in the gassing chamber. Where's your defib?' he asked.

'On the wall in the corridor,' replied Mrs Pritchard, first to react. 'I'll show you.'

The two of them headed for the door at the same time as Pete, with James and Stan close behind.

Joe grabbed the defibrillator off the wall and dashed for the yard. Everyone else followed in hot pursuit. 'Make sure security on the gate know an ambulance is on its way,' he shouted over his shoulder and Pete spun on his heel, back to the telephone.

Jim and Lukas were still working on Jonas when the office contingent arrived. James pushed to the fore.

'I'm trained on this,' he said, and took the defibrillator. Between them Jim and James pulled the overalls open and applied the pads. 'Stand clear.'

James tried once, then twice. Nothing. Jim restarted compressions as the defib recharged.

'Stand clear,' said James again, just as a car arrived in the yard at speed.

'Ben Asheton, first responder,' said the driver. 'Good job. Let me at him now.'

Lukas noticed that Ben was quick to reach a decision. He himself had already realised, reluctantly, that all the hard work was probably so much wasted effort. Jonas not only had no heartbeat and no pulse, but was stone cold and stiff. Lukas watched Ben test the eyelids and neck, although Lukas' own efforts at resuscitation seemed to have loosened the jaw. As he looked down at the smear of dry blood on his hands from where he had handled Jonas' head, he saw Ben glance up.

'You can stop,' Ben said to Jim; and to Lukas, 'I'm sorry but it's too late for your colleague. He's dead. I need to call this in.'

He ran to use the radio in his car.

'The casualty at Stalham Poultry is dead at the scene,' he

reported. 'No, no doubt about it. I'd estimate he's been dead for some hours. Could be the effect of the gas, but there is an injury on the back of the head.' He paused to listen, then replied, 'Yes, I'll wait for the police to arrive. There're some uniforms here at the gate, connected with the cull. I think they've been notified there's a problem but I'll update them too.'

He was interrupted by Pete, with James hovering at his elbow, the latter envisaging the mass of accident forms he would now need to complete.

'What's happening now?' Pete demanded.

'And you are?'

'Pete Willis, site manager.'

'Well, Mr Willis, I've notified my control that the casualty is dead and in my estimation has been for some hours. In the circumstances that makes this area a potential crime scene. The police are on their way and they'll take over from me.'

'Surely it's an accident. A terrible accident!'

'I'm sorry.' Ben was determined to stick to his guns. 'It may indeed be an accident, but at present all that can be said is that it's a suspicious death and therefore requires investigation. It's important there's no further disturbance of the scene until the police are happy to sign everything off.'

'What about the cull?' asked Pete.

'You'll have to discuss that with the police. For the present, everyone should remain on site until the police say otherwise, and no one should enter this part of the yard nor the gassing unit until they say so.'

'But how long will that take? I've teams catching and crating turkeys in Shed Two as we speak. They have to be dealt with.' Pete was aghast at the implications and foresaw some very difficult conversations with his head office.

'Nor can we postpone the cull indefinitely,' chipped in Jim. 'The infection carried by these turkeys presents a threat to the industry in the whole region, and possibly human health as well.'

'You'll need to talk to the police about that,' repeated Ben.

'I'll need to talk to our ROD,' said Jim.

Everyone headed for phones, leaving Ben and Lukas in sole ownership of the yard and the casualty.

The thin morning sun lit the early mist hugging the ground between the big sheds, glinting off the equipment lying useless and discarded in the yard.

'How well did you know the casualty?' Ben asked Lukas, forgetting for a moment that he was no longer a police officer, just a first responder.

'I'd worked with him for a while. For say three, four months. But I not say I knew him so well. Not meeting up in the evening well. I live with my family in Hemsby. He live with the teams in a company house I think. He'd only been here for those few months. His family are home in Lithuania. They will need to be told.'

'I'm sure the police will handle all that,' reassured Ben.

At that moment a contingent of two uniformed police came through from the gate.

'We've left Constable Nicholls to hold the gate,' said one. 'We've been told securing this area is priority. Don't I know you?' he said, turning to Ben.

'Ben Asheton,' said Ben, holding out his hand. 'We may

have met before I retired from Norfolk Police. Or at a darts match.'

'Both I think,' the policeman replied, shaking his hand heartily. 'I think I met you soon after I joined, and I definitely remember your darts. You're a bit greyer now though. You here as first responder?'

'That's right. One casualty, found when the team started to clear this gassing chamber' – he waved at the repurposed storage container, partially sealed by additional sheeting and taking up a substantial part of the yard – 'around forty-five minutes ago. I arrived on the scene at 0635. I checked for signs of life and they were all absent. More, I found what I believe to be signs of rigor mortis beginning. Your pathologist will have more to say on that I'm sure, but my guess is he's been dead for some hours. Lukas here is one of those who found him and was involved in the resus attempt.'

They both turned to look at Lukas, now perched on the low wall at the side of the yard.

'I'm Constable Davidson,' the policeman said to Lukas. 'I think I've seen you before. I've been on your gate on and off since yesterday. You'll need to stay on site until you've been interviewed, but you can go into the offices and get a cup of coffee while you wait.

'You too if you like,' he said to Ben. 'I gather the new DCI is on his way and there's nothing more you can do for this chap. I'll give you a shout when you're needed.'

By the time Ben entered the offices, they were nearly as crowded as for the early morning meeting, even though the disgruntled catching team were absent, having set up their base in the shed they had cleared the day before. Ben saw them all in the doorway, sitting round on empty crates, waiting to be told when they could get on with the job. The office was now crammed with vets and Stalham management, while Mrs Pritchard had risen to the occasion with instant coffee and gingernuts.

Ben accepted something hot and dark in a mug with a logo for poultry feed emblazoned on the side. 'Thank you.'

He sat down next to Jim Mackie who put his phone back in his pocket with an exasperated air.

'The ROD is talking to the police at Wymondham,' he said to his fellow vet Monica, perched on a desk near the door sipping milky tea.

She pushed dark hair behind her ears. 'Has anyone contacted the lorry on its way here for yesterday's carcasses?' she asked.

Pete Willis looked up. 'Mrs Pritchard rang, but it was too late to stop them. They'll be here in a few minutes but they'll be held at the gate. We'll need the police to ok the loading of the carcasses.'

'It's a mess,' said Monica. 'We need to ship those carcasses out and cull those already caught this morning ASAP, or we'll have rotting turkeys in the yard and the catchers will have to release the ones they've caught. You realise that if this whole site is a crime scene, we won't be able to proceed with the cull perhaps for days. The turkeys will carry on dying from disease, we'll have a centre of infection that is uncontrolled, welfare problems, an extended movement ban on this whole area – it's a complete nightmare!'

'I'm sure Emma is saying all that to the police command,' replied Jim.

*

She was, and more. By the time she came off the phone, Chief Superintendent Margaret Tayler, head of County Police, was very well apprised of the likely impact of an extended delay on the economics of East Anglia, animal welfare and human health. It was with Emma's last words on human health ringing in her ears that she turned to her new DCI.

Greg Geldard was sitting in his new boss's office in the HQ at Wymondham, all set to spend a morning meeting his new team and working his way through the, often tedious, processes of induction to a new force. However the rest of his day panned out, it didn't look like being tedious. He took a swig of his excellent coffee, recrossed his legs and wondered how his wife Isabelle was getting on, unpacking yet more boxes in their new rented home.

'It appears that we have a major problem,' said Margaret, putting the phone down. 'The possible murder reported to us a few moments ago is located on a turkey farm with a nasty outbreak of bird flu. The strain has been confirmed as,' she consulted her notes, 'H5N1, which apparently is not only very infectious and virulent, but also transmissible to humans. The NHS is being put on standby as we speak. So, you can imagine that dead birds sitting in a yard, and infected live ones hanging around waiting either to die or be culled, are a big headache.

'I have to say,' she added, 'the Defra comms seem to be as good as ours. Their HQ seem to have been briefed as quickly as me.'

DCI Greg Geldard looked up from his notes.

'Let me see if I've got this right, Ma'am. We have a

suspicious death at a poultry rearing establishment that's currently in the middle of a notifiable disease outbreak. The place the body was found also includes a few hundred dead and soon-to-be decomposing turkeys while the immediate vicinity contains around a thousand more which are also presumed to be infected by a disease transmissible to humans. Defra is panting at the leash to continue the cull before the rest of the East Anglian poultry industry approaches bankruptcy and the NHS are on standby for a public health emergency. I can see that preserving evidence at the site is going to be a challenge.' Behind his dispassionate demeanour, Greg didn't know whether to laugh or cry. A murder on his first day was one thing. A possible pandemic was another.

'To put it mildly.' Margaret Tayler grinned suddenly. 'I like your style DCI Geldard. Challenge is one word. Disaster is another. And that's why I've authorised additional budget for crime scene management and forensics. The only solution I can see is for you to get in there and grab every bit of evidence or potential evidence you can. I can only hold off the turkey killers for 12–24 hours, so get yourself to Stalham and work something out fast.'

When Greg arrived mob-handed at Stalham Poultry, the first face he saw was Ben's.

'Ben Asheton, as I live and breathe,' he said. 'I haven't seen you since our boat chase down the Broads. Does anything happen in Norfolk without your help?'

'Not a lot,' said Ben, striding over with his hand out. 'On the other hand, what the devil are you doing here?

What's North Yorkshire's foremost crime investigator doing down among the flatlands?'

'Hopefully making a success of a promotion,' replied Greg drily, 'but as I only started here yesterday and my first assignment has more complications than type 2 diabetes it's not looking so good.'

'Congratulations Detective Chief Inspector. Great news. How can I help?'

'Just give me a moment with the crime scene team, then I'd like your take on what's been happening here before I start interviews. My biggest problem's going to be preserving evidence without holding up the cull unnecessarily. The obvious thing to do would be to devise a plan with the help of the local site manager. But as he may be a suspect, I daren't let him guide what areas we release when. I think a three-cornered chat between you, me and the vet in charge might be useful.'

'They're all in the site office,' said Ben. 'Follow me.'

Leaving his crime scene coordinator Ned George in charge in the yard, Greg followed Ben through a nondescript green door, down a narrow corridor and into an office full of people drinking tea and coffee.

'This is Pete Willis, site manager,' said Ben. 'Lukas works here on site and Joe works for the contractor supplying the mobile gassing chamber. They and Jim here, were the first to spot the body. Jim and Monica are government vets, supervising the cull.' He indicated the two perched on the table wearing Defra-logoed protective clothing. 'And Mrs Pritchard supplies everything from defibs to gingernuts as required. The rest, I'm sorry I don't have names for yet.'

Pete Willis stepped up. 'This is James Metcalfe, company health and safety officer, and Stan Innes, biosecurity.'

'Thank you,' said Greg. 'I am DCI Geldard and I'm taking charge of this investigation. I appreciate at this point it's just a suspicious death,' he said, seeing from the corner of his eye that Pete Willis was gearing up for an intervention, 'but we have to take it seriously just in case a crime has been committed. Therefore, my men, and my men alone, will have access across the site for the time being. I understand that in addition to the eight of you in here, there's another team of four in one of the sheds. We'll carry out preliminary interviews with each of you and then take stock of how the farm can continue to work over the next day or so. And,' he added, looking at the vets, 'what progress can be made with the cull. Perhaps Jim, Monica, Ben and I could discuss that now. Is there another office we can use?'

'Next door,' said Pete Willis, and Mrs Pritchard leapt to show them the way.

'In here,' she said, 'there should be room for the four of you. Just let me know if you need anything,' and she sailed away, patting a loose hair back into the tight French pleat.'

It was a small room with walls covered in progress charts, graphs and printouts. Greg sat at the desk and the other three pulled up chairs.

'Believe me,' he said to Jim and Monica, 'the importance of the cull has been explained to me in painful detail. My problem is that if I let catching teams, poultry workers or anyone else trample over a crime scene before we've collected whatever evidence is available, my investigation is compromised and someone will have my guts for garters. Worse, a murderer may get away. So, I need your help to work out how we can meet both objectives.

'The pathologist and the crime scene investigators are in the yard as we speak. The body will be moved shortly, and the next priority will be the gassing chamber itself. After they've been over that thoroughly, I'd expect to be able to release the crates of dead birds for disposal. Say, by tonight, all being well. From your perspective, what are the priorities after that?'

Jim looked at Monica, then said, 'Shall I go first? The first issue is animal welfare. As long as we have live birds on the farm they need to be fed and watered which means some farm personnel having access to the normal systems. At the moment nothing is happening, and that needs to change very soon.'

Ben interrupted. 'If I can make a suggestion. My estimate was that the casualty had died in the early hours of this morning, say somewhere between midnight and 0300. If the pathologist comes to the same view, then perhaps staff from elsewhere in the company could care for the remaining stock. We know who was on site yesterday and overnight, because there were police on the perimeter as part of the cull arrangements. It's up to you of course,' he added hurriedly and belatedly, suddenly remembering which hat he was wearing.

Greg made a note. 'That might work for staff. But now, what about access to different locations? My starting point would normally be that everything was out of bounds until the crime scene staff have finished.'

'How long does that take?' asked Jim.

'That's the difficult question. It depends on circumstances. Here we have a large and complex establishment. If this was a factory or storage depot I'd just shut it down until we were finished, but I recognise I can't do that here. To be pragmatic, we'll focus on the yard and the gassing unit where the body was found first. Then we'll take a look round the sheds and offices and I'll decide at that point what might need to be quarantined for a longer period. But realistically, sheds full of turkeys are not going to remain static and you've all been messing around in the offices all morning, so those scenes are already contaminated. Obviously all this depends on the pathologist's verdict, but in the meantime we just have to crack on.

'So, thinking aloud, I would aim to be finished in the yard later today and at that point we'll allow the transport in to remove the crates of dead birds, under our supervision. Once it's empty we'll take a closer look at the gassing container, so I don't see that being available to you for at least 24 hours.'

Jim looked at Monica who nodded. 'We could live with that delay but no longer. If there's likely to be a further hold-up we'd look to bring a second container on site to take over from the one deemed out of bounds. I'll discuss that with our ROD. Could you live with that?'

'Subject to having a say over where and how it is sited yes.'

When Jim spoke to Emma, she listened in silence then came to a swift decision.

'Could be worse. I'll organise a second gassing container and agree a schedule for it coming to you. If the police let us use the first one then the second will help us make up the time we've lost, so the cost is still justifiable. I'll let you know the timetable. Keep me posted. And Jim, are you and Monica ok to carry on until your scheduled replacements arrive?'

'We're fine thanks. And I think that would be best as we already know the set-up and the people. A change in personnel might disrupt arrangements.'

Arrangements for care of the live turkeys were quickly resolved between Pete Willis and DCI Geldard. Two of the catching team were redeployed on feed and water duties under both the vets' supervision, and with police oversight. Ned allocated one of his team to keep a log of anything taken into the sheds or removed from them. Uniformed police collected names and addresses from everyone on site, and all were sent to Stalham Village Hall where the police had parked a mobile incident room.

Greg took a last look round the now busy yard. The team, whose names he hardly knew let alone their personalities, were all going about their appointed tasks. As the day warmed up and the morning mist lifted, the dilapidated concrete of the yards and roadways was leaking dust with every movement. Over in the corner Lukas was being slow to take his departure, still fussing about the welfare of his birds at the hands of the catching teams. Greg saw Ned tell him to get out of their way and Lukas went to his car with many backward glances. At the back of his mind, Greg worried about the commitment of resource on what was so far only a suspicion, but pushed the concern away. He had a great respect for Ben, knowing his background in both nursing and the police, and clearly Ben thought there was something not right. Greg's instincts were pointing the same way.

Heading for his car, Greg tripped over the edge of yet another raised concrete slab and only just saved himself from an embarrassing landing at full length. He scowled down at his polished-that-morning leather brogues, selected for a day of meetings and training courses and not at all suitable for a day on a farm, any more than was his smart jacket. This was not at all how he had meant his new job to start. He sighed for the loss of familiar faces and especially his old North Yorks sergeant. Ben, packing his kit nearby, recognised the look.

'This is the proverbial deep end isn't it?' he observed. 'I imagine you hardly know one of your team from another yet?'

'I haven't even met my sarge,' Greg remarked. 'Yesterday was just an induction day and he was on leave. They're meeting me in the village I hope, then coming here after.'

'Who've you got?'

'DI Jim Henning. At least I know him from last year. And Sergeant Chris Mathews.'

'Obviously I know Jim. Good chap, and not the sort to get his nose put out of joint. Sergeant Mathews is since my time. I only know her by repute.'

'In a good way?'

Ben hesitated. 'Marmite, I believe. I'm sure you'll get on fine, provided you remember she's a woman!'

Those words were still ringing in his ears when Greg parked his BMW by the police van at Stalham Village Hall.

'Not there,' said a pint-size commanding presence in bright red warm coat and boots. 'Don't be a numpty. There's a perfectly clear sign saying keep clear for disabled access. You'll find some space around the back.'

Greg wound his window down. 'DCI Geldard,' he introduced himself. 'And you are?'

'Sergeant Mathews. Pleased to meet you, sir.'

'Do you usually address members of the public like that?'

'Sorry, sir. Should have said, don't be a numpty, sir,' replied Chris with a cheerful smile. 'Space around the back as I said. DI Henning is in the mobile and we have our interviewees lined up in the village hall.' She whisked into the mobile and Greg drove round to the back of the hall.

'Marmite,' he muttered.

Inside the mobile incident room he found Jim, Chris and a civilian, Nate, manning the phones. Jim came forward with his hand outstretched.

'First chance I've had to say welcome and congratulations, sir,' he said.

'Greg will do,' said Greg, shaking the proffered hand vigorously. 'I'm delighted to work with you again.'

'And how's your wife? Isabelle isn't it?'

'Very well thank you. Currently rehearsing in the Norwich Cathedral song school.'

Jim Henning turned to introduce the others. 'This is Nate. Just sorted our IT and now sorting phone enquiries.'

Nate nodded, his attention on his headset.

'I think you've met Chris?' he went on.

‘In the car park,’ said Greg, still not sure whether he was going to be marmite-phile or marmite-phobe. ‘And I met Ben Asheton at the scene. I had a quick word with him there, but I hope he’s going to join us over here later this afternoon. His initial impressions should be useful. He was first responder on site, and I think he’s made some useful observations.

‘So, before we start the interviews, let’s make sure we’re all on the same page. Essential facts:

‘1. A body was found in the gassing container at Stalham Poultry around 0600 this morning.

‘2. The container, a sort of covered freight container, was supplied by Defra contractors yesterday and used for the first time overnight.

‘3. The dead man was named,’ he hesitated and consulted his notes, ‘Jonas Balciunas. Lithuanian national. Employed at Stalham as a poultry worker since he arrived in the UK last November. We need to talk to his family. At present we’ve not yet established cause of death, nor time, although Ben thinks it was very early this morning on the basis of rigor mortis already setting in when he saw him at 0625.

‘Still at the farm are two of the catching team, looking after the remaining turkeys under the supervision of two Defra vets and a couple of uniformed officers.’

‘PCs Bill Street and Jill Hayes,’ supplied Chris.

‘Yes. Thank you. Waiting for us here should be the site manager, the health and safety officer and biosecurity officer from Stalham Poultry, two more catchers, the poultry worker Lukas Jankauskas, and the Defra gassing contractor Joe Simkins. The last two, together with a Defra vet, found the body. Let’s see them first.’

3

Afternoon of 4 April

Chris went into the village hall and, looking round, beckoned to Lukas.

'Can you come through to our incident room please?' she asked.

Lukas followed her out into the watery sunshine and across the car park to the brightly liveried mobile office, where she ushered him into a small room near the entrance.

Greg and Lukas regarded each other. Greg saw a tall lean man with sharp features and fine hands. His dark hair was cut short, his eyebrows strongly arched in the tanned face. There were fine lines round his mouth and eyes, but while the former looked melancholic the eyes smiled. His hands showed the signs of hard work and his overalls had clearly had hard wear, but were clean and neatly mended. He sat quietly in the chair, attentive but not obviously nervous.

'Thank you for waiting, Mr Jankauskas,' said Greg.

'I appreciate this has been a distressing morning for you and I'll try not to keep you much longer. I am Detective Chief Inspector Geldard and this is Detective Inspector Henning. You've already met Detective Sergeant Cole. This is just a quick chat to establish some basic facts. I've been told you are a Lithuanian national and that you speak English, but if I ask you anything you don't understand, please say so. We can get an interpreter on the phone if need be. We'll need a statement in due course, but we'll do that more formally at our offices in Wymondham.

'Now, PC Hayes has already noted your name and address, so can you just talk us through what you understand happened this morning?'

'It was normal day,' said Lukas. 'At least, normal except for cull, but we'd been told about that. We'd helped load the gassing chamber last night.'

'What time did you finish loading the chamber?'

'Around 10. Was late arriving, so we late finishing.'

'Who did the loading?'

'Me and Jonas, told by the ministry man, Joe.'

'You mean he supervised the stacking of crates in the container?'

'Yes. He told us what to put where. How to stack. How to leave some spaces between rows. Then we left and he closed the sheets. I went away then. I didn't want to hear the birds dying. And I was late going home. My wife would be worried.'

'Did Jonas leave at the same time?'

'Not the same time. He helped Joe for a bit. He was still there when I left. No. Not quite right. I saw him going back into the changing rooms as I got in my car.'

'So you drive to and from the site. How does Jonas get there?'

'He comes in the work minibus. I should explain perhaps. I have worked here for three years. Since before the company changed hands. My wife and I came to England together. By car and ferry. My wife is an interpreter. She has a good job doing interpretation on the telephone. I couldn't find a job in my profession so I took this one with turkeys. It pays ok.' He shrugged. 'We can save and someday maybe we go home and I can do my proper work again.'

'Which is?' asked Greg.

'Teacher. I taught maths. Here, I am not qualified to teach, so I work with turkeys.' He shrugged again.

'What about Jonas?'

'Him, I don't know how he got here. He came with whole gang of workers. They all stay in company house. They all arrive together. All live together at a place a few miles from here. All work together, either here or other places. They are not with their families you understand. Not like me.' He looked at Greg very steadily.

'Are you trying to tell me there's something wrong about them?' asked Greg.

'I think,' said Lukas slowly, 'that there are things you want to look at. Where they live. How they pay. Where they work. They have not worked with me for long, but there is something not right. I have discussed with my wife. We wondered what to do, but if we are right, these are not nice people they deal with. We were not sure where to go. How to report, without getting into big trouble. My wife didn't want to make trouble. I am taking a risk now,' he added, 'but now there is a death. You have to investigate. I have to answer your questions.'

Greg thought for a moment. 'Are Stalham Poultry management involved? The bosses?' he asked.

'I don't know how much. They must know where the men come from. They must know that cheap labour is not good thing. Do they make the arrangements? That I don't know. At least, I don't think Pete is involved. I think he is just sent men. But other bosses?' he shrugged. 'I don't know. There's something else you should know. That night, Jonas said he had a way of getting away. A way of escape. I don't know what it was. That's all I know. He shut up pretty quick.'

'That's very interesting, given what happened next. Can you remember anything else at all? Anything else Jonas said or did?'

'No, nothing. He never say anything before. Just that one time.'

'Thank you, Mr Jankauskas. As I said, we'll follow up with a formal statement in our main offices. We'll let you know the arrangements for this. Meanwhile, I hope you have no plans to leave England.'

'No. No plans. I need to go back to the farm now. Make sure my turkeys are ok.'

'For now, you need to go home,' replied Greg. 'The turkeys are being taken care of, I promise.'

Greg, Chris and Jim Henning looked at each other after Lukas left the interview room, his footsteps shaking the mobile as he left the unit and clumped down the steps to the car park and his elderly VW Passat.

'Getting messy,' remarked Jim.

'You're thinking?' asked Greg.

'People smuggling, illegal gangmaster, modern slavery. Any or all of the above.'

'Not something we had a lot of in the Dales,' remarked Greg. 'How much is it a problem around here?'

'Illegal gangmasters? Quite a lot. Using teams of low-paid workers in jobs like veg or fruit picking is open to abuse, and there's lots of veg growing in East Anglia. Down towards the Essex coast there have been issues with shellfish picking, but we don't really have the beaches for that in Norfolk. Modern slavery? Like anywhere, we've had some car cleaning and nail bar outfits we've been keeping a very close eye on. And Border Force has picked up illegal immigrants coming in to our coastline. So all the ingredients are there.'

'I'm wondering if we need to shortcut our original plan,' mused Greg. 'Lukas said the place the workers lived was not far from Stalham Poultry. It shouldn't be too difficult to narrow down the possibilities with a bit of local knowledge. I think we should prioritise finding that location before anyone has a chance to do a clean-up job.

'Jim, can you take charge of that. Get a uniform team together, screen the possibilities and check out anything that looks interesting. You might need to go in mob-handed if you get a strong lead. While you're doing that, Chris and I will do some quick and dirty interviews with the Stalham Poultry local management. If we need to we'll jump to formal interviews under caution, but let's see where a preliminary chat gets us.'

*

A couple of calls to the Police HQ at Wymondham, and Jim had agreed a rendezvous with a uniformed patrol at Wayford Bridge Hotel. HQ had agreed that, if needed, crime scene experts could be diverted from Stalham Poultry to assist. While not ideal, and not exactly compliant with Greg's suggestion of 'mob-handed', it was the best they could do at short notice. By the time he arrived at Wayford Bridge the team of two burly uniformed constables was already waiting in the car park in their marked car, attracting one or two comments from passers-by about police having time for coffee breaks in hotels. Constables Steve Hall and Phil Coleman had ignored the comments, but had taken the opportunity for a takeaway cuppa each, which they had to slot hurriedly into the cup holders when Jim arrived, leaning in the open driver's window.

'Good to see you, Steve, Phil,' he said. 'Sorry you won't have time to finish those. We need to get moving sharpish.' He flourished a map. 'Priorities at present are here and here,' stabbing the map with his finger. 'What do you think? You know this area.'

Steve and Phil looked at the map. Not that one, said Phil pointing. 'I went there not long ago when someone reported an illegal rave. It's just one barn and it was empty then. And it's near a village, hence the complaints.'

'I'd add this one,' said Steve, also pointing. It meets the criteria of being isolated and I don't think its farmed very actively. May be worth a look.'

'Ok.' Jim rolled up the map. 'Let's get started. Bear in mind, we think this may be linked to illegal gangmaster activity, or possibly modern slavery, so keep your eyes open and be wary. If it's the latter, the inmates will be frightened and the organisers very bad news. Don't put yourselves at risk. Keep each other in sight at all times and we'll call for backup if needed. Ok. Let's go. I'll go in my car. You follow. No lights or sirens.'

Steve and Phil looked at each other and Phil put the car into gear. Both adjusted their stab vests and checked they had batons and tasers safely secured. This made a change from stolen quad bikes.

Their first two attempts were fruitless, unless you counted some cannabis growing in tattered greenhouses. They reported in, but pressed on with their search. The third was different.

The farm was only a couple of miles off the main road. All seemed quiet as they arrived. The main farmhouse was tidy and looked well kept, but although they knocked loudly on the door, they got no answer. The yard was typically farm-scruffy, piles of plastic waste from silage bales in one corner, a stack of old pallets and a rusting van in another, and a lot of vehicle tracks in the mud. As they came away from the unresponsive house, Jim examined the tracks.

'Look like Transits, or similar,' volunteered Phil.

'Rather a lot of movement for a small farm,' remarked Jim. 'The tracks all seem to be fresh. I would have said at least four or five vans have been in here this morning.'

Steve had been looking round and pointed to a row of old poultry sheds on the far side of the yard. 'How about I take a closer look at those?'

'We'll all take a look,' said Jim. 'There doesn't seem to be anyone about, but watch your backs just in case.'

The three men picked their way across the rutted mud to the silent sheds. They were long, low, windowless buildings, each with a feed silo at one end and ventilators on the roof.

'They don't seem to be in use,' remarked Jim. 'At least, I can't hear anything. Wouldn't you expect to hear something if they were full of birds?'

'They don't smell like active poultry sheds either,' said Phil.

The three looked at each other and round the yard again. Still no sign of anyone.

'Let's see if the doors are unlocked,' said Jim.

The double doors at the end of the shed held firm when pushed. There was no sign of a padlock. They were obviously intended to open inward and there was a keyhole but no key. Jim pushed again, then turned away to walk to the next shed. Behind him, there was a bang and 'Whoops, fell against the door and it's come open, sir' from Steve. Jim turned back, suppressing a grin, and went over.

'How unfortunate,' he said, 'but as it's obviously unsecured we'd better make sure everything is ok. We don't want hens escaping all over Wayford Bridge.' His voice tailed off as he cautiously pushed the door open and poked his head in. Then he went in, followed by Steve and Phil. 'Either of you got a torch on you?' he asked.

Steve produced his and shone the powerful beam round the shed. The light fell on rows of bunk beds, maybe thirty. The beds had clearly been in use very recently, possibly that morning, as they all had rumpled blankets and dirty pillows.

'You stay here, Phil, and keep an eye out. We don't want to be surprised in here. Steve, you come with me.'

'There's a light switch over there,' said Steve, and going over to it pressed it down.

A row of fluorescent lights down the centre of the shed flickered on. They went in and Jim had to suppress a desire to cover his face against the smell of unwashed bodies, cooking and dirty clothes. At the far end was a rudimentary kitchen with a table and chairs.

'Where the devil do they wash and pee?' asked Steve.

'Hopefully in one of the other sheds,' replied Jim, with a grim expression on his face. 'What a tip! Imagine having to live like this.'

'So where are they all?'

'Either scarpered or out at work. I imagine their working day starts pretty early and finishes late. We need to report this in. Ideally we can...'

He was interrupted by Phil at the door. 'Someone's just driven into the yard,' he reported. 'Old Land Rover by the look of it. It's stopped. No, it's turned round and driven off again. I think they were spooked seeing our car.'

'Did you get the number?'

'No, sorry, wrong angle. There are cameras on the main road through Wayford Bridge. We might spot it on them.'

'Unfortunately there's no shortage of old Land Rovers in Norfolk. But it's worth a try. Radio that through to Wymondham with the best description you can muster and ask for a warrant to search the remainder of these sheds. We have good reason to suspect a crime here. I'm going to have a chat with the boss. He needs to know what we've found.'

*

Greg, called out of the preliminary interview with Pete Willis, was excited by the news.

'Well done, Jim. That's going to be very helpful. I'll make sure you get the warrant ASAP and some more hands to help. Pity we didn't find anyone there, but lucky the first shed wasn't locked.'

'Yes, lucky,' said Jim, smirking, and rang off in a hurry.

Greg went back to the interview cubicle where Chris was still sitting with Pete Willis. He looked relaxed, leaning in his chair, one arm hooked over the back. He sat up with a jerk as Greg entered the room.

'I was just saying to the sergeant what a pain this cull is,' he began chattily but stopped when he saw Greg's face.

'I think we'll continue this at Wymondham,' he said. 'We'll run you there, Mr Willis. Something's come up.'

'Am I under arrest? he asked, suddenly pale.

'Not at this point, but we would appreciate you helping us with our enquiries. You don't have any reason not to, do you?'

'No, but do I need my solicitor?'

'That's up to you, sir. You've not been charged with anything, but if you want your solicitor along, that is your privilege. Sergeant Cole will make a telephone available to you. You can ask them to meet you at Wymondham. We'll be setting off in a few minutes.'

Pete hesitated, then said, 'Yes, I think I will. The company will provide a solicitor I'm sure.'

Chris got up from her seat. 'Perhaps you'd come with me then, sir.'

Outside the interview room, Pete Willis safely in his car,

she stopped Greg with a hand on his arm. 'Has something happened, sir?' she asked.

Greg looked down at her. 'Jim's found the men's accommodation. Judging from his description it's awful. That chap's got some serious questions to answer. He's either involved, or criminally negligent. The whole thing stinks.'

4

Parallel Enquiries

Engrossed in his own complicated enquiries, Greg Geldard hadn't appreciated the extent of the parallel, detailed investigation also underway at Stalham Poultry.

The Defra vets Jim and Monica were also asking a lot of questions and Emma Knight wanted some answers. Where had the avian flu virus come from? No pockets of infection in wild birds had been reported any nearer than Eastern Europe, so the most obvious vector for transfer was man: either by importation of live birds or movement of goods or men. Either way, something or someone must have come onto the Stalham site soon after visiting an infected area. Emma needed to know what or who, and when.

The first and most obvious source of infection was imported turkeys and turkey products for processing. On their first day at the plant Jim had questioned Pete Willis closely, and he had insisted that while there had been imports from Hungary, that had been months ago. Moreover, there had been no outbreaks in Hungary. Judging by the paperwork, Monica had also carried out an exhaustive and exhausting check of the records. It was wearing Emma out just reading the report and she had to concede that the link did not seem to be there.

'They've gone through months' worth of records and cross-checked with our databases,' she said to Bill, chief vet at Bury St Edmunds. 'Your folk have done a great job.' She stretched to ease the crick in her back and rubbed her hands down her face. Momentarily she appeared eerily clown-like as her eyes stretched downwards.

'They haven't turned up any imports after the pre-Christmas rush,' she said. 'None at all. And the material that came in December was sourced in Hungary as they said. None of our databases report outbreaks in Hungary at that time. The nearest were...' she flipped through several screens on her iPad, 'the nearest were further north in Poland, then Lithuania. Have we got the virus typed yet?'

'This one here? Not yet,' said Bill. 'Might have some results through tomorrow. Has there been any sign of people movements over recent months? Pete Willis claims there have been no new teams brought on site in the past few months and that all their workers are either locals or have been in the UK for some time.'

'It's clear there are quite a few Lithuanians,' remarked Emma, 'and I suppose they may have travelled through Poland. But as that oily git Collier has been at pains to point out, and I quote, "their meticulous biosecurity procedures" would have dealt with any risks from that route. We need another chat with Stan Innes. But the timings aren't right anyway.'

Bill flapped his way through another pile of paper. 'It's a pity the police have whisked away a lot of the people we need to talk to.'

'I wish they'd whisk Mr "I'm so important" Collier,' grumbled Emma. 'He really is a pompous twat.'

'Now now, you shouldn't be so dismissive of one of our key stakeholders,' admonished Bill with a grin.

Making a noise remarkably like 'Tchah!' Emma said, 'I know. I'll ring that Mrs Pritchard. She seems to be the only person there you can get a straight answer from.'

'Mrs Pritchard,' she said when she got through, 'I need to know who may have travelled to Europe in February and March, but there's no one to ask. Do you have any records that might help?'

'The only travel arrangements that I make are for the managers,' she said. 'I used to handle travel when I worked in head office and I kept the role when I moved here. I usually book their planes and trains, etc, if they're travelling on company business. I'll look them out for you. When do you want them?'

'Any chance of this afternoon?'

'I'll have them ready for you by 2,' she promised.

Two o'clock, after a sandwich lunch and more phone calls from Mr Collier chasing progress, Emma got a return call from Mrs P.

'I'm just hitting the send on some emails,' she said. 'And some scans of things I thought you might want to see. I'm off now. I have a half day today. If you want anything else you'll have to ring me tomorrow.'

'Thank you,' said Emma, but was cut off short.

'Sorry, need to dash! The lorry collecting carcasses is just arriving and if I don't hurry up my car will be blocked in for ages.'

It didn't take Emma long to find and discard the file that dealt only with travel before Christmas.

'This is the wrong time period,' she said. 'We need something more recent. Have you anything there, Bill?'

'No. This stuff,' he flapped more printouts, 'is all about pre-Christmas turkey imports. Not relevant to now.'

Emma went back through the email trail.

'The more recent stuff is back here,' she said. 'Mostly regular trips to and from the Hungarian unit. They seem to happen roughly every couple of weeks. Occasionally Stan, the biosecurity chap, goes. Most often it's that Austen Collier. I suppose that figures.'

She carried on digging through the papers with a sigh, then paused on the very last sheet.

'What the…? Well well,' she said to Bill. 'Look what we have here.'

'What've you got?'

'It looks like details of claims for travel expenses over the past month or so. Hundreds and hundreds of miles. But the interesting bit is the "other" column.' She drew quotation marks in the air. 'According to this, someone has claimed for repeated ferry trips to the continent. Harwich to the Hook of Holland. They seem to have gone more or less monthly since the beginning of the year. And on this scan, there's what looks like a pencil scribble that says "Mr C's car" on the top. Now why would Mr C be doing all that driving? Wouldn't getting on a plane be easier? Is that Collier as well do you think?'

'No idea. Seems pretty weird.'

'But this could be how an infection was picked up and brought here to Norfolk. Depending on where "Mr C" went and what was carried in the car.'

'We need those virus typing results. If it's the East European virus, then we can start to trace a route.'

'And we need to pass this on to the police,' said Emma, with a sudden realisation. 'This might be relevant to the murder inquiry.'

In Wymondham, Pete Willis was looking rather pale. Cautioned and cautious, he sat picking at the edge of the table in the interview room. Beside him the company solicitor, a grey man in a grey suit, looked down at his papers. Opposite, both Geldard and Henning were staring at him with very serious faces. The silence lengthened.

'Do you have an answer for us, Mr Willis?'

Pete Willis looked at the solicitor, who raised a non-committal eyebrow in what even Greg Geldard thought was an unhelpful fashion. Left to his own devices, Pete cleared his throat.

'I just take the men I'm sent,' he muttered.

'How do they arrive for work?'

'In a van.'

'A company van.'

'Yes.'

'And how do they go home at the end of their shift?'

'Same.'

'How are they paid?'

'They get a monthly pay packet from Mrs P.'

'In cash?'

'Yes.'

'And a payslip?'

'Yes, of course.'

'With deductions listed?'

Pete looked at the solicitor again. It was obvious to Greg that Pete wasn't comfortable with the questions. The solicitor was still playing with his pen, and didn't look up.

'What were the deductions for, Mr Willis?'

'Just normal expenses.'

'Such as?' Greg was losing patience. 'Suppose we go through some of these in this folder from your office? For example, what is "housing"?'

'The costs of housing them,' mumbled Pete Willis.

'Louder please, Mr Willis, for the tape.'

'Housing costs.'

'So you did know they were in company housing?'

Silence.

'And this other item. Miscellaneous expenses. What were those?'

'I don't know.'

'You were making regular deductions from these men's salaries, and you didn't know what for?'

'The pay is all handled centrally. I don't make the decisions. I assumed they were for food, transport, that kind of stuff.'

'Even if you didn't decide on the deductions, you could see them going out. You knew these men, on the minimum wage, were actually getting much less. Less than half in fact.'

Pete was still looking wretchedly at the floor.

'Yes,' he muttered.

'Again, for the tape please, Mr Willis.'

'Yes,' he snapped.

'And it didn't occur to you that something funny was going on? The words "modern slavery" didn't come into your head? You see, Mr Willis, from where I'm sitting it seems we have at least two crimes to investigate. One is the suspicious death that brought us on to the scene. He's in the pathologist's hands as we speak. The second is what looks very like modern slavery. At the moment, I don't know what your involvement was in the death of Jonas Balciunas. But you look very involved indeed in the slavery of these men.'

Pete looked at his unhelpful adviser again, and again got no help. 'In our company,' he said clearly, 'questions aren't encouraged. It was made clear to me that my job was to manage the production site and keep quiet.'

The solicitor was moved to intervene. 'I suggest you don't say any more, Mr Willis.' And to the police, 'I would like an opportunity to consult with my client.'

Pete interrupted. 'I am no longer *his* client,' he stated with more clarity than anything else he'd said all morning. 'I want my own solicitor. I don't think he's here for me.'

'Now just a minute, Mr Willis,' said the solicitor, rising

to his full, unimpressive height of just five foot, 'I strongly advise you…'

'You don't advise me at all actually,' said Pete, and sat back with his arms folded.

'I think we'll take a pause there,' said Greg, with some satisfaction.

After an interlude for sandwiches, coffee, and the hasty briefing of a local solicitor, they reconvened in the interview room.

'Interview recommenced at,' Greg looked at his watch, '1315. I need to remind you, Mr Willis, that you are still under caution.

'If I might summarise where we'd got to, I think you'd agreed that you knew the Lithuanian farm workers were living on company property, transported by company transport, and were paying exorbitant sums for the privilege.'

The new solicitor, a young woman with short blond hair in a pixie cut and pronounced cheek bones, interrupted. 'I have advised my client to cooperate with your enquiries,' she said with precision, 'but I think it will go better, and with fewer interruptions from me, if we avoid value judgments. Can we note, for the present, that my client was aware that deductions were being made from the farm workers' salaries.'

Pete nodded, then remembering, said, 'Yes,' for the tape. 'Except for Lukas,' he added. 'Lukas was already working for the farm before it was bought by Stalham Poultry. We kept him on, partly because the law gave us no choice, and later because he was a good worker. I argued he should stay on when the management wanted rid of him,' he said, a touch self-righteously.

'Oh well done,' said Greg sarcastically, then caught a glance from the pixie cut. Making a note to himself that he needed to learn her name he went on.

'So, we have established that all the farm workers except Lukas were living in company accommodation, being transported by company transport, and paying heavily for the privilege.'

The solicitor cleared her throat again, but Greg forged on.

'Had you visited the accommodation at Wayford Bridge?'

'No.'

'You are quite sure of that are you, Mr Willis? We are checking CCTV footage and our scenes of crime personnel are very thorough. If you were there, we will find out.'

'I had no reason to visit. Staff turned up on schedule and if they didn't I reported it to head office and they would make sure I got someone to cover.'

'Isn't it a little odd, for a farm manager to have no input into staff selection and management?'

'Not really, not in this sector. Teams are often supplied by a gangmaster. You specify what you want, and the gangmaster supplies the team.'

'Or in this case, the company does.'

'That's right,' said Pete.

'The difference being, Mr Willis, that gangmasters are licensed, monitored and controlled. Did your company have a gangmaster licence?'

'I don't know. Why should they? They were just recruiting staff for Stalham Poultry?'

'Oh were they? You just said you didn't know anything about it. It's my understanding that, in law, a person acts as a gangmaster if he supplies a worker to do specified work for another person. Someone in your company has been doing just that, it seems to me. Moreover, it's an offence to use an unlicensed gangmaster knowingly, and that seems to me what you have been doing.'

The pixie cut intervened. 'You would need to establish that my client knew his labour supplier was unlicensed, Inspector.'

'Chief Inspector, Ms?'

'Ms Milsom.'

'Thank you, Ms Milsom. You're quite right of course, and you can be sure that we will be looking very closely at all company communications with regard to the poultry workers. I think we'll take a break now.'

Outside the interview room, Greg exchanged glances with Jim Henning.

'Any news from Wayford Bridge?'

'Not yet.'

At the end of the day, Greg convened a team meeting at the Police Investigation Centre in Wymondham. He couldn't help looking round and comparing the facilities with the old offices in Malton, to Malton's loss. However, he did rather miss the coffee lounge of the Talbot Hotel, to which he had often retired for team meetings when in Yorkshire. Now he had a purpose-built Ops room, WiFi'd, phoned and radio'd up to the hilt, whiteboards and screens all round the room. He went to the end of the long table running down the centre of the room and rapped sharply to attract everyone's attention.

‘Right, for everyone’s benefit, let’s have a summary of progress made. I’ll kick off, as I’ve just had the post-mortem report.

‘The initial finding was a body in the Defra-supplied CO2 gassing chamber at Stalham Poultry, used to cull turkeys infected with bird flu. The first responder on the scene, Ben Asheton, confirmed death at 0625 and estimated time of death as some hours earlier. The pathologist agrees. His report here,’ he waved some notes, ‘estimates time of death as between 2300 the previous day and 0300 this morning. He ascribes cause of death to asphyxiation due to CO2 poisoning. He states there were some signs of a struggle or of violence. In addition to superficial scratching and bruising consistent with the body being dragged a short distance and manhandled into the gassing chamber, he found a contusion on the back of the head which could well indicate a temporary loss of consciousness. He couldn’t find any illness or other disorder that would account for the collapse of the victim. He is therefore offering as a theory that he may have been stunned by a blow to the head prior to being gassed.’ Out of the corner of his eye he caught sight of Jim Henning’s raised eyebrow and added, ‘Yes, the good old blunt instrument, of which there were a goodly selection on site.

‘The victim has been identified as Jonas Balciunas, a citizen of Lithuania. His family are being informed by their local police and we expect a report from them later. Now Jim, over to you.’

There was a stir as Jim recounted what they had learned at Wayford Bridge. ‘The conditions were just plain terrible,’ he finished. 'We have a team keeping an eye on the place, but no one has gone back there yet.'

'What about the workers we saw at Stalham?' asked Chris.

'One, Lukas, lives with his wife in Hemsby. The others we saw at the farm were catchers. They're a separate team. As I understand it, they're a specialist team called in when the sheds are to be emptied, normally at the end of the production phase. They do the job, then move on to the next farm. The normal workers looking after the birds would be Lukas and Jonas on this shift, rotating with four or five others as needed. We haven't seen any of the others yet. They may be among those normally living at Wayford Bridge, but we don't know. There are some records in the pay sheets, but we're still going through those.'

'Give them the rest of the update on the workers, Chris,' said Greg.

'Essentially, they seem to be bound in some way to Stalham Poultry. They live, if it can be called that, in the accommodation described by Jim. Payment for that, for transport and all sorts of other stuff is docked from their pay packets, so they're taking home rather less than half the minimum wage. Again, we're still going through the paperwork, but it would seem that Stalham Poultry is, at best, either using an illegal gangmaster or is acting as an illegal gangmaster.'

'And at worst?' asked Jim.

'At worst, they're running their farms with slaves. And their management will be looking at charges relating to modern slavery.'

There was a silence in the room as everyone contemplated the life those men had led. Greg shivered slightly. The loneliness, fear and isolation of those men working in a foreign land seemed even worse than in the most malicious domestic incident he had ever dealt with.

'What are the management saying?' asked Jim.

'So far, we've only interviewed Pete Willis, the site manager.' Chris looked at Greg, who nodded for her to carry on. He was interested to see how she performed in this role.

'Willis is not saying much, but has already taken steps to distance himself from what he calls head office. The solicitor they provided him seemed more interested in the well-being of the company than in that of Mr Willis himself. He spotted that pretty quickly and demanded his own solicitor.

'His version is, that he was sent staff by head office and was also obliged to follow their rules for terms and conditions of employment including arrangements for pay. He claims to have been discouraged from taking any interest in the well-being of the men, but there is little evidence that he did anything other than keep his head down. We'll be talking to James Metcalfe, health and safety, and Stan Innes, the biosecurity guy, later this evening. The chap we really want a word with, one Austen Collier, a company director, is apparently not available. We're chasing that up.'

'Thanks Chris. The last reports for today are those from the crime scene, and an update from the vet team. Crime scene first.'

Ned George stood up. This was another new colleague that Greg did not yet know much about, so he looked at the lean and grizzled expert in black T-shirt and jeans with some interest. He knew a lot of crime scene investigators who dressed with the frequent need to pull on coveralls very much in mind, and clearly Ned George was another.

'Not a lot to report I'm afraid. As you can imagine, or as some of you have seen, we are dealing with a very contaminated environment. The whole place has been awash with people and both dead and alive turkeys, before and after the body was discovered. We've taken samples for exclusion purposes, but it's pretty much a waste of time. The men, whether that be work teams or management, appear to have been pretty much everywhere, and with few exceptions that applies to the Defra staff too. The only person who seems to have confined herself to the office is Mrs Pritchard. We've taken samples in the yard and in and around the gassing chamber. Some of those may back up the picture of the body being dragged to the chamber, but it's too soon to tell whether they are of human body fluids or turkey.'

The report from Emma, the Defra ROD, did not take long. There was a reflective pause as the team assimilated the information about overseas travel, then Greg made everyone jump as he clapped his hands together.

'Right. Next steps. Jim, you continue to follow up from Wayford Bridge. Someone has to come home there some time. Find out who owns it now. I also want to know where the men have gone who were living there. They can't have just disappeared into thin air. If need be, start from where they were working. Other poultry units might be a good start. Once we find them, we can ask some pertinent questions about their arrival in England, their pay, etc. It seems we might have two related crimes here: modern slavery, and murder. You lead on the slavery angle, and we'll keep in touch to make sure we don't miss any connections.

'Chris, you and I will interview James Metcalfe and Stan Innes. We may need a follow-up chat with Lukas too. We need to know more about Jonas' last movements, who he saw, who he spoke to, and any possible motive for his death. Was he just in the wrong place at the wrong time, or was he killed because of something specific to him?

'Jill, please chase down the information available from Stalham Poultry. Follow the paperwork. How were the men recruited and paid? Chase the links back to Stalham HQ if you can, and particularly this Austen Collier. Establish what links there are, if any.

'Go to it!'

Greg did not find the interviews with Metcalfe and Innes fruitful. The deadpan solicitor commissioned by Stalham Poultry made his reappearance, and both men stonewalled – presumably in response to instructions. Innes was adamant that his biosecurity was tight, and professed himself mystified by the outbreak. Metcalfe was equally confident about his health and safety procedures and denied knowing anything about the men's living conditions. Both denied seeing Jonas on that last evening, and both claimed to have left the farm before the gassing chamber was completely loaded. Frustrated, Greg called it a day and went home.

He found Isabelle curled up on the sofa before the huge TV, which was showing a disregarded episode of Holby City.

'Darling,' she said, as he kissed her on the forehead and sank down in the chair opposite. 'Bad day?'

He dropped his jacket on the floor beside him and sighed as he pulled his tie loose. 'Not bad, no, but long and hard. Are you watching this?'

'No, not really, it just followed what I was watching and I was too lazy to do anything about it. Have you eaten?'

'No. Don't worry, I'll get something in a moment.'

'Rubbish. I may not be the typical housewife, but on the rare occasions I am here, I can rustle up something for the man of the house at the end of a tiring day.'

'Not an omelette!' he shouted after her as she disappeared into the kitchen.

'Actually no,' she said with a smug grin. 'A casserole I defrosted earlier.'

'Miracles will never cease!'

Late as it was, the reheated casserole and microwaved jacket potato, washed down with a glass of red, hit all the right spots, and Greg retired to bed a happy man.

5

5 April 2018, new outbreak – new problems

The morning had started well for Emma Knight. At the early bird table meeting at the veterinary HQ in Bury St Edmunds, they had all noted good progress with the cull at Stalham Poultry, and plans for the subsequent cleanse and disinfection were signed off. The dead body aside, which she was more than happy to leave to the police, Emma had the feeling of a job well done and retreated to her borrowed office with a smile on her face. It was still there as she answered the phone with a cheery, 'Regional Operations Director, how can I help?' but her smile froze in place a second later.

'Oh bugger,' she said. 'I thought we'd managed to contain this one. How big is the affected flock again?'

'Only a hundred or so laying hens,' replied Jim Mackie. 'Well, less now of course. It seems they had a couple of deaths two days ago, thought nothing of it, and then they found a lot of dead hens when they went in this morning. They got their local vet in, but with the Stalham outbreak well publicised, they had few doubts about what they were facing and called us in at the same time. The hens are normally free range, but once the restrictions were imposed with the original outbreak, they kept them housed except for access to a small wired enclosure. Luckily their stocking density was low anyway.

'I don't think they'll have had access to wild birds, or that wild birds will have had access to their feed.'

'Tracing the link between them and Stalham is a priority,' said Emma. 'Obviously we need to know how it got there and whether it's spreading anywhere else. God help us if it is! We'll have the farmer's union screaming blue murder about the industry and the NHS ditto about human health. We need to impose a new movement order. I'll get onto that and I'll talk to the gassing team about moving a unit to the new location. Where is it again?'

'Right by the River Ant, hence the name Riverside Hens.'

'Ok.' She went to the ordnance survey map on the wall and marked the second outbreak with a second red pin.

'We'd better ask Trading Standards to do another on-foot survey round the new area for backyard hens,' she added. 'Any clues at all about mode of spread?'

'None at the moment. There're no shared staff. In fact Riverside Hens don't employ anyone. The family do all the work and they are gutted.'

'Feed deliveries?'

'Checked those. Different supplier and as far as we can see, no shared transport.'

‘Waste removal? Remember the case a few years ago where the problem was poultry waste being transported to a power generator for incineration?’

‘Yes, and no. This small site composts their waste and then either uses it themselves or sells it bagged as fertiliser.’

‘Bother. Well, we’ll just have to keep looking. Wildlife vector? Like the fox carrying carrion into a duck farm?’

‘You’re scraping the bottom of the barrel now. Given the hens have been housed or inside a wire enclosure, no I don’t think that’s likely. The biosecurity at this place seems pretty good. They’ve been careful, which makes it all the worse.’

Emma had hardly sat down again when the comms girl burst in to her office, waving papers.

‘Yes I’ve heard,’ Emma said. ‘Is it in the news already? Just when we thought we were coming out of the woods too. With the first cull complete, I’d just started to relax. Silly me! We’d better plan a press release and press briefing, just as soon as we’ve defined the new restricted area.’

And Emma went back to the phone.

Back at Riverside Hens Jim and Monica were talking to the tearful husband and wife team who had invested their all in the small specialist laying flock and associated enterprises.

‘It’s not just the money,’ said Tina Williams, looking over the fence towards the immaculate shed and surrounding pasture. ‘We’ve worked day and night to get this off the ground, and the hens are integral to everything else. Their fertiliser helps feed the soft fruit and veg, and we have a loyal following for their eggs. They’re very popular in guest houses round here. It's not just that they're local, but the green and blue ones look so pretty on a breakfast table. And being free range, the yolks are amazing.' She sniffed back the tears and wiped her face with a grubby fist.

There was little hen activity in the worst hit enclosure, and Jim knew there were a lot of sick and dying hens in there. It had hit this flock hard.

'Have you any idea where it could have come from?' he asked again.

Tina opened her mouth and her husband Nick frowned, but she went on. 'No I'm going to say it, Nick. It's the most likely answer.' She turned to Jim.

'Down by the river you'll find a sort of shack. It's just over our boundary, but the bloke who uses it crosses our land to get to it. He even has visitors sometimes. Visitors with four-by-fours. They park just off our track, then they cross our fields too. We've put signs up saying "no right of way" and "private land", but it makes no difference. I've been saying for weeks we should tackle him about it, especially since the movement restrictions were imposed, but Nick won't let me.'

Nick looked uncomfortable. 'I thought we should live and let live. There's no point setting someone like that off. He could be very difficult and his friends are probably worse.'

'Someone like what?' asked Jim.

'Poacher,' said Tina, succinctly. 'He's not just fishing down there. He's poaching. Whatever it is he's catching, he seems to sell quite a lot.'

'Quite a lot of what?'

Tina and Nick looked at each other again, and Nick shrugged. 'I suppose we've got nothing left to lose now,' he said. 'I think it's elvers. I've seen some traps that look like elver traps and I read somewhere they fetch nearly as much money per kilo as drugs. So you can see why I didn't want to stir things up with this chap. You can't put a whole farm and 100 hens into witness protection.'

Jim reached for his phone. 'I think this is one for the police,' he said, and dialled the contact number he'd been given by Greg Geldard.

Henrik always stood the early watch on a Thursday. He parked his Daihatsu in the privileged position, privileged for Coastwatch and lifeboat crew that is, on the grass by the Caister old lifeboat station, and let himself in through the back door. He was first to arrive so had to turn the alarm off, before he found his way past the old lifeboat, nodded as usual to the spooky figure of a crew member in old-style life jacket, and scrambled up the precipitous iron stairs to the Watch Station. As ever, the stairs were a bit of a challenge for elderly knees, and he negotiated them with some care, reflecting on the unfortunate conflict between the need for a good view of the beach, and the average age of the qualified watchkeepers. Like him, most were comfortably retired and filling in their time with voluntary roles. And also like him, most were not particularly agile any more. Everything had been left tidy by the last watch the day before, and he was just updating the log when his fellow watchkeeper arrived.

'Wotcha,' said Big Dave, as his head appeared through the hatch. 'All quiet? I'll put the kettle on.'

Henrik was still taking the covers off the big telescope and mounted binoculars. 'Haven't had much of a look round yet,' he replied. 'I've logged on to Shipfinder and there's nothing much in our patch. Just a couple of ships coming out of the main Yarmouth harbour.' As he spoke, he focused the big binoculars and did a sweep of the sea between the Caister shoreline and the wind farm. The early morning haar was lifting, the white turbine blades on the offshore wind farm turning lazily.

'Nothing out there except the wind farm support boat,' he said, then paused in his sweep of the beach. 'Wait a moment. There's something at the water's edge, down towards the holiday camp.'

'Dead seal?' asked Big Dave.

'Could be. Can't get a good look at it at this angle. I'll try the telescope.' He moved the telescope to the side window overlooking the dunes and the racecourse, and refocused it on the beach. After a bit of hunting about he found the bundle again, just where the waves were breaking.

'Oh boy, oh dear,' he said. 'Dave, I think we've got a floater.'

'No,' said Big Dave. 'Are you sure?'

'Not sure no, but it looks like it. Definitely not a seal anyway. Could be something like an old display model or scarecrow, but why would one of those get into the sea. We're going to have to take a look.'

'I'll go. Have you had one of these before?'

'No.'

'Nor me. Well, there's a first time for everything. I'll take the radio with me, and let you know what I find.'

'Sure you're ok to go?'

'Course I am…'

'Better get a move on then, before a dog walker beats you to it.'

Big Dave went back down the ladder, radio in hand, and puffed his way over the soft sand onto the harder stuff nearer the water's edge. It was easier going there, and he speeded up to where the gentle waves were washing over the tumbled pile of old clothes. Watching through the telescope, radio to his ear, Henrik saw him pause as he got closer.

'Dave to Base,' crackled the radio. 'I can see what looks like a foot. I'll go a bit closer to make sure. Keep listening.'

Henrik watched as Big Dave moved towards the figure in the water, then turned aside and threw up on the sand.

'Dave to Base,' said the radio again. 'It is a body. God, it's worse than I imagined. It's been in the water a while and fish or crabs have made a bit of a mess. From the clothes it looks like a man in working gear, but I can't be sure. I'll stay nearby and keep dog walkers away. Can you ring the police please, Henrik? Out.'

Henrik reached for the phone and dialled 999. 'Police, this is Caister Coastwatch. We've found a body on the beach. Seems to have come in on the tide.'

Put through to the police, he repeated his message. Then, 'No, I'm not on the beach myself, I'm in the Coastwatch station, at the top of the old lifeboat shed. My colleague is on the beach, keeping the public away. No, he hasn't touched anything. In fact he hasn't gone any closer than he had to. He thinks it's male, but the sea creatures have been at it.

'No, it shouldn't be at risk of drifting away just yet. The tide is still coming in. But we are almost at high tide. I wouldn't waste any time getting here if I were you.'

'We'll be with you as soon as we can,' said the voice.

'Come down by the old lifeboat station. But don't venture on to the soft sand at the end of the ramp unless it's a four-by-four. And park to the side just in case we get a call-out for the lifeboat.'

'Got you,' said the voice. 'I'll pass it on.'

Two police cars and an unmarked ambulance appeared shortly after. Two uniformed police and two apparent civilians went straight down to where Big Dave was sitting, an appropriate distance upwind of the body. Looking through the telescope, Henrik saw one of the plain-clothes personnel go straight to the body and inspect it closely without moving it. The other stood back to take photographs and the two uniformed constables began erecting crime scene tape. There was a shout from the bottom of the stairs and a becapped head emerged from the hatch.

'Constable Fellows,' he introduced himself. 'Are you the chap who rang this in?'

'That's me,' agreed Henrik. 'How can I help?'

'I just need to take some details from you – name, contact numbers, etc – and what time did you notice the body on the beach?'

'All recorded in our logbook,' said Henrik, and pushed it towards the policeman. 'You're welcome to take a copy. It records when Dave and I came on watch, the time we noticed the possible body on the foreshore and everything else we did.'

'Brilliant,' said Bob Fellows, taking his cap off. 'That saves a lot of time. I wish all witnesses were so organised.' He used his phone to take photos of the relevant pages and said,

'That'll do for now. We may need a certified copy later. I'll just whip down and report in to the station.'

'Is the body going to be removed soon?' asked Henrik. 'It's still quiet at present, but we do get a lot of dog walkers and joggers on this beach. And the tide is close to turning.'

Bob Fellows looked through the window. 'Looks like they're fetching it now,' he said.

Two dark-clad men from the unmarked ambulance were heading on to the beach with a wheeled stretcher.

'That won't be much use to them on the soft stuff,' remarked Henrik, and was soon proved correct as the two men puffed and stumbled back to the ramp with an occupied body bag on the stretcher.

The ambulance was replaced by yet another police car, as the scenes of crime officers headed for the location where the body had washed up and began a search for any other remains. Big Dave, thankfully relinquishing guardianship of the scene to the police, returned to the Watch Station and his much-delayed cup of strong tea.

Henrik handed him his special mug, the one that read 'Keep Calm, then Panic' and pushed him towards a seat. It was clear that Dave had been shocked by what he'd found, his face pale and his hands shaking slightly.

'Sorry you had to do that,' he said.

'Tell you what,' said Dave, 'the next one's yours. That was not pretty. Not pretty at all. The crabs or something had had his eyes and quite a lot of his face. The doctor said that the exposed areas always go first. Obvious I suppose if you think about it, but it's not something you do think about is it?'

'Did they say what they thought?' asked Henrik. 'Suicide? Fishing accident? Drowned asylum seeker even? There've been a few boat sightings recently. On the other hand, I've been thinking about where he washed up and looking at the tide tables. It seems most likely he went into the water further south, maybe even in the river, then came north on the current as the tide turned. That's what I told Constable Fellows anyway. I guess they'll have their own theories.'

'I said something similar,' said Dave, round the rim of his mug. 'But I don't think it was an accident. At least, not unless the accident involved a knife. The doc seemed to think there was a stab wound in his chest.'

There was a clatter of heavy boots on the metal stairs and two other heads appeared through the hatch.

'What have you two been up to?' asked the midday watch.

6

5 April, the search for the missing

Jim Henning was getting frustrated. No one had reappeared at the Wayford Bridge farm for more than 24 hours. No one. No one had come back to the – what in his mind he was calling – SOMOs or sheds of multiple occupancy. No one had come back to the farmhouse, but by lunchtime his worn patience was rewarded with a warrant to enter the property. More door knocking and calling at both front and back was rewarded with more silence, Steve Hall wielded the ram with energy and relish, and they were in.

The house was dark, silent and damp. Jim, Steve and Phil went through the ground floor rooms with some caution. All were clear of everything except shabby furniture, faded curtains and worn carpets.

'It looks like my gran's,' said Phil, 'only damper and dirtier. No one seems to have been here for years.'

Only the kitchen was different. There were dirty plates and mugs in the sink, a flyblown milk bottle on the big kitchen table, and a rather dried-up loaf on the dresser. Steve opened the fridge and found more milk and a catering size margarine tub. It was half full of rather crumby and rancid marge.

Jim raised an eyebrow. 'Not a great diet,' he remarked, 'but obviously someone was here recently.'

'Probably cleared out around the same time as the blokes in the sheds,' added Steve.

'Right. Let's check out upstairs.'

The upstairs rooms were a revelation. Here, the general air of faded farmhouse disappeared. All the bedrooms contained multiple mattresses, scantily covered with tattered blankets. But it was the clothes hanging from the picture rails that were the real shock.

'These are girls' clothes,' said Jim, aghast. 'And small girls at that.' He picked up a skimpy dress on a hanger and held it near him. 'This would fit my youngest, and she's thirteen. What the hell have we got here?

'Right, count the beds and let's get a rough idea of how many were living here, then we'll report in and get the SOCOs back.'

The total of beds and mattresses had reached twenty-four when Steve said, 'There's another door here, and more stairs.'

He went carefully up the narrow stairs to what was obviously the attic floor.

'Christ,' the others heard him say, and then, 'It's ok. No

one will hurt you. You're safe now. Honest. You're safe now.

'Boss, you need to get up here quick. And we need an ambulance.'

Jim went up the attic stairs two at a time. The door at the top now swung open, but there were new-looking heavy bolts on the outer side. Just inside the door, he could see Steve hunkered down, talking to a shape crouched on the floor close to the eaves at the far end of the attic.

'It's ok,' he kept saying. 'You're safe now. You're safe now.'

The shape made no move other than to shrink away as Steve tried to approach. From the doorway, all Jim could see was the top of a balding head, some straggling brown hair, and the shoulders of a grubby sweatshirt. The room stank. It was apparent that part of the reason was its unwashed occupant. Much of the remainder of the smell came from the bucket of human waste overflowing in the corner.

'Steve, stay where you are, and keep an eye on things. I'll ring for an ambulance.'

It took the paramedics some time to get close enough to the attic dweller to reassure him, and eventually sedate him in order to carry him down the stairs. One of them paused as he climbed back into the ambulance cab.

'We'll be taking him to the Norfolk and Norwich,' he said to Jim. 'He undoubtedly has some mental health issues, but he's also suffering from malnutrition and dehydration. He's probably in his early thirties, but to be honest it's hard to tell in his current state. He's clearly been badly neglected. He's skinny, filthy, and hasn't had a shave or a haircut in a long time. He also seems to find it hard to walk, but whether that's weakness due to hunger or just lack of exercise?' He shrugged. 'God knows how long he's been locked in that room.'

'Did you get a name?' Jim asked.

'No, not yet. We must be off. Is anyone coming with him?'

'Yes. Constable Hall will follow in a squad car. I need to report to the DCI, but it's likely we'll want him under guard at the hospital.'

The report from Jim reached Greg just as Jill Hayes rushed in, flushed with success and waving a piece of paper.

'Just a sec, Jill,' he said, and then, 'Go ahead, Jim.'

On speakerphone, Jim's voice echoed round the office.

'...The big shock was when we got into the attic. A man had been shut in there with the door bolted from the other side. He'd obviously been there some time. A waste bucket was overflowing and a water jug was empty. Presumably he'd been locked in there untended for the last 36 hours at least. The paramedics said he was suffering from malnutrition and dehydration. God knows who he is. They took him to the N&N and Steve Hall is with him, in case he can be persuaded to say something.'

'I think I know who he is,' interrupted Jill, 'or at least who he might be. That's what I was coming to say, boss. I found out who owns the farm. The previous owners were a Mr and Mrs Potter. They both died last year, only a couple of months apart. They had one son, Tom Potter, and he inherited the farm. The records show there was some involvement with social services when he was younger, related to a diagnosis of learning difficulties. Once he passed eighteen he seems to have dropped off their radar and is assumed to have been living at the farm. Presumably on his own since his parents' deaths. But he's not as old as all that. Only thirty-eight.'

'The poor sod,' said Jim over the speaker. 'He's been cuckooed.'

'Sounds like it,' said Greg, 'but let's check some facts before we jump to any more conclusions. Jill, you get hold of social services and see what their records tell us about Tom Potter. Jim, I assume you have the SOCOs at the farm.'

'Yes,' said the disembodied voice.

'Then can you get back here and get a full-scale hunt underway? We now have several scores of men and a possible twenty-four women missing.

Jim and Greg gathered all the team not working at Wayford Bridge, in the Ops room for a full-scale planning session. Alerted by a request for additional manpower, the Chief Super slipped quietly into the back of the room to observe. Greg offered her a chair at the front, but she waved it away.

'I'm fine here,' she said. 'Just want to be apprised of what's going on.'

'Right,' said Greg, with what the team were beginning to recognise as his trademark introduction. 'You've all heard Jim on what he found at Wayford Bridge. The challenge is to find the men and women who were previously housed in the sheds and farmhouse there. We have two ways of tackling this, and I think we need to employ both. We can look for their new accommodation and we can look for their places of work.

'Let's take the workplaces first. Jill has put together a list of possibilities including poultry processing plants, fruit and veg farms and packers, fish processing, shellfish harvesting, nail bars, massage parlours and car washes. The Gangmaster and Labour Abuse Authority has been very helpful, but we need local knowledge too. Team A, that's those of you by the window,' – they looked at each other and nodded – 'will be responsible for checking out everything you can on all those establishments. Report back to Chris. She's going to manage data collection and correlation.

'Team B – you lot by the noticeboard – you're going to check out the accommodation possibilities. Start with the hostels and homeless charities, in case they've picked up any information, but I doubt we'll find them there. Judging by Wayford Bridge, they'll more likely be cuckooing somewhere else remote. Or possibly in one of the poorer housing areas in Norwich or Great Yarmouth.

'Ok we've a lot to do. Get to it.'

7

6 April, cases collide

Wednesday morning and Greg was barely back in his office before the phone rang.

'Emma Knight, Regional Ops Director, Animal Health Emergencies,' said the pleasant voice on the other end. 'We haven't spoken before, but I have good reports of you from my team at Stalham Poultry. I'd like to thank you for your cooperation.'

'That's good to know,' said Greg, itching to put the phone down and get on.

'I'm afraid I haven't just rung to be polite,' said the voice, perceiving the note of hurry from Greg. 'We have another bird flu outbreak and there seem to be complications that may be of interest.'

Wondering why civil servants always used 'seem' and 'may' rather than 'are' and 'is', Greg said, 'I'm listening.'

'The new outbreak is on a small poultry unit close to the

River Ant. The owners have suggested the spread may be due to poaching.'

'I can see that may be a police matter,' said Greg rather dismissively, his mind full of murder, mayhem and modern slavery. 'I'll pass your message on to the local team.'

'You misunderstand me,' said Emma. 'The poaching is alleged to be of elvers – glass eels – and I've done some looking up. They're extremely high value, weight for weight similar in price to illegal drugs, and their trafficking is widely linked to organised crime.'

Greg sat down.

'You're right,' he said. 'That puts a different complexion on it. I'll send someone over to look into it.'

Although Greg didn't know it, his life was about to get more complicated still. Over at the Norwich Mortuary, Professor Bell from the UEA was just completing the post-mortem on the body retrieved from Caister beach. As was his custom, he'd begun the task in the early morning so he would be finished in time for hospital and lecturing duties later in the day. The mortuary attendants had respectfully laid out the body ready for his arrival at 0600. Respect was high on their agenda after the incident some years before, when a body hit by a high-speed train had been laid out across several adjacent tables and someone had already pre-completed the beginning of the report form with 'Cause of death – blunt force trauma'. Professor Bell had chastised the perpetrators for jumping to conclusions, and then forced them to watch while he completed a very lengthy and meticulous examination.

On this occasion he'd reached several interesting conclusions before he turned his attention to the victim's alimentary tract. Constable Bob Fellows had already made copious notes and was itching to get to the phone. He was well aware that two of the findings were crucial. Professor Bell had pronounced the cause of death to be from drowning, subsequent to a stab wound to the chest that could also have proved fatal had the victim not been dumped into water before he died from it. He had also, in passing, noted that the water in question was probably not sea water, but more likely river water. Bob was so distracted by these two findings that he was looking the wrong way when Professor Bell made his next discovery, but his 'Well, well, what have we here' pulled the constable's attention back to the messy end of the table.

Professor Bell was carefully teasing a cylindrical shape from the corpse's rectum.

'I believe what we have here is known in some circles as a Kinder Surprise,' he said.

Bob came closer to the table and watched as the Prof carefully unscrewed the end from the cylinder and decanted the contents into a clean dish.

'Well well,' said the Prof again. 'That's not at all what I was expecting.'

'Drugs?' asked Bob, craning his neck to see.

'No,' said the Prof. 'That's what I was expecting, but what we seem to have here is,' he paused as he unrolled a tight wad of paper, 'money. It's euros. 200 euro notes. Looks like 2000 euros in total.

*

Once Bob Fellows fed his news back to base, it was a matter of minutes before Margaret Tayler summoned Greg to her office. He was joined by Jim Henning, and another DI he didn't know.

'Sarah Laurence, from intelligence,' she introduced herself.

'I've asked you all to come in because we have a number of cases running in parallel and I think we need to share what we know. It may be that they're all connected, or at least, I don't think we should overlook the possibility.

'Greg, this started with your case, the death of a Lithuanian national in a turkey gassing chamber at Stalham Poultry, and developed into a case of possible modern slavery or illegal gangmaster activity, now being investigated by Jim.'

'I have an update on the Stalham death,' interrupted Greg. 'The results are through from the lab. The victim had received a blow to the head which would have resulted in unconsciousness before being placed in the gassing container.'

'To continue,' said Margaret, 'we now also have a further death by stabbing and drowning. For those of you who don't know, a body was washed up on the beach at Caister yesterday and was found to contain a substantial sum in euros in a container secreted in his intestinal tract. The pathologist's view is that he drowned in fresh to brackish water, not in sea water, therefore the presumption is he entered the water in the River Yare and then was washed out to sea, before coming to land at Caister.

'Plus, we have a further case of bird flu close to the River Ant, which has thrown up possible links with organised crime and the smuggling of glass eels. Are they linked? Your views, Sarah?'

'In my view we can't ignore a strong possibility that they are all linked,' she said. 'There are a number of possible threads:

'First, the Lithuanian link. At least one of the victims was Lithuanian, the second may have been, and we know, from the evidence of Lukas Jankauskas that at least some of the workers brought in from the Wayford Bridge accommodation were also Lithuanian.

'Second, and most powerful, the likely involvement of organised crime. The possible offences we have listed include illegal gangmaster or slavery activity, glass eel smuggling, possible people trafficking, and cuckooing. All these are crimes usually connected to large and well-organised gangs. I think therefore that we should assume all three cases are linked until we prove otherwise. The interesting question is, where is and who is the governing intelligence? Who is masterminding these operations, and why did they resort to murder? Until the first death at Stalham they'd apparently been operating successfully under the radar. Something must have triggered that rather stupid act. I think that if we find out why the man was killed in Stalham, we'll find out who is responsible for this whole chain of activity.'

Greg looked at her silently for a moment. She was a muscular woman, probably in her late thirties or early forties he estimated: features finely drawn and dark hair tied back in a neat bun at the nape of her neck. Next to her, the rather more matronly Chief Superintendent looked positively blousy, her soft fluffy mid-brown hair escaping in a cloud as normal.

'That's a really helpful summary,' he said, 'and should

help focus our investigations. On that basis, we should prioritise solving the murder at Stalham. I agree, that may expose the driving intelligence behind the other cases. On the other hand, we can't ignore the potential human cost to whomever was displaced from Wayford Bridge. Fortunately, all roads lead back to Stalham Poultry. My plan is that we should go back to the start. Reinterview everyone involved there, find out where the men come from on all their units across East Anglia, and where they live, pin down the elusive Mr Austen Collier and follow up on the information the Defra vets flushed out about movements on the continent.'

'Not forgetting the glass eels,' added Sarah. 'I know they may seem a bit niche, but you would be surprised just how valuable they are. If someone has been smuggling them out of Norfolk to the continent and we can find out how, the route used might tell us a lot about who. And if that's the case, perhaps your victim in Stalham found something that threatened to expose the whole business.'

Margaret clapped her hands together. 'Good,' she said. 'So we have a way forward. Greg will prioritise his investigation as he has outlined, back at Stalham Poultry in the first instance but also keeping an eye on the glass eels link. Jim will continue to seek out the missing workers from Wayford Bridge. You'll both keep Sarah in the loop and she will liaise out of county as needed. If this is as big as we think, there'll be implications for other forces. I'll do my best to free up more resource, but don't hold your breath. We're already spending a lot on this one and I'll need to go upstairs.'

*

Chris and the rest of the team were waiting eagerly when Greg and Jim returned with Sarah in tow. Performing introductions, Greg noticed that Chris' marmite effect was to the fore. While it would be going too far to refer to anyone as bristling, there was little warmth between the two women.

'Chris, where are we at with tracking down the elusive Mr Collier?'

'According to the latest message from Stalham HQ in Hellesdon, near the airport, he's just arrived back from an overseas visit to suppliers in Hungary, and has kindly offered to meet us at the Stalham Poultry rearing unit at the end of this afternoon, after he has "caught up with himself" back at the office.'

'Very kind of him. We'll go to see him in his office as soon as we've finished here. Say 1100? Good. Jill, can you also call Messrs Willis, Metcalfe and Innes, and ask them to be available for a chat this afternoon at Stalham?

'Ned, can you get your team back to Stalham and have another look round – this time, specifically for anything connected with these glass eels?

'Steve, can you meet me at Riverside Hens at the end of the day, say around 1700? I would like to get the feel of the place and ideally to meet their mysterious neighbour.'

Steve nodded and chipped in, 'I know him by repute. He's a rough character, but not I would have said a criminal mastermind.'

'Before we see him, do a bit of digging around the neighbourhood: how he is living, whether there are any signs of him having visitors, or excessive and unexplained supplies of money? We have a busy day ahead. Go to it.

'Jim, can you stay behind a second please.'

*

As the rest vanished about their tasks, Greg asked, 'Jim, what progress on the missing men and women? I don't want you to feel that angle is being sidelined. It worries me a lot, what has happened to them. It's one of the reasons I want to catch Mr Director Collier on the hop.'

'It's worrying me too,' said Jim, 'especially if the new body on the beach is connected, and the euros would seem to suggest a European link at the least. We checked the homeless charities and some of the obvious sites in town, but no sign yet. The workers on the other Stalham Poultry sites we've visited, well I'm just not sure what to think about them. Most are housed in locations similar to Wayford Bridge, but although they're a bit rough, they're not dirty or unsuitable, and the workers appear to be getting the minimum wage with only reasonable deductions for costs. And they were hired through a licensed gangmaster who also checks out, so what was happening at Wayford Bridge? Why was that so different? And we still don't know where those folk have gone. We have a couple of leads from regular informants, but I'm not holding my breath.' He sighed, 'We'll keep at it Greg, but for the moment I think we're grinding to a halt.'

Greg patted him on the shoulder sympathetically. 'It's tough when it's like that,' he said. 'I know it's not for want of trying. Stick at it, Jim. You'll get a breakthrough soon, I have every confidence. And, I think it would make sense if you took over the enquiry into the body on the beach. There's a good chance it's connected, and until we find it isn't, I'd like the two exercises to move in tandem. Is that ok with you? Margaret has said you can have a Sergeant Peters seconded to you. It seems he's worked with the gangmaster licensing folk before.'

'Margaret is it now?'

'It's what she told me to call her,' said Greg, to his annoyance feeling himself begin to blush. 'Bugger off, Jim.'

8

Poultry Enterprises

Wymondham to Hellesdon was only thirty minutes on a good day. This wasn't a good day, and it was forty-five minutes later when Greg and Chris pulled in to the main entrance of Poultry Enterprises Ltd, a short distance from Norwich Airport. As they arrived at the security barrier a big helicopter clattered off overhead, en route to gas rigs in the North Sea. The noise made communication from car to gatehouse difficult, and it took two attempts before the guard got the message that they were here to see Mr Collier, no they didn't have an appointment and no, they were not prepared to go away without seeing him, no matter how busy he was. More inaudible chat on a phone and the guard lifted the barrier, waving them towards the few visitor parking spaces near the door marked 'Reception'.

Chris pulled up with an impatient flourish, and parked neatly in the bay nearest the door.

'If there's one thing that gets on my tits,' she remarked, 'it's men who think they're so important everything has to dance around them.'

'Not that we're prejudging anyone,' he replied.

And Chris said, 'Of course not, sir. Just saying.'

Greg hid a grin as he followed Chris up the short flight of steps into reception. Today she was wearing smart black trousers topped by an orange and pink, asymmetrically hemmed kaftan-style top and a black jacket. She looked a little like a traffic cone in a suit. Some day, he promised himself, he would ask about the vivid colour sense, but not just yet. Rather more urgent and potentially equally sensitive was a discussion about what she had against Sarah Laurence. There were only so many dangerous conversations he was willing to have in one day.

They were kept kicking their heels in the reception area for nearly half an hour. Chris' emotional temperature was mirroring her outfit by the time they were allowed upstairs by a receptionist with fingernails so long it was surprising she could reach her workstation keys. Greg would have been feeling the same, except one glance at their interviewee and he knew the delay had been both deliberate and a ploy to put them off balance. It wasn't going to work.

'Good of you to see us, Mr Collier,' he said to the man silhouetted against the bright window behind the desk and, without waiting to be asked, pulled one of the chairs on the visitor side of the desk round the corner, so the light fell over his shoulder rather than full in his face. He sat down and took out his voice recorder. 'I hope you won't mind if we record this interview. Sergeant Mathews will be taking notes, but a recording is so helpful. Oh, sorry, I haven't introduced myself. I'm Detective Chief Inspector Greg Geldard, Norfolk Police.' He didn't hold out his hand.

Wrong-footed, the man sat down behind the desk and leaned back to fiddle with the blind behind him. The light faded from glare to a more comfortable glow. Chris took the seat across the desk and got out her notebook.

'This really isn't very convenient,' the man said, in a pompous tone. 'I've a great deal to do today and I told your office I would come to see you at Stalham later in the day. I had thought such a simple message would get through. Perhaps I should have spoken to the Police and Crime Commissioner instead. I'm well acquainted with him.'

'Oh, the message got through all right,' said Greg with a cheery grin, 'but we have a great deal to do today as well, and in these circumstances we take priority. And by all means speak to your friend the Commissioner, but it won't make a jot of difference. He never interferes in operational issues.'

The man behind the desk swelled like an enraged toad and Greg was interested to note that the similarity did not end there. He had receding hair which left him with an extended forehead, from which he had a habit of sweeping away the non-existent hair, as though he had never adjusted to its loss. His pale blue eyes were slightly protuberant and his lips were unpleasantly dark, as though wearing lipstick. In fact, so persuasive was this impression that Greg took a closer look to make sure the colour was in fact entirely natural. It did seem to be.

'Well I hope you have a good reason for rearranging my entire day,' Collier snapped.

'Isn't murder a good enough reason?' asked Chris with a deceptive mildness.

'Oh, well, of course I'm aware of the very sad death at the poultry unit,' he replied, 'but I don't see how I can help. I don't work there. Moreover, I hadn't appreciated it had been definitely confirmed as murder. I thought there was a possibility it was a terrible accident.'

'Unfortunately that's not the case,' said Greg briskly. 'We have confirmation that the victim was stunned by a blow to the head before arriving in the gassing container. So unless he stunned himself, then dragged himself across the yard and into the container, subsequently sealing the container from the outside behind himself, it was not an accident nor even an elaborate suicide. It was murder.'

'No! How dreadful,' said Mr Collier, with mechanical smoothness. 'But I still don't see how I can help.'

'We'll get to that,' replied Greg. 'First of all, can you confirm your name, date of birth, home address and role within the company.'

'Austen Ralph Collier. 23 September 1965. Broads Edge, Neatishead, Norfolk. Company Director.'

'Director of what?'

'The company,' he replied tartly. 'What else?'

'No, you misunderstand me, sir,' replied Greg with ostentatious patience. 'What is your particular area of expertise or responsibility in the company? Finance? HR?'

'I suppose it's best described as Operations.'

'Covering what precisely?'

'Well, more or less everything to do with getting things done,' he replied.

Chris could feel the smugness rolling off him like haar off a winter sea, and wriggled in her seat with irritation. Greg shot her a look, and she stopped.

'I negotiate with suppliers, agree contracts with outlets, monitor performance at different sites and so on, and so on.'

'Good. Let's take those one by one. Suppliers of what?'

'Everything,' claimed the toad behind the big desk. 'Overseas suppliers of young birds for fattening, feedstuffs and other materials for rearing, energy supplies – you name it I deal with it.'

'Personnel?' asked Chris softly. 'Who procures the workforce?'

Austen Collier switched his attention, surprised she had spoken.

'Mostly that's the responsibility of the HR department. I would have thought you would know that,' he said condescendingly.

'Oh yes, I know that,' she replied. 'But "mostly" is the word that interests me. You see, the HR team told me yesterday when we spoke on the phone, that they recruit for management positions, on the rare occasions when they do recruit, and they make payments of wages, etc. But they don't procure all the manual workforce. I'm using their term you understand. They used to do all the staff recruitment but more recently, since Poultry Enterprises expanded into the Stalham site, it appears that the poultry worker teams for that site have been provided by a gangmaster under a contract arranged by you, Mr Collier.'

'And? Your point is?'

'Did you arrange the gangmaster contract?'

'I expect so.'

'You did or you didn't, Mr Collier. Did you arrange the contract that supplied the men working at Stalham Poultry?'

'It's likely. I'd have to check.'

'Perhaps you would like to check then, Mr Collier. And while you're at it, perhaps you could confirm their terms and conditions of appointment, especially where they were to live and how much they were paid.'

'Living arrangements are a matter for the gangmaster,' he responded. 'And they'd be paid the minimum wage or a little more depending on their skills.'

'If living arrangements were the concern of the gangmaster, why were they paying you for their living costs?'

'Presumably because the gangmaster was charging us and we needed to recoup the cost, but I'd have to look at the detail of the contract to be sure.'

'We look forward to seeing those details,' replied Chris. 'Perhaps you could send for it now?'

Collier looked sulky and answered, 'Perhaps you'd better ask your other questions first, then I can get on with some work while the office girls look out the paperwork for you.'

Greg took over. 'No problem,' he said. 'Where were you on the night of 1 April?

'What?'

'The question is perfectly clear. Where were you on the night of 1 April?

'I'll have to check in my diary.'

'Really? That's only three days ago.'

'I'm a very busy man. I have many commitments. Ah yes,' he said flipping through his iPhone screens, 'I was at home that evening.'

'Will your wife confirm that?'

'I'm afraid not. I think she was out. I spent the evening alone.'

'And what car do you drive, Mr Collier?'

There was a long pause, while the toad seemed to hold an internal debate.

'Look, what is this? I'm beginning to think I need my solicitor present. Am I a suspect?'

'At this point we are just seeking to rule you out, Mr Collier. You will note I haven't cautioned you. Yet. But we can continue this at the station if you prefer.'

Greg raised his eyebrow and his subject shuffled papers on his desk.

'Your car?'

'A Range Rover. Green.'

'Registration?'

'A1 COL.'

'Thank you. We'll pick up that contract on our way out, if that's ok with you, Mr Collier. Oh, and we may need to speak to you again.'

Back in the car, Greg flicked through the paperwork they had collected, while Chris rang the office with the number plate details of Mr Collier's car.

'Now to the poultry unit?' she asked.

'Yes please. Thanks Chris.'

'They'll check the ANPR for the cameras on all the routes in and out of Stalham for that night. We should know by tonight if he drove there.'

'You don't believe him then?'

'No I don't.'

'Nor me. Have them check the roads around Riverside Hens while they're at it.'

9

Turkeys to Hens

Arriving at the Stalham Poultry unit, Greg and Chris were surprised to see a low-loader in the yard and a frenzy of activity round it. Greg stuck his head out of the window and hailed the nearest workman.

'What's going on here?'

'The cull's finished and we're removing the gassing chambers.'

'I hope the SOCOs had finished in the yard.'

'No idea, mate. I suggest you ask one of them,' pointing to the two Defra vets coming round the corner, clipboards in hand.

'Hi Jim, Monica,' called Greg. 'How's it going?'

They waved and came over to the car.

'Going well for us,' said Jim.

And Monica chipped in, 'Cull finished, about to start on C&D.'

'Clean and disinfect,' translated Jim, 'provided of course we get the go-ahead from your chaps.'

'Any idea where my chaps are?'

'One in the offices, the other, I saw him last in the quarantine area.'

'Remind me which that is.'

'It's the space where the workers come in to change into work clothes. There are strict rules about outdoor clothes one side of the room, shower, changing facilities, and work clothes the other side. It's part of the biosecurity precautions. You may not have had a good look last time you were here, as we were still restricting access to avoid cross infection.'

'And the biosecurity has been pretty good here,' said Monica. 'At least, I've seen a lot worse.'

'So, how did the bird flu get in then?'

'Don't know. We'll be interested in anything your chaps find that might shed some light. We've had confirmation that the strain is identical to the one in Poland, but no idea yet how it got here or where the breach in biosecurity was. Their chap Stan Innes is spitting feathers. He's furious at the mere suggestion someone broke his rules.'

'We're about to talk to him now. I'll let you know if we turn up anything that might help you.'

'And likewise,' said Jim.

'I'll check in with Ned first,' said Greg. 'Chris, can you set us up in one of the offices his team have finished with, then line up our interviewees.'

'Any preference as to order?'

'Let's have the biosecurity chap first, then health and safety. Pete Willis last.'

'On it,' said Chris and locked the car doors, her notebook and recorder in hand.

When Greg reached him, Ned George was just finishing up, stripping off his paper coverall and overshoes in the yard.

'Anything of interest?'

'Hard to say at this point, but we've a lot of samples and traces to analyse. Hope the budget stands up to it. One thing I'm taking a bit of a punt on,' and he waved to a plastic crate sitting in the biggest sample bag Greg had ever seen.

'What is it?'

'A box. Yes I know,' he laughed at Greg's expression, 'you can see that. But it's a box with an odd smell, and I'm not talking metaphorically.'

'What sort of smell?'

'That's just it, I'm not sure. Sort of earthy and slightly fishy, but not really fishy. Anyway, it also has some traces of liquid in the bottom. I've taken samples and I'll be taking more. We've found a couple of fingerprints on it, so we can check those against the ones we've taken from staff.'

'Any other traces of blood?'

'Can't tell you yet. As I said we've sampled everything. We'll have to see what the analysts can find.'

'Right. Good, thank you.'

Stan Innes was bristling and defensive. He sat forward in his chair, hands clenched on his knees, white knuckles showing.

'I've been through this so many times. There was nothing wrong with our biosecurity measures. The staff were trained and their performance monitored. It was made very clear to them that a failure in biosecurity might well mean the sack. Look, I even had the advice and the posters translated into Lithuanian for God's sake, to make sure there was no confusion.

'And it's not very complicated. You come in one side of the room. You strip, cross the room, shower and dress in the working kit. Normal outdoor clothes one side never touch working clothes on the other. I generally find that once folk are in the routine it becomes automatic. They don't have to think about it any more than they think about breathing. Part of that is how you set the space up. It prompts good behaviour. For example, there is a physical barrier across the centre of the room. You sit on it to take your shoes off, then swing your legs over to the clean side to put your clean white wellies on. You can no more just walk in with dirty shoes, than you could walk on a kitchen table.'

'And yet, the disease got in.'

He sighed and sat back. 'Yes I know. And it beats me. I suppose someone could have done it deliberately but why? Anyone working here has too much to lose. The only other possibility, to me, is someone not familiar with our biosecurity measures. But who? Even Mrs Pritchard knows the basics, which is precisely why she never goes beyond the offices.'

'Perhaps our fingerprint experts will find something that might suggest an unusual visitor?'

'You know, I really do hope so, but I doubt it. One of our rules is a thorough cleaning of the quarantine space every day. It will have been cleaned every evening. Not much chance of fingerprints.'

*

The discussions with Jim Metcalfe and Pete Willis were repetitive and, as Greg remarked, dull in both senses of the word, being both boring and unilluminating. They stuck firmly to the line they had taken previously: procedures at Stalham Poultry were perfect, the men perfectly trained, and there were never any breaches of either biosecurity or health and safety. A scrutiny of the accident book would seem to bear them out, although Chris was doubtful.

'It's too empty,' she commented, ruffling through the pristine pages. 'You're not telling me there's any farm environment where no one ever gets a cut, or a bruise, never trips or falls, never does something stupid up a ladder or with machinery. It's too good to be true. If we were to believe this, we'd have to conclude that the most dangerous environment on this site was Mrs Pritchard's office. And all she's reported is a paper cut and a trip over a filing cabinet drawer she left open herself!'

'You sound as though you're speaking from experience,' remarked Greg.

'To an extent I am. My family are farmers. And with the best will in the world, when you're handling machinery, livestock and dangerous chemicals, accidents do happen. The whole point of recording even the minor mishaps is to help prevent something worse, and with agriculture having the worst record in the country for workplace deaths, that's important.'

'Has it? I didn't know that.'

'Yes it has. And this sort of ignoring everything because we're all big boys here is just not on.'

'So, you think the empty accident book is more of a sign of a macho culture than a safe workplace.'

'I do, when you take it together with a health and safety officer who goes home with a potentially lethal activity still underway on his site.'

'That's a good point, Chris. Remind me, what time did he leave?'

'He states at 2130, and that fits with the record kept by the officer on the gate. The lead poultry worker, Lukas, didn't leave until 1015. Metcalfe's version is that in his view the responsibility for the gassing lay with Defra and the Defra specialist. That may be so but personally, if my staff were still working, I would've expected some senior management to stick around. Neither Metcalfe nor Willis did.'

'It may be worse than just macho,' said Greg, reflecting on the other evidence relating to the workforce. 'I think it has more to do with an underlying attitude that the men working here had little or no value. No one cared how they lived, what they were paid, or even it seemed, whether they lived or died.'

He was interrupted by Chris' phone.

'Sorry, sir,' she said, 'I should take this.'

There was a silence, while Greg went back through his notes of the recent interviews and Chris listened to the tiny voice on the other end of the phone. After a while she made one short note on her pad, then rang off. She looked excited.

'Now, that is very interesting indeed. Very. It's the data from the ANPR cameras on the routes between Irstead, Hellesdon and Stalham for the night of 1 April. Incidentally, the chaps have worked really hard on this. They must be bog-eyed by now.'

'Yes, absolutely,' said Greg, 'but what've they turned up?'

'First, they've logged A1 COL moving between Hellesdon and Irstead in the early evening, around 1820 to 1900. They couldn't find anything on that car later that evening. It seems it stayed in Irstead until the following morning.

'Oh,' said Greg, disappointed.

'No, it gets better. Some bright spark noticed something else. A car with a similar number plate moving on the main road near Stalham. The number was F1 COL. He did some checking, and a car with that plate belongs to a Mrs Fiona Collier, of Broads Edge, Neatishead. It was in the vicinity of Stalham around 2230, then back on the road, heading in the opposite direction, between 0100 and 0200.

'Now why was Mrs Collier driving to and from a poultry unit in the early hours of the morning?'

'Unless it wasn't Mrs Collier at all, but Mr Collier in his wife's car. Chris, we need to make some enquiries about Mrs Collier's movements, then we need another chat with her husband, this time under caution.'

10

Great Yarmouth

The seaside resort that was Great Yarmouth was having a busy day for so early in the year. Some tourists were wandering the seafront and Sea Life had queues, mainly of grandparents, restraining accompanying grandchildren with varying degrees of success as they waited for the opportunity to see sharks, turtles and other attractions. Judging from the fluffy and brightly coloured items clutched in the hands of the smaller visitors as they exited further along the road, the gift shop was doing well too.

In the centre of town, the marketplace was heaving with tourists, locals and predatory herring gulls enjoying chips with everything. A few early cruisers were on the river heading towards Bredon Water while down Stonecutters Way there was a long line of folk waiting outside a nondescript office. It didn't look much of a tourist attraction, but a closer scrutiny would reveal a different function. Citizens Advice Great Yarmouth was also having a busy day.

Aileen, on reception, was handing out forms and clipboards as fast as she could go to the sudden rush of people that followed the opening of the door. This was only her second week of volunteering, and she was feeling the pressure. A lifetime career as a librarian had, she thought, prepared her for a mixed bunch of customers; but nothing had prepared her for the sheer desperation of some of the CA clients.

'If you could just fill in as much as you can,' she was saying. 'The more you can explain what help you want, the quicker we can help you.

'Yes, I know you filled one in last week,' she said to another client, 'but we still need your consent to hold your information if you want us to help.'

And to another client, 'Hello Mary, nice to see you again. I'll just get someone down to help you with your form.'

A quick call on the phone and an adviser trotted down the stairs to take Mary on one side and help her complete the necessary. Mary was a regular and, as the receptionist well knew, could read little and write less.

The first rush over, Aileen sat back behind the reception desk and started collecting the completed forms. New clients were registered on the system, old ones updated, and interview times allotted. As usual, there were more people than there were interview slots available, and some of them were panicking about rapidly approaching deadlines for benefit claims. Rob came down from the office to help triage urgent problems from those that could wait for another day. Aileen was hesitating over one scantily completed form, and handed it to Rob with a raised eyebrow.

The form was completed in a hand that suggested the owner did not write much, and the space for outlining the problem that had brought him there just said 'in my house not want be'.

'Whose is the form?' asked Rob quietly and Aileen indicated a small man sitting in the corner by the door. He was dressed only in sweatshirt and tracksuit bottoms, with tattered trainers, no socks, on his feet. No coat or jacket against the brisk wind. He had a beanie in his hands and he was turning it round and round as he waited. His hair was long around a central bald patch and shaving was not something he had done recently.

Rob took the form over to him and pulled another chair over. 'Would you like to come upstairs and I'll see how I can help?' he said.

'No. Need Bill,' said the man.

'I'm sorry, we don't have an adviser named Bill,' said Rob. 'If you can come with me I'll do my best to help.'

'No,' said the man again, 'not me. Bill. Need Bill.'

'I'm sorry,' said Rob again, but the man interrupted him, becoming agitated and his voice getting louder.

'NO! Not me. Need talk to Bill. You need to talk to Bill.'

'Oh I see,' said Rob, enlightened. 'You want me to talk to Bill. But where is he?'

The man looked round the room and dropped his voice to say, 'Outside. Round the corner.'

'Well, why don't you ask him to come in and I'll see you both?'

'He won't come in here with all these folk. He's too frit.'

'Of what?'

'Too frit,' said the man again.

'Ok,' Rob looked at the form, 'John isn't it? Ok John. How about you and I go to find Bill and then bring him in through the back door. That way he won't have to come in through reception. What do you think?'

'Ok,' said John and stood up.

'Hold on,' said Rob, 'I'll just get the key for the back door, then we'll go and find Bill.'

He went quickly to Aileen and, reaching behind the desk for the key, said, 'I've got a feeling about this one, Aileen. I think there's something wrong. I'm going to take this chap and his friend into Interview Room One and I'll see what I can find out. Can you just let Sara know what's happening?'

She looked up quickly. 'Are you ok?'

'Yes fine. Not that kind of problem. I'll keep you briefed.'

The short man in the tracksuit and sweatshirt had gone, but when Rob went swiftly to the front door he found him just outside.

'Here,' he said. 'Round here,' and he went round the corner of the building into the alley behind. Following, Rob found a man leaning on the side wall in the alley. He was tall and lean, with a labourer's hands and wearing a donkey jacket over green overalls with a logo on the pocket. He stood up sharply as Rob came round the corner and looked as if he might run away.

'S'ok Bill,' said John. 'This uns one of the nice chaps. He's ok. He'll see us right.

Won't you?' he said to Rob.

'I'll certainly try,' he answered. 'Would you like to come in Bill and have a sit down in one of our offices. You can come in this way,' indicating the battered old back door, 'and up the stairs to our office.'

'That's ok,' said John. 'It's ok isn't it, Bill? I told you these uns be ok.'

The man nodded and followed Rob through the door and up the stairs, John bringing up the rear. Rob settled them both in Interview Room One. It was one of the small rooms at the back with only a skylight. With the door closed, the atmosphere immediately became rather ripe. It was apparent that one or both of the two guests had not bathed any time recently. Rob went to push the door ajar, but Bill immediately made a sound of objection and Rob subsided into his seat by the desk.

'No problem,' he said. 'We'll keep the door closed. Only it might get a bit warm. Now, how can I help?'

John looked at Bill, who looked back silently. Then John looked at Rob.

'He don't speak much,' volunteered John. 'Not as you can understand any road.'

'Ah,' said Rob, looking at Bill, who looked back impassively. 'Do you speak English?' he asked.

'Little,' said Bill, with a heavy accent.

'Would an interpreter be helpful?' asked Rob, and Bill looked at John for help but got none. John seemed to feel that having got Bill there, he had done his bit.

'What language do you speak?' asked Rob, pursuing his hunch. Bill looked at John again and said slowly, 'Lithuanian.'

'Great. We can help with that,' and Rob reached for the phone. He dialled a number, gave the respondent a code and stated 'Great Yarmouth Citizens Advice', then gave his own name and said 'Lithuanian.' Then he sat back and put the phone on speaker.

A voice issued from the phone in Lithuanian and Bill immediately brightened as he replied at some length.

Rob leaned forward, and said into the phone, 'Thank you for your help today. As you have discovered, we have a Lithuanian-speaking client here. Could you ask him his name please, and how we can help him?'

The voice on the phone chattered on for a moment, then Bill replied with some caution evident in his voice.

There was a pause, and the interpreter on the phone line said, 'His name is Matis. He doesn't want to give a surname. He says he's been forced to live in someone's house, someone named John, and has only just escaped. He wants to go home but he has no money and no papers.'

There was another pause, while Rob looked at John.

'S'right,' said John cheerfully. 'We got out today while they weren't lookin. I knew to come here. I knew you'd find us some help. I bin here afore.'

'While who wasn't looking?' asked Rob, forgetting about the interpreter on the phone. He was taken aback therefore when she interpreted his question and Matis/Bill answered.

The interpreter said, 'Matis says he was taken to John's house by the, I think he said gangmaster, and told to stay there.' Matis interrupted and she went on. 'There were ten of them but one disappeared a couple of days ago. Matis doesn't think John had any say in the matter. He was forced to stay in one room until Matis and his friends let him out.'

'S'right, said John again. 'They let me out.'

The silence in the room was echoed by a parallel silence on the end of the phone, then Rob said to the interpreter, 'We need to establish all the facts we can, then I'll need to involve the authorities. Are you ok to help me?'

'Yes,' she said. 'I'll help all I can. But can I just warn you of something? Tread warily around authorities. He'll be nervous of the men in blue coats.'

'Understood,' said Rob. 'Let's get all the facts we can first, then I'll address that issue carefully. First of all, I think some coffee and biscuits. Can you ask Matis if he would like some?'

After an enthusiastic yes, Rob stuck his head round the door and shouted down the corridor, 'Sara, any chance of coffee and biscuits?'

Rob watched as the hot strong coffee and sugary biscuits put some colour into the thin face of the man opposite. John was enjoying them too, although his face was far from thin and he did not exhibit the signs of long-term hunger in the way Matis did.

'How long have you been staying at John's house?' he asked, and waited for the to and fro with the interpreter before he got the answer.

'Three days.'

'And before that?'

'On a farm somewhere.'

'Where have you been working?'

'On a poultry farm, with turkeys. But now in a,' the interpreter hesitated and then said, 'I think it translates as processing plant.'

'Meat processing?'

'Yes.'

'How can I help?'

'I want to go home to Lithuania. But I have no money and no papers. I have nowhere to go in England that is safe.'

'Haven't you been paid while you were working?'

'Yes, but they took most back to pay rent and for food. And for work clothes. There wasn't much left over.'

'Were you all treated like this?'

'Yes. I think so.'

'Why didn't you object?'

'Some did. One of us, Tomas, ran away two days ago. He had some money hid and he said if he got home he would send help. I don't know what happened to him.'

'You know that how you have been treated is illegal in this country?'

Silence, then a spate of words to the interpreter and she said, 'He says the men who brought them here and made them work are very bad men. Very dangerous men. He says they are not men to cross and he is afraid of them, not just here but also at home in Lithuania.'

There was a silence as Rob thought hard, then he said to the interpreter, 'All sorts of alarm bells are ringing for me. We can help find somewhere for Matis to stay, we can supply him with food vouchers and so on, but none of that addresses the central issue. I'm pretty sure a crime has been committed here. Several crimes by the look of it. Modern slavery, illegal gangmaster activity, cuckooing at John's house, and that's just for starters. I need to help Matis and John report this to the police. Can you explain that to him?'

At the mention of the word police, Matis jumped to his feet and John looked up from where he was dunking his ginger nut into his milky coffee.

'He won't like that,' he said. 'I tole him he should go to the cops but he wun't.'

The interpreter interrupted in soothing tones and spoke at some length. Matis replied and sat down, and the dialogue went on for some time, then the interpreter came back to Rob.

'He's agreed to stay and he's agreed to talk to the police. I was able to tell him about my dealings with the police and I think I reassured him a bit. I am Lithuanian myself. Also,' she added, 'he likes that you are going to help him report the crime, not just take it all out of his hands.'

'Right, that's good. Thank you for your help. Are you able to stay on the line until the police come?'

'Yes of course. I'm not ringing off with the story half done,' she replied.

Rob stuck his head into the corridor again and shouted for Sara.

'Sara will sit with you and get some more details from you,' he explained, 'while I go and organise some lunch and ask the police to come here. Then I'll help you explain everything. Is that ok?'

Matis and John nodded. Rob swopped seats with Sara, then stuck his head round the door.

'Forgot to ask, is there anything you don't eat?'

Matis smiled wanly and shook his head.

John said firmly, 'Not cheese. Hate cheese.'

'Ok, not cheese it is. Back soon.'

*

Rob was surprised how quickly he got a response from the police. He had anticipated a long wait and lots of arguing with civilian telephone operators before he got anywhere, but as soon as he mentioned modern slavery and turkeys he was put straight through to a police sergeant.

'We'll be straight round,' he said. 'Try not to lose them. We've been looking for them for days.'

They were as good as their word and Rob was surprised again when a plain-clothes detective and a uniformed constable were ushered upstairs from reception.

He met them in the corridor and explained, 'The room is a bit small I'm afraid, but we've got an interpreter on the phone and you *will* need her help as Matis doesn't speak much English. As most of our clients have left now, I suggest we leave the door open and one of you stay in the corridor if that's ok. I know Matis would like me to be with him at least for the moment.'

'That's fine,' said the plain-clothes man. 'I'm Detective Inspector Jim Henning and this is Constable Steve Hall. We're very grateful for your help. Let's get started shall we, and see how we get on.'

Sidling into the small room sideways, Jim introduced himself to Matis, John and the live speakerphone. Sara murmured her excuses and made herself scarce. The room was strewn with the remains of a meal, packets of crisps, sandwiches (not cheese) and cans of coke all over the desk. Jim sat down in one of the remaining chairs and Rob in the other, while Constable Hall perched on a chair in the corridor.

'Sandwich?' asked Matis, proffering a couple of packets.

'Don't mind if I do, thank you,' said Jim, selecting an egg and cress. 'Had no lunch today,' he lied. 'That's very kind of you.'

His guess was correct. Matis visibly relaxed as the feared policeman took a substantial bite out of the sandwich and leaned back in his chair. John, on the other hand, looked a little aggrieved and made haste to grab the last sandwich before it was given away too.

'I'm so pleased to see you, Matis,' said Jim. 'We've been trying to find you and your colleagues ever since we saw the accommodation at Wayford Bridge Farm and no one came home to it.'

The phone translated the comment, but Matis still looked puzzled.

'Here,' said Jim, producing his phone and scrolling through some photos. 'Was this where you were staying?'

Matis took the phone and looked through the photos of the farmyard, the sheds, and the accommodation inside.

'Yes,' he said. 'I lived there for six months.'

'Did you go straight from there to John's house?'

'No, not quite. That evening, two, three days ago, we were picked up from work but not taken home. We spent the night in a shed, a sort of warehouse, near the river. One of the men fetched us a burger and chips each, then locked us in with the vans. We slept where we could and were taken to work the next day. Most of us that is. Some said that evening they hadn't gone to their usual place. Then we were taken to John's place.'

'Were there any girls with you?'

'No. Just men.'

‘Where did you work?’ asked Jim.

‘I usually worked on a poultry farm, but that day I was taken to a factory, a processing plant, and worked there instead, mainly carting boxes about and loading lorries. Some of the others at the big place, Wayford Bridge you said,’ he stumbled over the name, ‘they’d been working in a car wash, somewhere near a village. Several worked there.

‘One man, Tomas, escaped while we were at the warehouse, but when we arrived at John’s place they got very strict about locking doors and keeping an eye on us.’

Jim exchanged a look with Steve and asked, ‘What did he look like, the man who escaped?’

‘About my age, about my shape, dark hair. Have you seen him?’

‘I’m not sure. We may have. Can I come back to that, Matis? First, can you talk me through how you arrived in the UK and exactly where you have been working?’

After half an hour of intensive questioning, the telephone interpreter was sounding exhausted, the crisps had all gone and even the cola supply had run out. Jim looked at Matis, John and then at Rob.

‘I think that’s as much as we can do for now,’ he said, ‘and you have been amazing,’ he said to the telephone. ‘Can you ask Matis if he is willing to come to the station with me? I would like to take a formal statement, and we can provide him with a shower, clean clothes, and somewhere safe to stay. Will you stress to him that he is not under arrest in any shape or form. He is the victim of a crime, or several crimes, and we want to bring these criminals to justice.’

He hesitated, then he went on, 'Can you also explain to him that we found a body on the beach yesterday. When he is rested, we would like him to take a look at it for us, just in case it is the man Tomas who escaped from the warehouse.'

There was a pause, then a torrent of rapid Lithuanian on the phone, followed by a few words from Matis.

'He says yes. Yes to both,' said the tired interpreter. 'And he asks, what about the men at John's house? And what about John?'

'Tell him we already have the house under observation, and if anyone returns to it this evening, we will be ready. As for John, we will talk to him some more at the station and make sure he is looked after until we can return him home safely.'

11

By the Ant, morning of 7 April

The proprietors of Riverside Hens looked distraught and exhausted. With only small numbers of poultry involved, the cull team had already been and gone. Even the Defra vets, Jim and Monica, had completed their reports and departed, promising to return to check the cleanse and disinfection processes. Now the paddocks were empty, the sheds echoing and bare. Greg and Chris looked round, noting the immaculate fencing, the neatly gravelled drive and pathways, the professionally lettered signs advertising fruit and eggs, and the boot-dipping troughs at the entrance.

Nick followed his gaze, and snorted. 'Much good that did us,' he said. 'We were so careful with our biosecurity, even if we did have visitors calling for eggs and so on.'

He sat down next to his wife on a straw bale near the gateway. There were the tracks of tears on Tina's dusty face, her hair pulled back in an untidy ponytail and the 'Riverside for Happy Hens' sweatshirt she was wearing was also dusty and grubby at the cuffs. Looking at Nick, Greg noted the same sweatshirt, the same dust layers and that he wasn't far off the same tear tracks. He looked round, and spotting another bale pulled it over to sit opposite them.

'I'm sorry,' he said. 'This must have been a horrible day for you.'

'The worst,' replied Tina. 'It's not just the money. We've been caring for those hens every day for years. We tried so hard to treat them well – fresh air and space to scratch and sun themselves. We tried so hard to look after them well. Now I feel we let them down. They've all died horribly and it was our fault.'

Another tear crept slowly down her face. Greg rummaged in his pocket, by some miracle found a clean hanky, and offered it.

'It's ok,' said Tina, wiping an arm across her face and smearing the dust some more. 'But thank you.'

'I'm sorry we have to bother you right now,' said Greg, 'but the quicker we follow up, the more chance we have of identifying how this happened. How about we go into the farmhouse and Chris here makes us all a cup of tea? Would that be ok?'

Tina started to get up, but her husband interrupted. 'I'm surprised this is a matter for you,' he said. 'Isn't this usually a Defra-only issue? Why are the police getting involved?'

Greg got up from the bale and replied, 'You may have heard there was a suspicious death at the farm where the first outbreak was identified. The death is now presumed to be murder.' He paused. 'Your wife suggested that your outbreak might be due to trespass by a poacher or his customers. We need to follow that up.'

'There, I told you! Stirring things like that,' Nick exclaimed. His round red face reddened still further as he glared at his wife. 'Now look what you've done.'

'Let's have that tea,' interrupted Greg, 'and then see where we get to.'

The farmhouse kitchen was as neat as the rest of the establishment. Clean tea towels hung drying on the Rayburn and the only things on the kitchen table were salt and pepper and a jar of chutney.

Greg noticed an array of wellingtons of various sizes by the back porch and asked, 'Do you have children?'

'Two. Boy and girl, ten and eight,' said Tina, banging the kettle onto the hotplate. 'They're with friends at present. We didn't want them to see the cull. They're very upset as it is. They're having a sleepover tonight and coming back tomorrow.'

Nick sat at the head of the table, still glowering as Greg sat opposite him and Chris pulled out one of the chairs on the side.

She got out her notebook as she asked, 'Why are you so worried about your neighbour, Mr Williams?'

Tina put a teapot, mugs and milk on the table as she sat down and said, 'He thinks I shouldn't stir it with him. I've had a couple of run-ins with him over the past year, and he can be quite unpleasant.'

'Run-ins about what?'

'Mainly about him trespassing on our land at night.

We had a fox trying to get to the hens a few months ago, and when I went out to check, Jackson was crossing one of our paddocks, on his way to the river I assume. I challenged him and he gave me an earful. When I went to see him the next day, he was even more horrible. Said that incomers should mind their own business if they knew what was good for them and theirs.'

Tea over, but no biscuits, as Chris had mournfully remarked to Greg, and the two police made their way down the track, pointed out by Nick, towards the riverbank. Greg was looking at his watch as they went. Almost 5pm, and the light was already beginning to fade as storm clouds gathered.

'We'll have a quick look, Chris, and a quick chat if possible then, depending on what we find, I think we need to get back to Wymondham for a debrief before heading home.'

The well-maintained trackway changed markedly as it reached the boundary of Riverside Hens. The dividing line was marked by a rickety gate, held up by baler twine rather than hinges and with most of its crosspieces hanging loose at one end, rotted away from the uprights. In consequence it sagged heavily at almost every point when Greg tried to pull it to one side, and he was panting by the time they could continue down the now deeply rutted track between heavily overgrown hedgerows. They could see their destination ahead of them, a ramshackle tin shed perched close to the riverbank.

Measuring only around twenty feet by twelve, both the walls and roof were made of corrugated iron. Most was an elderly rusted red, but in places it had at some time been patched by a newer version coated in grey, which gave the whole thing a diseased, leprous appearance. The door was padlocked, and there were no windows. After a frustrated circuit of the construction and a bang on the door, Greg gave up.

'Seems there's nobody home,' he remarked.

Chris had been giving her attention to an elderly white van parked on the track. It too was locked, and little could be seen by peering in through the windscreen. There was a certain amount of clutter on and around the passenger seat, mostly newspapers, takeaway cartons and cardboard coffee cups.

'Can't deduce much from this either,' she said, 'except that Mr Jackson appears to patronise McDonalds. I'll get a check run on the licence plate, but I don't think we're going to get much further here. At least, not just now.'

'I agree. We'll get someone down here first thing in the morning. Now it's back to Wymondham for us.'

The two took a last look round. Greg thought to touch the bonnet of the van, but it was cool. No sign it had been used recently. One last shake of the padlock and they turned away to tackle the rutted path and the rickety gate.

'Anything on the licence plate, Chris?'

'No signal. I'll have to try again nearer the road.'

'That explains why mine has been so silent too.'

'It's a notorious problem in Norfolk. One of my old friends was a community nurse. It used to drive them mad, trying to find patients in out-of-the-way places, and then not being able to contact the GP.'

Once on the Riverside Hens roadway, both walking and talking were easier.

‘What do you think about this poacher angle, Chris?’

‘I’ve been looking up glass eels or elvers,’ she replied. ‘It’s true they are incredibly high value, pound per pound, and in big demand in the east. Short of rhino horn, it seems there’s not much to match them. And according to the River Trust, the populations of eels have been recovering, so it’s not beyond the realms of possibility that Jackson has added them to his poaching repertoire. The difficulty will be catching him at it. It’s the same with all wildlife crime. Lots of open space the chummies know better than us, and too few of us to police it. If we are serious about following up these accusations, I think we’ll need some good intel, a helicopter and a dog team.’

Had they but known it, Greg and Chris had missed Jackson by less than an hour.

A short, square man, Jackson exuded a generalised aggression that tended to keep most people at a safe distance. He had short hair, short beard, and a short fuse which meant that even in his local pub, both those who knew him and those who didn’t would pass by on the way to the bar with great care not to jostle him and no more than a quick word of greeting. While he had never been heard to demand of someone ‘What you lookin’ at?’, he definitely looked as though he would, on the slightest provocation. He lived in a small terraced cottage on the edge of the village, his only companions his ferrets, which spent much of their time mooching round his kitchen. He maintained, to the few who had the temerity to ask, that they kept down the pests. They certainly added to a particular, pervasive atmosphere.

That evening, as his planned enterprise was to be aquatic rather than terrestrial, the ferrets were left behind and he loaded his van with the fine mesh net that he used to catch elvers. He drove down the track through Riverside Hens with an internal sneer at the effort they had put in to creating a smart layout.

'Much good it did them,' he muttered as he levered his old gate aside and pondered leaving it open for his return journey. The recollection of the row he'd had with Tina Williams deterred him, and with a scowl he heaved it closed behind him. Once on the riverbank, he shouldered the lightweight net, the long aluminium handle he used with it, the plastic box for his catch, and the old haversack with his snack and bait in it. Thus encumbered he set off along the riverbank through the failing light. Despite his burdens he moved silently and negotiated most obstacles with the ease of long practice.

The light was fading fast by the time he reached his spot just where a brook joined the Ant. Here the bank was clear for a few feet between heavily overhanging elders. Well hidden under the branches he sat on a log to eat his thick cheese sandwich and drink his flask of hot sugary tea. He had hesitated over a can or two of beer, but long caution over mixing rivers and alcohol had decided him on leaving it behind for, he hoped, a celebratory drink later. The half-moon was a dim shimmer tracing a path downriver when he began fishing with his net, and he grunted with a dour pleasure when a reasonable yield of elvers were dropped into his keep box. They wriggled over and round each other like animated spaghetti, no doubt wondering why, after so many thousands of miles from the Sargasso Sea, their journey upstream had now been interrupted by a smelly Norfolk man with net, box and insurmountable greed.

He was just about to plunge the net back into the river for another scoop when he heard the quiet splash of a paddle. Freezing into stillness he listened and watched the water. He was too old a hand to make the mistake of moving away into the trees, knowing that movement was much easier to see than stillness. However, on this occasion the man in the kayak knew where to look, knew where his prey was to be found. Jackson was surprised to see a kayak very like the one he had left in his tin shed, and astonished when he saw who was paddling it.

'What the fuck you doin' in my canoe?' he exclaimed. 'I niver giv you permission ta…' then saw, too late, just what the paddler was pointing at him. 'Oh shi,' he said, trying to back off, but hampered by the net with the long handle. Then something hit him hard in the chest and the last thing he knew was cold water on his face.

Earlier that evening, with the moonlight glimmering softly on silky water, the kayak had pushed off from the bank. Unlike most of its ilk on the Broads, this one was camouflage green rather than passion pink. Mindful of how well sound travelled over water, the occupant paddled with extreme caution, one slow stroke after slow stroke. The fact he was moving with the current helped, and as he slid downstream the kayak hugged the bank, even disappearing under low willow branches from time to time. An otter, disturbed by a foreign smell and foreign shape, plopped into the river just ahead, provoking a muffled expletive from the startled paddler. The rings of the otter's passage spread on the calm water as the kayak slowed for a moment, the person on board listening intently, then the double-ended paddle lifted and dipped once again. The kayak moved forward.

As it approached its destination, progress slowed some more. Slowly, slowly, it moved through the water, only a faint whisper audible from its passage. Ahead could be seen the light from a muffled torch, and there were sounds of grunting, as someone hauled something heavy from the river. More grunting and some disgruntled muttering hid the sounds of the approaching kayak so effectively that the grunter on the bank was completely taken by surprise.

There was a loud click, a rushing noise and a thud. The man curled forward, hung still for a moment, then fell into the river. The kayaker back-paddled and waited to see if anyone had heard the shout or the splash. Nothing. Where the man had fallen there was a confused swirl of current, a brief glimpse of an arm, or was it a leg? Then nothing. The river closed over the gift, as if it formed some recompense for all that he had taken from it, over very many years.

The man in the kayak waited for a moment, then pulled up to the bank to see what had been left. He pulled the box into the water and the newly released elvers arrowed upstream, relieved to resume their long journey. The net he took with him, balanced awkwardly on the deck of the kayak. The grubby haversack and the vacuum flask went unnoticed, half hidden as they were by the dead tree trunk. He paddled off, the handle of the net trailing in the water and skewing his progress downriver.

12

Wymondham

The Ops room was in moderate turmoil when Greg walked in. Two of the civilian assistants were talking on the phone. Jim was at the whiteboard, adding photos and scribbling comments in red. Sarah Laurence was making copious notes on her iPad and a small knot of constables was arguing and gesticulating in the corner.

'Right, let's have some order,' snapped Greg in a voice designed to carry, as he crossed the room towards Jim. 'We have a lot to get through before we knock off. Jim, sorry I've been out of touch. The mobile signal is horrendous by the Ant, but if I understood the garbled message correctly, you've found the missing workers from Wayford Bridge.'

'I've found some of them,' said Jim, 'courtesy of Citizens Advice Great Yarmouth. I can't claim a lot of credit. We were lucky that the chap, John, who was cuckooed by the Wayford Bridge team, is a long-term client of Citizens Advice. He calls in there regularly when he needs help and has a lot of faith in them. So when he and one of the workers saw a chance to escape from his house in Cobham he persuaded him to go with him to CA. And they called us.'

'So what's the story?'

'In short, the day of the murder at Stalham, all the men who'd been living at the farm in Wayford Bridge were taken to a warehouse near the river in Yarmouth, and the following evening some twenty of them were taken to John's house. Each day they were delivered to a workplace, not always the one they'd worked at before, then back to John's to sleep. We're currently following up two leads. The warehouse, the poultry plant Matis has been working at, and we've a team watching John's house. In addition, and this has only just come through, Steve has just reported back from the mortuary. Matis has identified the body found on Caister beach as one of his fellow workers at Stalham. He knew him only as Tomas.'

'What about the women?'

'Matis didn't know. He says the men and the women at Wayford Bridge never mixed. They knew there were women in the house, but they were never allowed out except to get into one of the Transit vans that took them to work.'

Greg tapped his teeth with a whiteboard marker. 'So, that makes two murders of workers connected with Stalham. What the devil is going on?'

Between them, Greg and Chris were reporting back on their interviews with Stalham Poultry management, Riverside Hens, and the abortive attempt to contact the poacher, Jackson, when one of the civilians held up a phone.

'Report from Cobham,' he said. 'They got ten men and a van driver. All of them claim to be unable to speak English. All seem to be Lithuanian, but they're waiting on an official interpreter.'

'If Matis was right, there's another ten on the loose somewhere,' remarked Jim, 'but it's probably reasonable to assume there was a second vanload and that it will have been warned off. We need to step up the pace on the riverside warehouses right now, just in case they've gone back there.'

'Understood. Jim, get going. If you're ok I'm going to leave the gangmaster end of this investigation with you and I'll see if I can get you some more help. As well as the warehouses, see what you can find out about how the men were recruited, transported to the UK, and the range of places they worked. We have some very pointed questions to ask in their workplaces. We also still need to find the girls.'

Jim left the room briskly, picking up Steve Hall and Phil Coleman en route with a glance.

Greg continued, 'Busy day tomorrow for all of us. Chris and I will follow up the intelligence we got from the ANPR and we'll go back and try a chat with the poacher fellow tomorrow morning. If we're at all unhappy, we'll bring him in for questioning. Sarah, I'm just going to brief Margaret before I head for home. Do you want to come?'

Margaret had clearly spent much of the early evening running her fingers through her hair, as it was now standing out around her head in an aureole.

'I've had the local press in the shape of the Eastern Daily Press and the Mercury on the phone this afternoon, both wanting to know what we were going to do about the serial killer wiping out migrant workers.'

'I didn't think two deaths counted as a serial killer,' commented Greg incautiously, and as Margaret glared at him he added hurriedly, 'Not that two isn't bad enough.'

'Two in Great Yarmouth qualifies as a serial killer for the Mercury', she snapped. 'Our normal crime rate leans more to minor drugs violations, TDA and scraps outside pubs on a Saturday night. Anyway, the press are my problem for the moment. I'll keep them off your back for as long as I can, so bring me up to date.'

Greg did so, Sarah chipping in from time to time with detail. At the end of twenty minutes, silence fell. Margaret was tapping her pen on the desk, first one end, then twisted it over and tapped the other, over and over, her eyes fixed on the rotating pen. After a moment she sighed and, putting it down with a click, ran her hands through her hair again.

'What d'you need from me?'

'Ideally,' replied Greg, 'more manpower to follow up with probable employers of the men, and to find the missing women. That means trawling nail bars, massage parlours and the like, certainly all the way from here to Norwich. Possibly further afield too.'

'Ok. I can ask local teams to follow up on that. Local intelligence would be helpful, particularly in places where they have good contacts. Give me a brief ASAP and leave that one with me. Who should they report to?'

'Me,' said Sarah, just as Greg said 'Jim.'

'Me,' said Sarah again. 'Jim has a lot on his plate with warehouses, meat plants, etc. Let me coordinate and I'll brief

Jim as soon as something turns up.'

'Ok,' said Margaret. 'What else?'

'We need to follow up some issues with the Poultry Enterprises senior management. That's likely to rock some boats, if Austen Collier is to be believed.'

'What exactly are the issues?'

Greg started to count them off on his fingers. 'One, his wife's car being caught on ANPR near the plant late on the night of the first murder. Two, some unexplained journeys by Austen Collier in Central Europe round about the time the bird flu virus may have been brought to Stalham. Three, the possible link between the poacher Jackson, the transport of the virus from Stalham to Riverside Hens on the Ant, and the smuggling of glass eels.'

'Be careful you're not doing Defra's job for them. Routes of transmission of avian flu are for them, not us.'

'Absolutely. My concern is not the bird flu itself, more that it's an indicator of some odd movements that may be linked to the transit of materials and/or workers and possibly eels. A sort of trail, marking where goods have moved.' He hesitated. 'I don't have the proof yet, but it seems to me that what may be happening is a two-way traffic. Men and women into Norfolk, glass eels out. And someone has quietly been making a lot of money out of this, possibly for years. Enough that they are willing to kill to hide their involvement.'

As they left Margaret's office, Greg's phone rang. Excusing himself to Sarah he stepped aside and answered it.

'Me,' announced the familiar voice. 'Are you home for supper this evening?'

'I hope so,' he said, 'but I'll be late. I'm still in Wymondham and I haven't finished here yet.' He looked at his watch. 'God, it's 8 already. I'm sorry Isabelle. Don't wait for me, have yours now, and I'll get mine when I get in, whenever that is.'

'Actually, I was ringing to say that I've been held up too, so if you don't mind picking up a takeaway or something on your way home, don't worry about me. I'll see you later. Ok?'

Sighing, Greg rang off, reflecting ruefully that he was in no position to complain, but that he seemed to see Isabelle less and less. He caught up with Sarah further down the corridor.

'Sorry, it was my wife. It seems I'm on my own for supper this evening, so would you fancy catching a quick bite with me? I think there's one or two things we could usefully go over.'

'What did you have in mind?'

'A pub supper?' he hazarded. I have to admit I don't really know my way around Wymondham's hostelries yet, so I'd be happy to take your advice.'

'How about the Green Dragon?' she asked. 'Good pub and good food. In the middle of the town.'

'Sounds perfect. Let's go.'

A few minutes and some tricky parking later, they were both seated in the pub restaurant, menus in front of them.

'Prawns to start, then Chicken Caesar salad with a side of chips,' said Sarah to the waitress.

'Soup and a steak and kidney pie,' said Greg, handing back his menu. 'And a pint of low alcohol lager. You?'

'Diet Coke,' said Sarah. 'It's a bore having to drive after,' she added, 'but I never drink and drive.'

'Me neither. Where do you live, Sarah?'

'Acle. It's a market town down the A47.'

'Yes, I know it vaguely from when I was here last year. Nice little place I thought.'

'Quiet, and does at least have a few shops, unlike most of the villages. What about you?'

'Still renting at present. In Norwich, near the cathedral.'

'Wow! That must be costing you an arm and a leg. How do you manage that on police pay? Sorry,' she said catching herself up. 'That was rude.'

'Not at all,' he replied with a laugh. 'My wife's a singer. She has contacts at the cathedral. We're renting for a while from the diocese, but only for a short while, then I'll need to buy something sensible. The house is great, but I don't like renting. It makes us both feel so,' he hesitated, 'so temporary. Sort of displaced. It makes me think about those men. If I feel like that in a luxury house, how on earth do they feel confined in a filthy dormitory?

'Anyway, in York we had a flat by the river, but I quite fancy something in one of the villages here.'

They were interrupted by the arrival of their starters. Sarah's prawns looked plump and juicy. For a moment Greg had a bad attack of menu envy, but only until he dipped his spoon in his soup.

'So. Back to work,' announced Sarah around a prawn dripping in aromatic butter. 'I had the impression you weren't pleased with me butting in back there.'

Greg put his spoon down and hesitated over his next words. 'No, I wasn't at the time,' he admitted. 'I thought you risked undermining Jim. And I still think that's something to guard against. But I've had time to think further since then. You were right. I overlooked your potential contribution and risked overloading Jim.'

'So we're all square then.'

'All square.' He finished his soup and put down his spoon. 'Who do you favour for it?'

'By it, you mean the mastermind behind the whole set of crimes, or the murderer?'

'Ah, well that's the question isn't it? Are we looking for one person, or one controlling mind using tools to do his bidding?'

'So you think it's a he?'

'At the moment, my money is on Austen Collier. He's the one who took the side trip to Central Europe. It was his wife's car spotted near Stalham on the night of the first murder. He's the director with overall responsibility for the hiring of workers, so he must have known what was going on there.'

They paused as the main courses were delivered along with the usual enquiry made to check everything was ok.

'Don't you hate it when they come back in a few minutes, just as your mouth is full, and ask the same question again?' she said. 'Anyway, before they do, what about the body in Caister?'

'We don't know nearly enough about that yet. No weapon, no idea where he went into the river, no idea why he had money on him, or rather in him.'

She grimaced. 'Not an image I wanted with my salad thank you very much.'

'Yes, I was wondering about that too,' he said. 'Salad *and* chips, so not a diet choice then. Not that you need it,' he added hurriedly and then, 'Oh God, now I'm being creepy and inappropriate. Sorry.'

She laughed. 'Don't worry. Almost anything you can say these days can be taken the wrong way. As it happens, I just like salad and I also like chips. A lot. In fact I like savouries full stop. Hence my choice of starter and no pud.'

'What, no pud! But I saw sticky toffee pudding on the list.'

'So you have it. I'll happily keep you company with a coffee.'

'It's a deal.' There was a pause and he went on. 'I feel I've been neglecting the Caister body. That's the problem with such a multi-faceted case. It's hard to keep all the plates spinning at once.'

'That's my job,' she said briskly. 'To tell you when I think one is slowing down and might fall off.'

'So, what you're saying is?'

'Jim has a good grip on the Yarmouth end of the gangmaster and modern slavery case. I was worried the girls were being overlooked but Margaret has just ok'd more help, so I'd say that angle is ticking over nicely. You and Chris have been following up on Stalham Poultry and the possible link to eels and to Riverside Hens so, ok for the moment on that one too, at least until we know more about Mr Collier's movements. That leaves the Caister body, Tomas. Thanks to Matis' statement we know he was linked to the gangmaster case, but we don't know much else, hence my mentioning it.'

'You're right. Thanks Sarah. I know Jim has it on his to-do list, but you're right. There is too much on his list.'

'Add it to yours,' she suggested. 'If we're right, and the murders are about someone covering up their involvement in the movement of men and eels, then the Caister case has a lot in common with Stalham. Let Jim focus on running to earth all the organisations that have been using these gangmaster teams. At the least it will result in prosecutions for use of an unregistered gangmaster, and it may lead us to the gangmaster management team and prosecutions for modern slavery. I can help with that by coordinating data on those businesses and hopefully finding all the affected men and girls. That would leave you the space to concentrate on the murderer and the governing mind.'

'Who may be one and the same.'

'Who may be one and the same,' she agreed, and picking up the last chip with her fingers, ate it and pushed the plate away. 'So, sticky toffee pudding and coffee?'

'Actually, after all that soup and pie I'm pogged. I think I'd better get on with following up your suggestions. Do you mind if I settle up and make tracks?'

'Not at all. But we'll split the bill.'

'Ok, and thanks for the suggestions. They've all been good ones, from the Green Dragon on.'

'My pleasure,' she said, and realised she meant it.

It was after 11 by the time Greg got home and he was only a little surprised to find that Isabelle had already gone to bed. She tended to the owl rather than the lark, late to bed and late to rise, but on this occasion she was already under the covers and back turned to the door. He crept in and undressed quietly, all the while hoping that she would wake and turn over with a question about his day. He was disappointed. He slipped under the covers, checked his phone was silent and the alarm set for the morning, then slowly slipped off to sleep.

13

The Farmer's Lady, morning of 8 April

Farmer's Lady was one of the old-type Broads boats. Long and low, she had a cross section highly reminiscent of a bar of soap, well designed for the shallow lakes and low bridges of her natal waters. Her owners Rob and Anne, as her name indicated, were farmers from Essex. Firm believers in 'no such thing as bad weather, only the wrong clothes', they were untroubled by the East Anglian climate even in spring, and were looking forward to a week of quiet fishing.

That night they'd tied up at one of their favourite spots on the Ant, where an eddy in the river had cut out a shallow curve of bank shaded by willow and alder, with just enough space clear of nettles to allow them to park a couple of folding chairs ashore. They'd spent a pleasant evening playing dominoes, eating griddled lamb chops (their own of course, brought with them from their farm shop) with a salad of young spinach, spring onions and radishes, also from their shop, and retired to bed with ritual complaints about the feeble dribble from their onboard shower. They were disturbed in the early hours by a bump against the hull and a volley of barks from their black Labrador, Flint. They assumed it was a swan or other water bird, told Flint to pipe down and turned over to go back to sleep. With a few muttered grumbles, Flint piped down and they had been undisturbed until morning.

Morning was one of those when the right clothes were definitely needed. A steady rain cut visibility significantly and pattered complex designs into the water. Rob, rubbing his hand in turn over his balding head and neat beard, proposed staying put for a while to see if it would let up. Anne, consulting the weather app on her phone, argued against on the grounds that it looked set in for the day and they were running low on water. So they togged up for rain and set to their normal tasks, Rob at the wheel and Anne, hair covered in an unbecoming rain hood she wouldn't be seen dead in under any other circumstances, unmooring the boat. They'd tied the bow to a handy tree stump, and she had no problem casting that off, allowing the boat to nose out into the river. At the stern, however, she'd dropped the mud weight, and here she had a problem.

'The mud weight's fouled,' she shouted to Rob. 'Try moving her ahead slowly to see if that frees it up.'

It did, and Flint started barking again as something rose and bobbed behind the boat. Anne gulped and sat down hard as she came the closest she ever had to falling in the river.

'Stop,' she bellowed. 'Stop, Rob. Stop engines.'

Rob cut the engines and turned round to shout, 'What's wrong? Flint gone in again?'

'No. Oh God. Oh my God, Rob, there's a body round our mud weight.'

'A body?'

'A man. I think.'

'Jesus.' He abandoned the helm and ran back through the boat to look for himself. 'Hells bells, you're right. Ok. We have to report this.'

The sound of shouts and a siren drew his attention back to the fact that Farmer's Lady was drifting down the Ant without power, and as such was a hazard to navigation. He ran back to the helm and shouted to the boat coming upriver, 'Sorry. We have an emergency. Give me a moment and I'll get out of your way.' He reached for the key then stopped as he thought about what even Farmer's Lady's small propeller could do to the dead body tangled with the rope at the stern.

The other boat had cut her engine too and the helmsman shouted, 'Can we help?'

'I've a dead body tangled with the mud weight and I daren't start the engine. Can you push me into the bank? Gently!' he added.

'Bugger!' said the man on the big hire boat. 'Jessy, make sure the children stay below. What is it? A dog? Have you reported it?' he asked as he used his throttle to nudge Farmer's Lady back where she'd come from.

'Not a dog, no. My wife's reporting it now,' said Rob. 'If you could just stay there a moment while I tie her up? And thank you.' He threw a cable over the nearest tree branch and secured it hurriedly. 'There, that'll hold her for the moment. Thank you.'

'I'll get going then,' said the other man. 'Don't want the kids to see anything unpleasant.'

'Thanks again,' said Rob, clambering back into the cockpit. He made a note of the other boat's name – Champagne Charlie – before he forgot it.

The 999 call was swiftly channelled to the Coastguard and a first responder was despatched by inshore lifeboat at the same time as police were alerted. As luck would have it, the nearest available first responder was Ben Asheton.

Whatever the circumstances, a trip upriver was always a pleasure. The lifeboat nosed upstream through the steady drizzle as Ben chatted to the crew.

'So, a floater?' asked the cox.

'Sounds like it. If we're lucky it won't have been in the water for too long. The lady who reported it in said it had fouled their mud weight. They noticed it when they tried to move on this morning.'

'Should be there soon. They're at what3words location designated *wet/occasion/feather*, and according to my GPS that's just round the next bend.'

When the lifeboat arrived, Rob and Anne were sitting in the prow with their dog, as far as they could get from the bundle tied to their stern. Ben went aboard while the lifeboat crew took a look at the recovery challenge.

'Morning. I'm Ben Asheton, first responder. Just tell me how you found out about your little problem back there, then we'll see about retrieving it.'

'I think it's a him,' said Anne. 'Sorry, I should have offered you a tea or coffee. You and the crew. What would you like?'

'It's ok, thank you. Perhaps later. Why do you think it's a man?'

'When I first pulled the cable in, he rolled in the water and I caught a glimpse of his face. That's how I knew it was a body. Before that, I just thought it was a bundle of old clothes or rags, or even a scarecrow.'

'Ok. I'll go and take a look now and we'll see about recovering the body to the lifeboat. In the meantime, perhaps that tea would be good,' he said, partly to give them something to do.

At the stern of the boat, he consulted with the lifeboat crew. 'What I'm thinking,' he said, 'is that I try pulling in the mud weight cable and you stand by to retrieve the corpse if it comes loose. We don't want to have to chase him down the river.'

He pulled gently on the cable. The body bobbed up towards the surface, and twisted as it did. Ben found himself looking into the face of the dead man.

'I know this chap,' he said. 'Seen him in a pub quite recently. Bit of a poacher if I remember rightly.' As the water eddied, more of the body floated towards the surface. 'Hang on,' he said, and stopped pulling. 'Do you see what I see?'

The cox, hanging over the side of the lifeboat, also took a closer look. 'Arrow, or dart?' he hazarded.

'Possibly. More likely a crossbow quarrel. Radio it in, Bob. This is a violent death, probably a murder. We need the police to take a look before we go any further.'

A brief discussion on the radio, and the lifeboat set off to meet the police at Sutton Staithe and ferry them to the scene. Ben stayed aboard the Farmer's Lady to reassure her owners and to make sure no one interfered with what was now, potentially, a crime scene.

The radio message to Wymondham caused a scramble. Getting SOCOs, a pathologist and a couple of officers to a remote location on the River Ant was never going to be easy. The limited space on the inshore lifeboat was also an issue, and some of the crew found themselves stranded at Sutton in order to make room for the police contingent. Indeed, Greg, squashed onto the boat in a borrowed life jacket and waterproofs, had to leave Chris behind. She was still muttering, not in the least under her breath, when the lifeboat pulled away.

Once at Farmer's Lady he took one look at the situation and had a swift chat with the SOCOs while the pathologist took a preliminary view over the side of the boat at her semi-submerged subject. Then the three of them put their heads together.

'Clearly, from my point of view, the best option is to retrieve the body from the river, bag it as it is, and take it to the mortuary ASAP for a proper examination.'

'And you, Ned,' asked Greg.

'We need a closer look at the mud weight and cable, and

indeed most of this boat, probably mainly for exclusionary purposes. But we don't want to do a sloppy job just because it seems the owners have been super unlucky. We need to look along the bank too, both here and upstream, to see if we can find where he went in.

'As far as the boat is concerned, it would be easier to do a proper job if we took her back to Sutton Staithe and moored her in a secure location. The search along the banks – well that's not going to be easy and will take some manpower.'

Ben chipped in, 'I may be able to help with ID. I'm pretty sure I recognise the corpse. I think it's a bloke named Jackson. He was well known as a poacher even when I was in the force. If I'm right it shouldn't be too hard to find someone to do a formal identification, and you could start the search for his entry point at his place near the river.'

Greg swung round so fast the boat swayed and he had to grab a handy cleat to avoid an early bath. 'Jackson?' he said sharply. 'Not the chap who has a place near Riverside Hens?'

'That's the one.'

'Too much of a coincidence,' and he got on the phone. 'Chris, the dead man here is tentatively ID'd as the poacher Jackson. Get someone over to his place near Riverside Hens ASAP. Make sure no one gets into that shed, and secure all access to the riverbank from there. I'll be back as soon as the lifeboat can run me back to Sutton, but don't wait for my return.'

'On it, boss,' she said. And rang off.

'Ok. Retrieve the body ASAP and bag it. Ben, can you keep an eye on the lifeboat crew doing that? Ned, as soon as you've finished with photos here and have recovered the mud weight and cable, we'll get this boat to the Staithe for a closer look. I'll have a word with the owners now. Bill, when we go I'll need to leave you here to secure this location until we've scoured the bank for anything that might be there. I'll get you some reinforcements as soon as I can.'

Returning to Farmer's Lady, Greg said, 'Mr and Mrs Bailey, we'll need to take this boat to Sutton Staithe for a more thorough examination than we can do here, and we'll also need statements from you please. I'm sorry to wreck your day, but I'm afraid there's no alternative.' He hesitated and then said, with a smile that Anne privately found quite charming, 'When I say take your boat to Sutton, actually I mean could you please drive her there? It would be a lot easier than having to tow her.'

'Of course I'll take her,' said Rob, 'but I hope we'll be able to carry on with our holiday after that.'

'One thing at a time,' replied Greg. 'Hopefully we won't need to keep you too long. So, we'll just wait for the lifeboat crew to recover the body, then we can set off. I'll let you know when we can move.'

'You're not bringing the body on here I hope,' exclaimed Anne.

'No. No, not at all. The body will go aboard the lifeboat, and so will the mud weight and mooring cable. Then we can make a move.'

14

Riverbanks

Wide grey clouds hung low over the river as Ben stayed with the lifeboat crew and the pathologist to retrieve the body. Farmer's Lady, with the Baileys, Greg and Ned on board, set off through the persistent drizzle to Sutton Staithe, Greg with his phone apparently spot-welded to his ear as he tried to keep up with the many swift-moving threads of his investigation. The lifeboat crew let them get out of sight around the first bend before setting to the task of hauling the sodden last remains of Ted Jackson, poacher of this parish, from the slow-moving river.

'At least we don't have to worry about him coming to pieces in our hands,' remarked Dr Sawston. 'I remember one corpse hauled from a river – every time we got a grip on an arm or a leg it came off in our hands. By the time we finished it looked…'

'With all due respect, doctor,' interrupted Ben, 'I think

we'd all be glad if you could save the more gruesome reminiscences for later.'

He winked at Bob the cox as they bent over the stern in an attempt to free the trapped clothing from the cable to the mud weight. 'Not sure why it got trapped here,' he muttered.

'The current sets in to the bank just here,' answered Bob. 'You can see where it's cut a small bay. That's why he drifted in here.'

'No, I mean why has this bit of his jacket caught on the cable? Oh, I see now. There's something tangled in the jacket, a piece of line or something. Fishing line perhaps, and that's what wrapped round the cable. Be careful, don't drop it in the river or you'll have to go after it to get it back.'

His threat was not needed. Bob unwound the line carefully and dropped it into the evidence bag held out by Bill. Then the crew, Bob and Ben all got a firm grip on the body and raised it over the stern with a certain amount of grunting and effort. Putting it down on the open body bag, they paused as Dr Cawston held up a hand.

'Just before you zip him up, I'd like a closer look at his chest.'

They all paused while the doctor, precariously perched on the gunwale, peered closely at the end of the crossbow quarrel protruding from the victim's chest.

'Interesting,' she said. 'I'm willing to bet that it missed the heart and got him through the aorta. He'd have bled out in minutes. Anyone like to take my bet?' She looked round cheerfully at the crew. They all shook their heads. 'Spoilsports,' she muttered. 'No one got any sporting instinct?'

'I'll take you, doctor,' said Ben. 'A tenner says it's through the heart.'

'You're on,' said the doctor. 'And you're wrong. I'll let you know after the PM.'

The mortuary van met the lifeboat at Sutton Staithe and the sorry bundle in the body bag was manhandled over the thwarts and onto a stretcher. A little down the bank, Greg stood near the Farmer's Lady while Ned and his team completed their checks. Rob and Anne, having given their statements and contact details, had retreated to the comforts of the Sutton Hotel for a restorative coffee and cakes.

'Thanks for getting to Riverside Hens so quickly,' Greg said down the phone. 'What did you find at Jackson's place?'

'All quiet when we got there,' replied the disembodied voice of Phil Coleman. 'We had a good look round but couldn't see anything other than discarded nets and fishing line. And the remains of a bonfire. We broke into the shed and that was more interesting. Most of the space was taken up by a kayak in camo colours. What's really intriguing is that there were no prints on it. Not one. Unless Jackson was obsessive about cleanliness, that suggests that someone wiped it in the very recent past.'

'Nothing I've heard about him so far suggests obsessive cleanliness as a characteristic,' remarked Greg. 'What else?'

'Well, this is the other interesting bit,' said Phil. 'On the walls of the shed where the wooden framework crossed the galvanised metal walls were lots of nails with things hanging on them. Tools, netting, and some distinctly illegal traps. But some of the nails were empty and the wall behind was marked as though various items had hung there in the recent past.'

'What about the bonfire?'

'That was just a small pile of ashes when we got there. Still warm, so a recent fire. Nothing much left and I think it may have been started using an accelerant. We found a can smelling of petrol in the hedge.'

'Any sign of where Jackson went into the river?'

'According to the lifeboat crew, we need to look further upstream for an area where he could have been taken by the current to where he was found. Certainly there are no signs on the bank here, other than one place where someone, probably Jackson himself, had obviously cleared a stretch of shrubs and so on. There are marks on the grass that would be consistent with the kayak having entered the water there.'

'Can you tell when?'

'Not with any precision. But there are several marks, some apparently old, some fresh, so certainly recently. I've sent a couple of chaps with dogs along the bank in each direction to see what we can find. If that doesn't turn up anything we may need bigger teams for a more thorough search.'

'Let's hope the dogs come good. I'd be surprised if he'd gone too far on foot, especially carrying traps or nets.'

On the riverbank, a couple of springer spaniels were having the time of their lives. One heading upstream and one down, tails were exhibiting all the signs of perpetual motion and heads were down, sniffing busily. The chauffeurs of the partnerships followed through the undergrowth with rather more difficulty.

On the upstream bank Meg, an excitable four-year-old, was quartering the ground with enthusiasm. Suddenly she gave one sharp bark and stiffened, her nose pointing at an old log. As Constable Jenny Warren came up to her, the dog made a little dart with her nose at the space under the log, then pointed again.

'Good girl, good Meg,' said Jenny, and threw an old tennis ball down the bank for Meg to play with. Pulling on gloves, Jenny pulled foliage aside with care and peered into the dank cavity under the tree. Stepping back and taking her phone out, she took some photos in situ of the items Meg had found. Only then, she pulled on the thin plastic gloves and picked up the old haversack and the vacuum flask. She examined both with care, sniffed the remaining contents of the flask, and dropped them into evidence bags. Then she collected Meg and her ball and looked round her once more.

The grasses at the riverbank were trampled and she took more photos before moving cautiously to the edge and examining the ground for footprints or scrapes. She could see nothing and was about to turn away when something caught her eye. Under water and a few feet from the bank she could see something bright blue. Its shape distorted by the ripples, it was hard to see exactly what it was, and it was too far for her to reach unaided without going into the river. She made the call to her sergeant and took advice. Then she sat down to wait. Meg, after a drink and a refreshing paddle in the water's edge, sat down beside her and appeared to go to sleep.

Back at Sutton Staithe, Greg was just in time to intercept the lifeboat before it departed. 'You couldn't do us a favour could you?' he asked.

15

Southtown, Great Yarmouth

Down by the River Yare, the search was continuing for the warehouse that had housed the Lithuanians. Jim and his team were working their way along the riverbanks between the confluence of the Bure and Yare and the sea. As most of the South Quay was open space, offices and rather sad, light industrial units it did not take long to check and decide that there was nothing to find there. The Southtown side was another matter. This was where the bigger vessels moored when they came upriver rather than using the new port. Historically, the only harbourage had been on the river and there were therefore large numbers of warehouses and storage depots, many now out of use since the construction of the new deepwater port. At one time there had clearly been even more, as there were acres of elderly concrete marked by the shadows of long-gone constructions. After searching the first six rust-streaked warehouses with their broken-surfaced and puddle-strewn yards, the team was visibly tiring.

'Time for a break,' announced Jim. 'There's a decent coffee van in the car park at B&Q. Let's pop up there for a quick one then back to work.'

They loaded into the car and van, and drove away from the river to B&Q. There, as promised, was the dispenser of hot coffee and Jim, after a quick look round, decided that a sugar boost was probably a good idea and added doughnuts to the order. A number of the team showed signs of sneaking off to B&Q to top up with DIY supplies and one, Jess, did manage to get as far as the van selling farm fresh eggs before Jim put a stop to such peregrinations.

'This was going to be a quick one,' he reminded them. 'So no wandering off. Sup up, as our new boss would say, and we'll get back to work.'

'Aren't we wasting our time?' complained a uniform drafted in to help and by all the signs not particularly pleased about it. 'According to the briefing we know they moved on from the warehouse. Surely the team looking into the poultry processing plants is likely to have more luck finding them.'

'You don't seem to have listened to the briefing very carefully,' interrupted Sergeant Peters, 'or you'd know we're also looking for the place Tomas, the body found on the beach, was murdered and entered the river. And we don't know they've stopped using a warehouse. We only know that some men were transferred from there to the house in Cobham. If you're looking for the wrong things, that might perhaps explain why we haven't found anything.' He glared round.

The rest of the team hastily dissociated themselves from the skinny uniform with bad teeth and a morose expression.

He scowled too, and downed the last of his heavily sugared coffee before getting back into the van.

'Ok,' said Jim. 'Back to the river. Just to recap the briefing, we're looking for evidence of space being used to house migrant workers, evidence of a violent crime being committed and of a body being deposited in the river. Hence, the probability is we're looking for an unused, or little used, warehouse with easy access to the river but reasonable road access. The warehousing in active use is therefore low priority at this point, unless something strikes us as odd. We're also not interested in the storage further from the river, certainly nothing on the wrong side of Southtown Road. Is that clear? Ok, let's carry on working our way towards the river mouth.'

They drew a blank at the warehousing in the first rank between Haven Bridge and Bunn's Lane, which ran down to the water. All were either in active use and well maintained, or dilapidated and empty. None of the latter showed recent signs of access or of having been used by anything other than pigeons, rats and seagulls.

Moving on to the areas accessed via all the other side lanes leading towards the river was similarly unproductive. Jim could sense the team flagging again, and was about to call for another stop and refresh, when something near the end of Ferry Lane attracted his attention. Behind a ramshackle wire fence some ragged sycamores and shrubs loomed over single-storey sheds arranged in a makeshift quadrangle. The rickety gate was clad in rusty corrugated iron and padlocked. So far, so normal, and Jim was about to turn away again when he realised what had caught his eye.

Through the rusty holes in the corrugated metal, he had a glimpse of something shiny.

'Stop here,' he said, and the car pulled up with the van behind.

'What's up, boss?' asked Phil Peters.

'Not sure yet. Just hang on a minute while I take a closer look at those gates.'

He climbed out of the car and walked over to the gates. Beneath his feet the rough earth was churned and muddy, only partially hardcored. Once at the gates he shook them firmly, but the big old padlock, attached to what looked like a motorbike chain, held firm. He walked along the gates, trying to see what had caught his attention, then stopped. He looked again, and realised that the bright flash he had seen was new metal. There was a second, reinforced gate behind the old one. Moving more swiftly he went to the fencing beside the gate to see what else was visible. Nothing. The fencing was a mixture of old wall and wooden fence at least seven feet high. He turned to the team who had got out of the car and van and were watching him.

'Send the drone up,' he commanded. 'There's something not quite right here.'

Jim and Phil Peters crowded round the operator with the iPad screen. The drone hovered low over the gate which had attracted Jim's attention, and then over the yard beyond.

'Don't go too low,' said Phil. 'It would be embarrassing to lose it.'

'Sort of a "can we have our ball back?" moment,' agreed the operator. 'It has been known.'

He brought the drone up again, but not before Phil pointed at the screen.

'Looks like there's been some traffic in there. Look. Wheel tracks. Quite a few turning in that space before the sheds.'

'Or one making repeated visits,' agreed Jim. 'Can we take a closer look at the sheds?'

Unlike most of the warehousing in the vicinity, these sheds were long low units, more like old-style cattle sheds than storage. Definitely too low for lorries to drive in. There were three of the sheds arranged around the sides of a square, leaving one side open to the perimeter fence and the gate. Two were clearly old and ramshackle, their asbestos-sheeted roofs covered in moss, and plants growing in their broken gutters. The third was newer, the roof bright steel and the walls solid brick. There were no windows. The single door was also bright metal and, when the drone operator focused the camera, they could see another strong padlock on the door.

'All quite normal,' muttered Jim, 'so why am I getting a gut feel about this place? Apart from the vehicle tracks there's nothing out of the ordinary here. It would fit the description Matis gave, but that was so vague almost everywhere would fit. I can't see anything that would justify a warrant.

'Do we have a record of the owners or tenants?'

Phil scrolled through the list on his phone. 'It looks like it's down on here as Bridges Agriculture.'

'Aren't they the grain merchants down at the main port?'

'That's right. But they also seem to hold leases or own property in these old port areas by the river. I've got their name next to several of these Southtown units.'

'Got a contact number?'

'Yes. A Yarmouth number.'

'Let's give them a ring then and see if they'll give us permission to go in and have a look round.'

The phone call to Bridges was productive. The man in the head office at the new deepwater port seemed pleased to be asked to help. He joined them at the locked gate in only the time it took for him to drive upriver from the port, cross Haven Bridge and make his way downriver to Ferry Lane.

'Sorry for the delay,' he puffed as he extricated himself from his pickup. A tubby man with forearms like hams, more hair on his face than his head, and a ruddy complexion, he looked more like a farmer than an office boss.

'Ian Rhodes,' he introduced himself. 'Sorry to keep you waiting,' he said again. 'I was only a short distance away as the seagull flies, but I had to trek all the way round by the Haven and you know what the traffic's like.'

'No problem,' said Jim. 'Thank you for coming. Can you open the gate for us?'

'Well, let's see,' said Ian, producing a huge bunch of keys. 'I don't think anyone has been in here for an age, but one of these should fit.' There were multiple rings on the bunch, each with a different type of key. 'These look the right sort,' he muttered, 'right for a padlock anyway,' and tried each in turn. No luck.

'Oh,' he said, surprised. 'Well let's see what else we've got.'

He tried multiple keys from a range of options. Nothing worked. The police waited in silence. After some time he admitted defeat.

'I'm sorry,' he said, 'but I don't seem to have the key to this padlock. And that's odd because I've got all the keys to all the Yarmouth warehouse properties here.' He jangled the bunch at Jim. 'I'm really sorry. I don't understand it, unless this is not one of our padlocks and that doesn't make sense. Why would someone else lock up one of our yards?'

'When were you or anyone else last here?' asked Jim.

'Oh, not for ages. Probably six months at least. Maybe more. It's a long time since we used this area. It's a hangover from a company we took over a few years ago, and it was pretty derelict even then. The old company, Kay's I think it was, had inherited them from an earlier incarnation that used to ship livestock. But we've never done that and these sheds are completely unsuitable for modern grain storage, so they just sit here until we might need the space for something else.'

'If this isn't your padlock, do you have any objection to us breaking in?'

Ian hesitated. 'Well, I'd need to fetch a replacement in order to secure the site again, but I suppose not. No. Ok. Go ahead.'

'To be clear,' said Jim, 'you are giving us permission to break into this site?'

'Yes,' said Ian. 'You have my permission to remove that padlock,' he pointed, 'provided you'll keep an eye on this place while I go and fetch a replacement.'

'That's agreed then,' said Jim, and to Phil, 'Let's get the bolt cutters.'

One sharp snick, and the padlock fell to the ground. One good push, and the chain unravelled as the gate creaked open.

Jim looked round. The general topography was as indicated by the drone, but seen close up, the contrasts between neglect and renewed were more obvious. Two of the three sheds forming a rough courtyard were dilapidated. Brickwork was loose with rotting mortar and metalwork showed rust-red in more places than not. The muddy yard was rutted with wheel tracks. An area towards the river was overgrown with buddleia and willowherb, while a lanky sycamore overshadowed all.

'Steve, you come with me, we'll have a preliminary look round. Phil, you keep the drone up and let me know if anything changes,' and as Ian pushed towards the open gate, 'Sorry Mr Rhodes, would you mind keeping back for the moment? I'll call you through as soon as we need your help.'

'Oh, Ok,' said Ian, and stepped back. 'I'll wait in my car then.'

Jim and Steve stepped into the yard and looked round.

'These van tracks look recent to me,' said Steve.

'Yes. Let's keep over to the side and avoid trampling anything. I think our first port of call should be the newer looking building.'

To their surprise, the sliding door was unsecured. A chain hung from a hasp on the adjacent wall, but there was no padlock. Jim pulled gloves on and slid the door to one side, far enough to permit him to pass. He and Steve peered in, then recoiled from the smell. The space was only dimly lit by greenish light from algae-covered skylights. As their eyes adjusted to the poor light after the bright day outside, they saw a pile of thin foam mattresses in the corner, topped by a jumble of what looked like sleeping bags or duvets. In the opposite corner were two or three buckets, which appeared to be the source of the smell. Adjacent was a pile of pallets with another bucket on top.

'I'm going to go in alone, to minimise disturbance. You stay here for the moment, Steve.'

Jim slid round the door, stepping carefully to avoid touching anything. Using his phone he took photos of the mattresses and the bucket arrangements, then stepped back outside.

'The buckets appear to be toilet and washing facilities respectively,' he said, 'and they haven't been emptied, which explains the smell. This is consistent with the description by Matis of the temporary arrangements for the one night they stayed here, allowing for the fact that any personal stuff was removed when the men were moved on. We need the SOCOs here to crawl over this in detail, but I'm satisfied that this is the place, or one of the places, where the men were taken when they suddenly couldn't go back to Wayford Bridge. Come on, I've taken some photos. Let's go and show them to Ian Rhodes.'

'None of that's ours,' said Ian positively, when faced with the evidence of occupation. 'Those sheds should all be empty. Hang on a minute, can I see that last one again?'

It was the one of the shed door and hanging chain. In the top of the picture was also a strip of roof.

'It wasn't like that when I saw it last,' he said. 'That roof – bits of it look new. When I saw it last, it was all old asbestos sheeting. It was one reason why we hadn't got round to demolishing the sheds. Someone's patched it with corrugated iron.'

'Show him the sheds on the drone footage, Phil.'

Phil proffered the iPad and Ian stared at the footage of the sheds, two roofed entirely in asbestos, one showing leprous patches of brighter metal.

'There,' he said, pointing. 'All three should be like that. Just old asbestos. Someone's been mucking about with the third.'

'Which suggests,' said Jim, 'that they have used that shed on more than one occasion. Otherwise, why bother repairing the roof?'

'Or someone else has,' said Steve.

'True,' said Jim. 'When did you last see this yard, Mr Rhodes?'

'Not sure exactly, without checking my diary, but I'd say at least six or seven months ago. Possibly nearly a year. Like I said, we don't have any use for this yard nor any plans for it.'

'Ok. Get the SOCOs here, Steve, and while we wait for them, we'll have a quick look in the other sheds. You can go now, Mr Rhodes. You've been very helpful. We'll let you know when we've finished here, but you can be sure it will be secure. We'll be treating it as a crime scene.'

The other two buildings proved to be empty of everything except dust and broken pieces of timber which might have come from fencing or hurdles. Steve was just poking about among the weeds in the corner of the yard when there was a shout from the gate.

'Hi,' shouted Phil. 'Ian Rhodes says to be careful of the manhole. He's just remembered that the cover wasn't safe when he was here last. He put a pallet over it at the time, but the weeds have grown up a lot since.'

'Ask him where it was.'

'He says in the corner by the sycamore.'

Steve and Jim approached the ragged tree with considerable caution, but the manhole was easy to spot when they got closer. The nettles had been crushed and straggly buddleia bushes had broken branches. The rusty cover was more or less in place, but a gap was visible round the far edge.

'Something's been dragged here,' remarked Jim.

Steve agreed and, as Jim took more photos, he stepped sideways to take a closer look at the flattened nettles.

'Look here,' he said. 'Is that what I think it is?'

On the edge of the manhole's concrete surround was a dark stain, partly obscured by the squashed nettles.

'Don't get any closer,' instructed Jim. 'We need the SOCOs to look at that too. But yes, I think there's a good chance that's blood.'

'Phil,' he said raising his voice, 'ask Mr Rhodes what's under the manhole cover.'

There was a pause and then the reply, 'He says there's a big drainage channel that took waste water from the yard to the river.'

'I think we may have discovered how Tomas got into the river,' said Jim.

16

The riverbank and Stalham Poultry

Greg was back in the lifeboat and on his way to a rendezvous with the search dog team when his phone found an ephemeral signal and rang.

'Hi, Jim,' he said. 'Any progress?'

There was a long pause while he listened, struggling to hear over the engine noise and the flickering signal.

'That's great, well done, Jim,' he said. 'What led you to it?'

'The inappropriately reinforced gate in the first instance,' replied Jim. 'It took me a few moments to work out what alerted me, but everything else was old, dilapidated and dull. Bright metal was incongruous. At the time, I just knew something didn't fit, but thinking back, that was the trigger.'

'And what's the latest on the drain?'

'Our local contact, Ian Rhodes, has turned up some old maps. The drain runs in a straight line from the manhole in the old lairage yard to the riverbank. I've had officers check it out. The outfall measures three feet in diameter and there's no grid or grating that we can see. I've got the SOCOs checking around there and along the riverbank, but they don't think they'll find anything after multiple tides. One man has been down to the bottom of the shaft at the yard end and shone a torch down the drain. He couldn't see anything except a shallow trickle of water. We're waiting now on borrowing some kit from the water board. They have a sort of probe they use to check drains and pipes. We can send that down pretty much all the way to the outfall. No one is keen to send a man down as we don't know how structurally sound the old pipe is.'

'That all sounds great. Thank you, Jim,' said Greg again. 'I'm on my way to see where we think the poacher Jackson went in the river. After that, I'll head back to Wymondham. I think a general catch-up this afternoon would be good.'

'How are they getting on with checking out possible employers?'

'I'm not up to date on that. Last thing I heard they were checking on poultry units and processing plants near Thetford. I'll make sure we have a report back from Sarah this afternoon.'

The lifeboat rounded the bend to see Jenny Warren and her dog partner sitting on the bank. Both rose as the lifeboat approached – Jenny to catch the line, Meg to bark. Jenny waved frantically to prevent the lifeboat steering straight over the blue item she could see below the water.

'There,' she shouted. 'That's what I think we should retrieve. Over there.'

The boat turned sharply and then reapproached the bank from a different angle. Greg stepped out, reflecting as he did so, that he was getting rather better at this, just before he stepped heavily into a cowpat. Jenny tried, with limited success, to hide her smirk as he dragged his feet, trying to clean up his shoe on the rough grass. Even the spaniel had a superior expression.

'The items Meg found are over here,' she said, pointing to the old tree trunk. 'I used some clothes from the victim's home to give her a scent, and she signalled on these.'

Ned stepped forward. 'We'll take these,' he said.

Jenny nodded, then turned to the river. 'The other item I thought might be worth checking out was the blue box in the river, over here.' She pointed to where the lifeboat had made its original approach.

Ned looked up. 'We won't find much on that now it's been in the water for hours,' he said. 'But it's worth a closer look. Can the lifeboat team get it?'

'No problem,' said the cox.

And Ned added, 'If you can keep it right way up as you pull it out, that would be great.'

They moved the boat over to the blue shadow under the rippling water using oars only and after some effort from two crew hanging over the side, they retrieved the box. As in most parts of the Ant, the water was shallow: little more than three feet deep at that point. The lid, which was some distance away, was harder to reach, but they got it out after some splashing around and more wetting of arms and upper torsos. Returning to the bank, they handed their booty over to Ned.

He studied the box with care, showing particular interest in the small holes drilled at regular intervals round the top end of the box.

'What are those for?' asked Greg.

'My best guess is that this has been used to contain something alive, like fish. I think these are air holes. The lid would fit on tightly so whatever it was wouldn't jump out, but there would still need to be some air exchange to keep the water aerated. The victim in this case was well known to be a poacher, so it's a reasonable guess. We can test the box and the sludge in the bottom of it for anything that might indicate what, if anything, had been kept in it. But, after this time underwater, it's a long shot. Most importantly, this box is almost identical to the one we found at Stalham Poultry.'

'You're sure of that?'

'Oh yes. I'm sure. We'll see what we can find and we'll test the vacuum flask and haversack. We'll do the usual analytics on the fluid in the flask, but it looks and smells like milky tea. We can also test both items for DNA. There's a chance we might find some inside the haversack and on the lip of the flask.'

'What about the riverbank. Is this where he went into the water?'

'Can't say. It seems possible someone was sitting on the bank just here.' Ned pointed out marks in the shorter grass on the edge of the river. 'Those look like marks of a fishing stool. If these other items are linked with Jackson, then it's possible it was him on the bank. If he'd toppled in from his stool, we wouldn't expect to see much else. Bearing in mind where he ended up, this is the right area for the body to have started off.

But even if the DNA evidence is there, connecting Jackson to the picnic and proving this is where he was killed are two different things.'

'No blood then?' said Greg hopefully.

'Not that I can find. Bummer, isn't it?'

The day had started normally enough for Lukas. An early breakfast alone, a cup of coffee delivered to his wife in bed, then off to Stalham Poultry on the first shift of the day. He arrived in good time and was changing into his unit overalls when his assistant arrived. His heart sank. Dragan Bakalov did not normally work with the poultry. Mostly he drove the vans that delivered workers to the farms, but Lukas had come across him before when the firm was shorthanded. It was never good news. He looked at him now from the corner of his eye, as they both sat on the bench which divided the 'dirty' outward side of the changing room from the 'clean' inward side that led into the units.

Dragan looked as bad-tempered as normal. He was a burly man with a neck as wide as his head and tattoos covering his arms and shoulders. The drawings on his skin seemed to be mainly of daggers and guns. At least one looked to Lukas like a gang symbol, and he took care not to look too closely.

'Morning,' he said in a neutral tone.

Dragan grunted, then pulled a packet of cigarettes out of his pocket and made to light up.

'Smoking is not permitted here,' said Lukas boldly.

Dragan paused with the packet in his hand. For a moment Lukas thought he was going to kick off and reflected that, on this day, it seemed they weren't even going to make it into the sheds before there was a row. He tensed, but the moment passed.

'All rubbish. All waste of time,' grunted Dragan. 'No birds here. No risk. Rubbish.' He snapped his fingers, but took his cigarettes outside.

Lukas finished changing and went through into the deserted sheds. They were indeed echoingly empty. The formal cleanse and disinfect had been completed under official supervision. Now they were to do a final clean before the next batch of turkey poults arrived on the morrow. He got out the stiff brushes and the disinfectant, and started the hose down of the floor and walls. It was almost an hour before Dragan joined him. Lukas guessed that his arrival in the shed was probably connected with management arriving in the offices, although judging by the sounds of a car driving off, whoever had come in had gone again pretty swiftly.

'Rubbish, all rubbish,' grunted Dragan again, and marched across the wet floor towards Lukas. 'I hose, you brush,' he said, as he put his foot squarely in the middle of a puddle and went down hard, the back of his head striking the concrete floor as he landed.

For a moment Lukas gaped, expecting a swift and irate return to the vertical and preparing to get out of the way in a hurry. But Dragan did not get up. Cautiously, Lukas went over to the recumbent bully, then bent down to check the pulse in his neck. To his relief there was a strong heartbeat. The last thing Lukas wanted was to have to resuscitate Dragan, particularly if there was any risk he might regain consciousness during the process. The probable reaction just didn't bear thinking about. He took hold of Dragan's shoulder, preparing to roll him into the recovery position, but just at that moment his eyes flickered and he shook his head. The return to awareness was swift.

Dragan swore in what Lukas assumed to be Romanian, and shook Lukas' hand off his shoulder. For a moment he lay where he was, then tried to regain his feet. He was clearly unsteady, but when Lukas reached out to help him, he shook him off again and cursed some more. Lukas stepped back, and watched cautiously as Dragan did eventually manage to get up and leaned heavily on the wall.

'You should come and sit down,' Lukas said, and after a long delay and many fits and starts, he managed to encourage Dragan to stumble back into the changing room and to sit on the bench seat.

'Wait there,' he instructed, 'while I get Mrs Pritchard to ring for an ambulance.'

'No,' said Dragan, but Lukas ignored him and hurried off to the office.

Mrs Pritchard was enjoying her first cup of tea of the morning. She was so startled by Lukas' arrival she dropped her biscuit on the floor.

'Tchah,' she exclaimed, and blew the dust off before putting it back on her desk. 'Now what's the matter, Lukas?'

'Accident,' he said tersely. 'Need to ring for ambulance.'

Mrs Pritchard went a little pale. 'Not another death,' she spluttered round her tea.

'No, nothing like that, but this man Dragan, he fallen and banged head. Hard. Must ring for ambulance.'

At that point Dragan arrived in the office. Never an attractive prospect, his clothes were now covered in muddy water and he had a trickle of blood descending the back of his neck.

'No,' he exploded. 'No ring. No ambulance.'

Mrs Pritchard looked from one to the other, the phone in her hand.

'Well do I ring or don't I?' she asked, exasperated.

'Ring for ambulance,' insisted Lukas.

'No,' insisted Dragan.

'He's upright, and conscious,' said Mrs P, giving way to the more forceful personality. 'Perhaps we can deal with the cut here. I have the first aid box. Or someone can drive him to A&E.'

She looked at Lukas hopefully, having little desire herself to share a small space with Dragan and his tattoos.

'Ring for ambulance or I will,' Lukas put his foot down. 'He was unconscious. He have concussion, probably. It's big issue for health and safety. Ring.'

At the mention of the dreaded H and S words, Mrs P gave way and made the call.

Dragan glowered and made for the door, taking the keys to his van from his pocket. Lukas took them from him neatly and passed them to Mrs P.

'Definitely not drive,' he said, and with a swift push landed Dragan into a chair. 'I stay here until the ambulance,' he assured Mrs P and stood over Dragan in the chair.

The latter seemed to be in a temporary difficulty and, correctly guessing the next eventuality, Lukas grabbed up a waste bin just in time to catch Dragan's vomit.

'Ugh,' exclaimed Mrs P and recoiled towards the office door. 'I'll just, I'll…' and she retreated further. 'I'll wait for the ambulance outside,' she said faintly, with one hand over her nose.

Ben got the call just as he was loading his car for his morning's work.

'What? Stalham again,' he exclaimed. 'Not another dead body I hope.'

There was a squawking from his phone, and he gathered that this time the body was up and walking.

'Suspected concussion,' he confirmed. 'I assume you want me to assess whether he needs to come in? Ok got it. On my way.'

It was only twenty-five minutes between making the call and Ben arriving in the office. Lukas was relieved, as Dragan had been getting increasingly stroppy about being kept in the chair and had made repeated efforts to leave. Lukas had only won the argument because Dragan was clearly not firing on all cylinders. There had been no repetition of the nausea and Mrs P had ventured back to her desk in order to begin completing an accident form on Lukas' instructions. This had necessitated a thorough search of her filing cabinets as the forms, for some reason, appeared to have been mislaid.

'I don't know when I last filled one of these in,' she muttered, as she shook some dust off the curling papers from the bottom of a drawer. 'Not for ages.'

'Yes,' said Lukas. 'Is problem. Should always be filled in when there is accident.'

‘Well of course,’ said the harassed secretary. ‘And I always do. The last one here is from when I tripped over a filing cabinet drawer. But I can’t fill forms in for accidents I’m not told about. That’s your responsibility, Lukas.’

‘I always report to Mr Metcalfe. As told.’ he said. ‘Always.’

‘Well he hasn’t reported anything to me. How strange. Are you sure?’

She was interrupted by Ben’s arrival. Lukas was pleased to see an old friend and strode forward with his hand out.

‘Hello. Good to see you again.’

‘Hello,’ returned Ben, shaking the outstretched hand.

For a moment as their hands were joined, the two men almost looked like brothers, despite the disparities of nationality, age and occupation: both dark, both lean and fit, both with sharp-cut features and a smile that somehow shone with goodwill.

The illusion vanished as Ben turned to his patient. ‘What have we here?’

Dragan said nothing and continued to glower.

Lukas explained. ‘This is Dragan Bakalov. He slipped on wet concrete in the shed and banged his head here.’ He pointed to the back of his own head.

‘Did he lose consciousness?’ asked Ben as he looked at the abrasion on the back of Dragan’s head. He got out his small torch and tried to look into his eyes, but his patient wasn’t cooperating and kept twisting his head from side to side. He looked again at Lukas.

‘Was he unconscious at all? Out of it?’ he translated.

‘Yes,’ said Lukas. ‘For a few moment only. Then he got up.’

'Can you look at me please,' said Ben to Dragan, who snapped, 'Is all rubbish. No need.'

At least that gave Ben chance for a quick look at his pupils, then he took another look at the back of his head.

'He was sick too,' said Mrs Pritchard with a look of distaste. 'In my wastepaper basket.'

Ben suppressed a grin and stood up. 'I think he probably has a mild concussion and he should have the cut on the back of his head cleaned up and sutured. He should be checked over at A&E just in case there are other problems I can't see. Can someone take him into the hospital?'

Mrs P and Lukas looked at each other.

Lukas sighed. 'I can take him if it's ok with Mr Willis,' he said. 'But I can't wait there. I'll need to come back and finish preparing the sheds for tomorrow's delivery. And I have no help now.'

'Not going,' said Dragan.

'Yes you are,' said Ben. 'It's important you're checked over and that cut needs attention. What about family? Does he have any family locally? Where does he live?'

'Not going,' said Dragan again. 'Mind own business.'

Mrs P and Lukas looked at each other again.

'I don't know of any family, nor where lives,' replied Lukas. 'He not work here on normal day.'

Mrs P, feeling obscurely guilty, said, 'I don't have an address for him. I think he works for the contractor who provides labour and, as Lukas says, he doesn't usually work here. I assume Mr Willis or Mr Metcalfe would know more.'

Ignoring Dragan's contribution Ben said, 'If you can take him in Lukas, I'll let them know to expect him.' Then to Dragan, 'I appreciate you don't want to go to the hospital, but it *is* important they check you out. It is possible you could have a bleed on the brain and if that went unchecked it could do a lot of damage. Much the best to be checked over, believe me.'

'I'll let Mr Willis know, and Mr Metcalfe,' interrupted Mrs Pritchard. 'I'll see if they have an address or family contacts for him. And I'll talk to them about who should join him at the hospital and see him home. As for taking him in, I do think the best answer is you, Lukas.' She looked at him approvingly, more than a little relieved it wasn't her taking Dragan in her car. 'I'll make sure we sort something out so someone else collects him. That way you can get back to work here as soon as you drop him off.'

'Ok. Let's get going.'

Ignoring the grunts and resistance from Dragan, the other two men shepherded him out to Lukas' car and put him in it. It was a measure of his current weakness and dizziness that they were able to do so without a fight, reflected Lukas. After two attempts to get out of the passenger seat were thwarted by Ben pushing him back down, the two men exchanged glances and Lukas got behind the steering wheel.

'Good luck,' said Ben, and added quietly, 'Is he usually as difficult as this? Irritability can also be a symptom of a head injury.'

Lukas grinned. 'From what I know, this is normal,' he said, and nodded as the car pulled away.

Dragan glowered through the window.

*

To Lukas' relief, his reluctant passenger was totally silent during the drive to Norwich. Whether the motion of the car was partially responsible for a return of the queasiness, or there was some other reason, Dragan seemed more quiescent. Lukas thanked his stars for the temporary truce. He had no wish to be responsible for Dragan's death, even by inaction, but having the viscerally violent Romanian in his car felt rather like holding a rattlesnake by the tail.

At the hospital he was lucky enough to grab a dropping-off space and escorted Dragan into the A&E waiting area. It was busy, and it seemed likely there would be a long wait. He sat him down near the reception desk, reported his arrival, then looked at him for a moment. Dragan did not look up.

'You go,' he muttered.

And Lukas did, heaving a heartfelt sigh of relief.

The moment his back was turned, Dragan got out his phone and pressed a predial number. He listened for a moment, then said, 'Had no say.'

The voice on the other end said, 'Well don't hang about there for too long. Get the cut fixed and get out. Take a taxi. And don't give them any information you don't have to.'

'Ok.'

17

Debrief

By the time the team gathered in Wymondham for a debrief, the corridors were already buzzing with news. When Sarah dashed in her eyes were alight. Greg, about to begin the meeting, paused at sight of her.

'Looks like you've something hot off the press. Let's start with you.'

'We've found the girls,' she said, sitting at the front with an air of triumph. 'Two nail bars and a massage parlour in Norwich, and another two nail bars, one each in Cromer and Great Yarmouth respectively. We've worked in liaison with the Gangmasters and Labour Abuse Authority. They're picking this up as part of a wider investigation in East Anglia with links to shellfish picking and a veg farm.'

'And were they underage?' interrupted Chris.

Sarah hesitated, irritated at having her flow interrupted. 'It seems not. I know we were all a bit worried about the apparent size of the clothes found at Wayford Bridge, but it seems these were petite, young adults, not children. However, as I was about to say, the girls were not Lithuanian. They seem to be mainly Thai, so there are issues about illegal immigration in their cases. As I said, the GLAA are now in the lead.'

'And the rest of the men?' asked Greg.

'Not yet. Some suspect sudden vacancies in poultry processing across the East, but no proof. The men from Wayford Bridge seem to have gone to ground, or been taken out of the area. I've alerted other forces, but most likely they're hidden among similar populations elsewhere in the country. We have colleagues checking the most obvious places nearby, such as Wisbech, but understandably it's not top priority for them.'

'What about the links to Stalham?'

'Only indirect at this point. Several of the girls identified photos of the farmhouse at Wayford Bridge as the place where they were kept. They say they were taken in vans from there to the place of work and brought back again. They never had an opportunity to wander round the farmhouse or the yard, but some were aware there were men kept nearby. We have descriptions of the men who drove the vans. There seem to have been three regulars, but the descriptions are vague, perhaps deliberately so. It's clear the girls are very afraid of the van drivers.

'The GLAA is liaising with immigration authorities about what the girls want to do next – and with the police in Lithuania about the probable route across Europe.'

'What about CCTV footage near the places the girls were dropped off at work?'

'We're checking that out. In most cases they were dropped in back alleys where there's no CCTV, but there are a couple of possibilities in Norwich that may be more promising. In particular, the massage parlour itself had CCTV. The managers were not particularly cooperative and one can't help being a little suspicious of its purpose, but we have some footage that's being scrutinised as we speak.

'The unexpected bonus is that the search for the girls also turned up five locations where smuggled people were being coerced into tending cannabis plants. Our Norwich colleagues are checking that out too.'

'Great news all round, Sarah. Ok. Now Jim, let's have your update on the warehouses in Yarmouth.'

As Jim reported on what they had found in Ferry Lane, Greg, who'd heard it before, found his attention wandering a little. He'd been texting and phoning Isabelle since lunchtime but had no response. It was not like her to ignore his messages unless she was rehearsing, and as far as he was aware she had a free day. He brought his attention back to Jim as he got to the data from the water company robot.

'At first, it seemed we had nothing except confirmation that the drain did go all the way to the river without grids or blockages, but since then we've run the footage through some clever software at UEA and significantly improved the imaging. We think we can see something, a tool of some sort, half buried in silt at the lower end of the drain. We've no idea what it is from the imagery, but if the budget will stand it and the divers are happy, I'd like to get it checked out. If we're lucky it may be the murder weapon. I'd like permission to send a diver down and pretty soon, before any more rain washes anything that's left out to the river.'

'Have you done a risk assessment?'

'Yes,' said Jim. 'I considered a potholer, but as the biggest risk is a sudden influx of water owing to rain, I felt a diver with air supply would be safer. The drain itself seems to be structurally sound. At least, the chap from the water board seemed satisfied with its condition.'

'Ok. Have a word with their commander, with my blessing. Show them the enhanced footage you have and see what they say. If they're happy to risk it, I'll clear it with the Chief Super.

'Next, what did the PM on Mr Jackson show up?'

Chris consulted her notes. 'A single crossbow bolt to the chest went through his descending aorta. Fresh river water in his lungs, so he was alive when he went into the river, but not for long. Shot at close range. The doc's estimate is that he would have bled out within minutes. He'd eaten and drunk lightly not long before his death. Tea and sandwiches the doc reckoned, probably cheese. No signs of alcohol in his bloodstream. No drugs found. The bolt was still in the wound, so we have that, but forensic don't reckon it'll tell us much about the bow. It doesn't leave signs on the bolt the way a gun does on a bullet. On the other hand we do have the make of the bolt. It's written on the side. I doubt that's going to help us much though. Both bolts and crossbows can be bought off Amazon and a hundred other websites. They don't even cost very much.'

'Any forensics from the riverbank location?'

Ned spoke up. 'Matching fingerprints from the shack near Riverside Hens and on the thermos at the other location.

Definitely Mr Jackson's. The haversack didn't provide such a good surface but a wrapping inside it also had partials that match Jackson. The DNA report is still outstanding but I think we can be pretty confident the picnic was Jackson's and that the flask and haversack mark the location where he went into the river.

'And I was right about the blue box we asked the lifeboat crew to retrieve from the river. It's an exact match for the box we found at Stalham, the one with the odd smell and the sludge at the bottom, even down to the holes round the rim.'

'Any proof the two are linked?'

'Not so far, just the similarity in structure.'

'And do we know yet what was in the box at Stalham?

'Not yet. We know what wasn't in it, for example no trace of drugs or chemicals more generally and no prints. We've sent samples of the sludge off to specialists to see what they can find.'

Greg tapped his pen on his teeth, trying to pull all the data into a single picture in his head. He looked at the whiteboards and sighed. 'So, finally, our interviews with the management of Stalham Poultry. Chris, can you summarise the key points please?'

Chris took out her notebook and cleared her throat. 'First, Mr Austen Collier, self-described as director of operations. Says he's responsible for all supplies into the rearing units such as poultry, feedstuffs, energy and so on. At first claimed manpower was the responsibility of HR but subsequently admitted that he had agreed the most recent contract with the gangmaster supplying labour to various sites.

'According to paperwork found at the Stalham site, he

seems to have made a number of trips by ferry from Harwich to the Hook of Holland and to have driven a substantial mileage. One of those trips fits the timing for the transfer of bird flu from Eastern Europe to the Stalham turkeys. On the night of 3 April, the night Jonas Balciunas died in the gassing chamber, Collier's wife's car was caught on CCTV in the vicinity of the unit.'

'So, a person of interest then,' commented Jim.

'Yes,' said Greg, 'if by that you mean the guiding mind. I think it unlikely he would be directly involved in the murder of Jonas, and even less so in the murder of Tomas in Great Yarmouth. There I think we will be looking for one of the bully boys used to keep the coerced workers under control. But he may be a candidate for the man pulling the strings.' He caught an odd expression on Chris' face and asked, 'You don't agree, Chris?'

'I don't know, boss. To talk to, he's a pompous twat. If you met him in a pub you'd assume that he was, at best, roughly half as important as he claimed to be. But what little information we have does seem to point his way. He just doesn't seem to fit, personality wise.'

'You have a point, but I think he's our best bet for a follow-up so far. I think we should get him in for an interview under caution.'

'Before you move on, boss,' added Chris, 'there's one other thing from Stalham. The forensics team found a set of overalls with blood on them. It could be turkey blood of course, but in view of the injury to the victim's head, they're doing a DNA check. The overalls had a name on them. James Metcalfe.'

‘Oh did they? Interesting. Obviously a name tag isn’t evidence of who was wearing them even if it does turn out to be human blood, but perhaps we should keep an open mind on Mr Health and Safety. As for Collier, I think your character assessment is pretty accurate, but let’s see how he reacts to further questioning.

‘Other action, to sum up:

‘First, we keep in touch with the GLAA but leave them to mop up the work connected with the abused workers we have found so far. However, we do need some intelligence from Lithuania on the victims. Anything they can tell us about them would be helpful. Can you keep on that please, Sarah, either through the GLAA or directly if need be?

‘Second, Jim you’re going to organise a diver to see what’s down that drain.

‘Third, Ned we’re waiting for follow-up forensics on Jackson’s place, on the blue box found at Stalham and now the overalls.

‘Fourth, Chris we get Collier in first thing in the morning for an interview under caution.

Well done everyone.’

‘And Mrs Collier?’ asked Chris.

Greg considered. ‘Yes, I think so. But we’ll interview them separately.’

Greg had a quick word with most of the team individually on his way out. All were tired but there was a strong sense of purpose. Progress had been made, even if they felt a long way off resolving the question of who murdered either Jonas or Tomas. He clapped Jim on the back as he passed him, said ‘well done’ to Jenny as he got to the outer door and made a fuss of Meg. He was crouched down stroking the dog when Ned stopped alongside.

'I've got something back from our fish expert,' he said. 'That blue box. He found traces of eel blood. It had definitely contained eels.'

'Eel blood?'

'That's right. Apparently eel blood contains a strong toxin, so it's relatively easy to identify. That's why you should never eat eels raw.'

'I didn't know that,' said Greg, 'but then I've never fancied eating eels any way, smoked, fried or jellied. They look too much like snakes for me. Eels. So, that's what Jackson was after in the river that night.'

'Now we know what we're looking for, we can look again,' said Ned. 'If he'd had eels anywhere at his home or workshop, we'll find traces.'

'Defra suggested there might be eels involved,' said Greg. 'Looks like they may have been right.'

Jenny looked back from where she was loading Meg into the back of her pickup. A little diffidently she said, 'Excuse me, sir, but at this time of year it may well have been glass eels, and they're very valuable. Over 1000 euros per kilo in some parts of the world.'

Greg gaped for a moment. 'I knew they were valuable, but over 1000 euros per kilo. Are you sure?'

'Yes, boss. I've seen figures of up to 1500 euros quoted in East Asia. I'd like to join the wildlife crime team,' she explained, 'so I've been doing some research.'

'How big are they, these glass eels?'

'Oh tiny. No bigger than my little finger. They're an

early stage in the eel's life cycle, and later turn into elvers, then fully grown eels. They look more like transparent worms than fish, hence glass eels.'

'Elvers I'd heard of. How do they catch them, do you know?'

'In nets, a bit like shrimping really, but you have to be licensed to catch them. The price of glass eels caught legitimately is only £150 per kilo. The price of the same eels smuggled out of the UK illegally is up to ten times higher, so you can see the motive.'

'Wow,' said Greg. 'Thank you, Jenny. I think you have just given us some very important intelligence. This could well be the key to what's been happening at Stalham. Ned, can you prioritise that hunt for eel traces? I'll have a word with Chris and Jim about further enquiries.'

In her car by now, Jenny stuck her head out of the open window. 'If you're making enquiries locally, you might want to bear in mind that they have a slang name round here. Folk often call them glass arrows.'

Greg rushed back in and just caught Jim on the verge of leaving. Chris emerged from the ladies as they went down the corridor and they scooped her up on the way.

'Anyone seen Sarah?' he asked, as they sat down in his office.

'Gone home,' said Chris. 'She left just before you went out.'

'Oh, ok. I'll give her a ring later.' He passed on the information from Ned and Jenny's insight into wildlife crime. There was a short silence.

‘That might be the answer,’ said Jim softly. ‘Slave labour brought in, glass eels smuggled out. Just like the mediaeval smuggling trade, only that was wool out, brandy in.’

‘Pretty much as we speculated early on,’ agreed Greg.

‘I assume the trade in glass eels would be seasonal?’ asked Jim.

‘I think so. As they grow into elvers and then eels, the trade would be over for this year.’

Chris had been thinking. ‘This could explain some of the links. Trading eels via Eastern Europe could have been the source of the infection that came from Poland to the turkeys at Stalham. Movement of people between Stalham and Jackson’s place on the Ant, to collect eels or handover instructions or cash, would explain how the infection was transferred from Stalham to Riverside Hens. Perhaps exposure of the leading light in eel smuggling at Stalham was the motive for the murder of Jonas and of Jackson. But is it Mr Austen Collier? I’m struggling to see him heaving crates of eels about, let alone stalking Jackson on a dark riverbank and shooting him with a crossbow.’

‘Lots of questions to answer, agreed,’ said Greg. ‘And we’ll ask them tomorrow. Chris, organise someone to collect Mr and Mrs Collier from their home at 0630 tomorrow. Jim, can you take control of further enquiries around Jackson? You know what we’re looking for: any information regarding his income, what he may have been poaching, and who or where were his outlets. Thanks. See you both tomorrow.’

18

Domestic interludes

Notwithstanding a long and busy day, Ben was looking forward to an evening out with his wife Paula. It seemed ages since they'd had time for a relax and a catch-up, and a table had been booked at a favourite restaurant by one of the Trinity Broads near Rollesby.

They arrived at the Boathouse comfortably early. The evening was so pleasant they decided on a drink outside by the water before taking their reserved table indoors. A pint in front of each of them – bitter for Ben, cider for Paula – they settled at a picnic table nearest the water's edge. Paula pulled her jacket close as she looked out across the broad, its waters completely still except where a passing swan had left a widening vee of ripples.

'I'm glad we're eating indoors,' she remarked. 'It's not as warm out as it appears.'

'Are you cold?' asked Ben.

'Not quite, but one drink and I'll be glad to go to our table.'

The long evening shadows cast by the trees were joined by another, and a voice strange to Paula but familiar to Ben said, 'Good evening.'

Ben looked up, surprised. 'Hello Lukas,' he replied. 'You do get some time away from work then?'

'I was about to say same to you,' said Lukas. 'This is my wife, Esther.'

'And this is mine, Paula,' replied Ben. 'Would you like to join us for a drink?'

'We don't want to intrude,' said Esther in precise and only slightly accented English.

'Not at all. Look, there's plenty of room. Do please join us.' Ben looked round for a waiter as Lukas and Esther wriggled into the seating attached to the table. 'I'll get drinks from the bar,' said Ben. 'What're you having?'

'Oh no,' said Lukas embarrassed.

But Ben waved him down and said, 'No definitely this one's on me. I'm delighted to see you in happier circumstances.' He took their orders, then went in to the bar.

Paula looked at the two new arrivals. 'Do I gather Ben met you at work?' she asked.

'Yes,' said Lukas. 'Twice. The first was very sad, but this week not so bad. It was at Stalham.'

'Oh, I see,' said Paula, enlightened. 'So what happened this week, or shouldn't I ask?'

'This week an accident. A very nasty man slipped and banged his head. I insisted on ambulance and Ben came. But when I took the man to hospital he did not stay.'

Returning with full glasses Ben said, 'Are you talking about the accident this week? Dragan wasn't it? Do I gather he didn't go to hospital?'

'He went all right,' said Esther. 'Lukas took him himself and made sure he was registered at reception. But while Lukas went back to work the man walked out. He is not a good man. Not nice at all. A bully.'

'Oh dear,' said Paula. 'Will he come to harm, Ben?'

'Probably not. He looked like a man with a very hard head, and I would guess he's had worse. But it wasn't very sensible all the same. It's always wise to get a head injury checked over.'

'I think you have a saying,' said Esther. 'Something about a horse to water?'

Paula laughed. 'Yes, that's right. Your English is amazing. What do you do?'

'I am a translator and interpreter,' said Esther. 'And you?'

As the two women put their heads together Ben said quietly to Lukas, 'I got the impression you were the one insisting on good health and safety. Did you get any hassle as a result?'

'Hassle?'

'Trouble.'

'No. I don't think Mr Metcalfe was pleased, but he couldn't say anything, especially with Mrs Pritchard listening. I may find my shifts are not good for a few weeks, but probably nothing else. They need me,' he said simply. 'There many men missing and the ones who are coming know nothing.'

'And Dragan? He didn't look like a man to cross.'

'Not seen him since the accident. He's probably driving vans and by the time they arrive at the farm I am usually in the sheds with the turkeys. I've found out some more about him though, something that might help explain why he is the way he is. You know he is Romanian?'

'Yes,' replied Ben. 'He said so before he went to the hospital.'

'I spoke to one of the men who had come across him in Lithuania, in Vilnius. It seems he was from an orphanage.'

'In Romania?'

'That's right.'

'One of those awful places where the children were tied to beds and had no proper care?' asked Paula.

'That's right,' said Lukas again.

Ben whistled quietly. 'That really would go some way to explaining some things about him,' he said.

There was a pause, then Lukas asked, 'Do you know what is happening about Jonas?'

'That was the man who died? No, I don't know. Except that the police are still looking into it.'

At that moment, Paula interrupted. 'Our table's ready, Ben. Lukas and Esther, are you having supper here? Would you like to join us? I'm sure they could make it a table for four.'

Esther looked at Lukas who said, 'We don't want to…'

'Intrude,' supplied Esther.

'You won't be,' said Paula. 'But equally, we don't want to bother you either, if you have other plans.'

'It would be very good to have a meal with you,' said Esther.

And Lukas added firmly, 'Provided I get the next drinks.'

'Done,' said Ben, and the four moved into the restaurant together, laughing at the ducks and swans squabbling over titbits.

A man sitting at a distant picnic table in the shadows under the willow picked up his phone and took a photograph. Then dialled.

Greg rang home three more times during his drive to Norwich, but still no answer. Perturbed, he pulled into their drive with a scatter of gravel and looked up at the house. There were no lights he could see either upstairs or down. He checked his watch. 9pm. Unusual for Isabelle to be out in the evening without him knowing where or why. Perhaps she was having an early night but no, her car wasn't in the garage. He went into the silent house and foraged in the fridge for his supper. The pickings were slim. Out-of-date ham, tired cheese and an empty egg box. He thought about a takeaway but couldn't be bothered and decided to settle for toasted cheese. Isabelle's car drew up outside just as he finished.

He heard the door open and close, then sounds from the hall of a bag hitting the floor and a coat being taken off. There was a long pause and he was just rising from his chair when Isabelle called, 'Hi, you're home then?'

'Yes, a bit late but not so bad considering. How about you?'

He waited for her to come round the door, but the next thing he heard were footsteps on the stairs.

'Off to bed.' Her voice floated down to him. 'Bit tired. Night.'

Greg put his glass down on the table and considered it. He rejected the idea of an hour or so in front of the TV. An early night would be the thing, then at least he'd be able to have a few words with Isabelle before sleep. But when he went upstairs the light was already off in the bedroom and she was in bed, turned towards the window.

'Gosh, that was quick,' he said.

'Sorry, very tired. Do you mind?' and she pulled the duvet up round her ears.

There was no further movement as he quickly showered and climbed into bed.

'Night then,' he said, but got no response, so he sighed as silently as he could and lay down beside her. Sleep did not come quickly.

At the Boathouse, a convivial evening was coming to an end. Both couples found they had a surprising amount in common considering their respective backgrounds – enough to make the differences in their experience fascinating. By the time they got to the sticky toffee pudding stage, they were firm friends; and when they parted in the car park it was with kisses between the women and matey slaps on the back between the men.

'We should do this again,' called Paula across the car park as they moved towards their cars.

And Esther replied, 'We'd love to,' as she and Lukas got into theirs.

Lukas watched as Ben's car headlights came on, then he turned on his ignition and followed the car in front of him, up the winding drive to the main road.

'That was a good evening,' said Esther. 'The best so far. Do you think they meant it? That we should meet again I mean.'

'Yes I think so,' said Lukas. 'I think Ben is a very straight man, very genuine. And I liked Paula too. It would be good to see them again.'

'Funny isn't it?' said Esther.

'What?'

'Funny that our first friend in England – our first real friend I mean – should be an ex-policeman. I can't imagine being friends with a policeman back home.'

At the back of the grassy overflow car park a man in a pickup sat silent behind an open window. He heard every word of the exchange, and filmed the two cars on his phone as they rolled up the gravel drive. Then he dialled again.

'They've gone,' he said. 'Spent the evening together.' Then in answer to a question from the phone replied, 'I think it was arranged. They met up like it was arranged. Like old friends. And they've just arranged to meet again.'

The voice on the phone said, 'And he's definitely the one who came to Stalham twice and to the River Ant?'

'Yes. Him. Definite.'

There was a pause and the man in the car asked, 'Do I fix him?'

'No. I need to think. I'll let you know.'

*

From Greg's point of view, the morning was little better than the night before. Conscious of his early start with Austen Collier he had set his alarm, but even so Isabelle was out of bed first and quickly into the shower. By the time he had showered and shaved she was downstairs eating cereal.

'You were very tired last night,' he said. 'Are you ok now?'

'Yes of course. Don't fuss, Greg.'

'It's just unusual for you to leap into bed without a chat first,' he said mildly. 'I wondered how your day had been?'

'Fine.' Her attention was still on the cereal and the morning paper.

Greg looked at her, but she didn't look up. 'I need to be off,' he said, 'and I'll probably be late back tonight. Don't wait up for me.'

'Fine. Ok.'

'Isabelle, is everything alright?'

'Fine. I said don't fuss. Bye. Have a good one.' And she looked up briefly before returning to her paper.

He didn't have time to pursue it and got into his car still worried.

Hearing the car leave the drive, Isabelle folded the newspaper slowly and sighed. She leaned back in her chair, sipping her coffee, and wondered drearily what she had done. And what she should do next.

19

9 April, interviews

As Greg dashed through en route to his office, he was waylaid by Steve Hall.

'The Colliers are in the waiting room, boss,' he said. 'They've made it clear they're not speaking without their solicitor present and he's on his way from Norwich. Should arrive any time now.'

'Good. Thanks Steve. Any problems this morning?'

'Just a lot of strop,' said Steve with a grin. 'Along the lines of "didn't I know who he was, didn't I know he's chums with the commissioner and how dare I". He swells up like a toad when he's cross doesn't he?'

Greg grinned back. 'Yes I've noticed that. What about Mrs Collier?'

'Good as gold and silent as a mouse. Never said a word in the car or at the house, beyond "I'll get my coat". Oh and, "What have you done now, Austen?" But he shushed her at that point and started on about the solicitor. We had to hang about while he made the phone call.'

'Ok. I think I'll see Mrs Collier first. Let Mr Collier stew a bit more. He should be brewing nicely after an hour or two's wait.'

Sticking his head round the Ops room door he spotted Chris and said, 'With me please, Chris. We'll see Mrs Collier first. Would you like to lead?'

'Yes boss,' said Chris with enthusiasm. 'Under caution I assume.'

'That's right. Ok.'

Mrs Collier was sitting in the interview room with her solicitor, the same man as had appeared for Pete Willis a couple of days earlier.

She was an elegant woman, dressed in pale camel from head to toe with a striking chunky silver necklace and hoop earrings. Chris estimated her ensemble as costing around the two to three thousand mark. Clearly Mrs Collier had money to spend. She crossed smoothly nyloned legs under the straight camel skirt and pushed the arms of the matching cashmere sweater up from her wrists. Chris noted that there was a chunky silver bracelet or two as well. She administered the caution and Mrs Collier raised an ironic, beautifully drawn eyebrow but responded only to state that she understood.

'Your full name and address please, Mrs Collier.'

'Fiona Louise Collier, Broads Edge, Neatishead, Norfolk. Why am I here?'

'We're making enquiries into the murder of a man at

Stalham Poultry on the night of 1 April and we think you may be able to help us.'

'I can't imagine how. Do I look as though I get involved with rearing turkeys?' She raised the eyebrow again.

'Nonetheless, we have a few questions we would like to ask you. First, what were your movements on the evening of 3 April?'

'I attended my book club in Norwich and had supper there. Then went home, had a nightcap and went to bed.'

'Can anyone vouch for your attendance at the book club?'

'Most of the other members I should think. There are only twelve of us.' She provided the name and phone number of the secretary.

'What time did you leave the club?'

'Around 10pm.'

'And did you go straight home?'

'Yes of course. To save you the next question, I got home around 1030, had a drink of brandy as I hadn't drunk all evening – I don't drink and drive – and went to bed.'

'Did you see your husband during the evening?'

'Hardly, it's a ladies book club.'

'Did you see him before you left for the club?'

'No.'

'And after?'

'He was in when I got home. Watching TV I think. I told him I was back, sat down for a few moments while I drank my brandy, then went to bed.'

'Did he follow you to bed?'

'Not immediately. I heard him come up the stairs later,

but I don't know what time as I was in bed by then and half asleep.'

'Did he go out again?'

'No idea.' She smiled coolly at Chris and remarked, 'You surely don't imagine we share a bedroom?'

The solicitor twitched, but said nothing.

'What's the registration of your car, Mrs Collier?'

'F1 COL.'

'What was it doing in Stalham around 1050 that evening?'

'It wasn't there. It was in our garage by then.'

'It was caught on CCTV camera at 1049 that evening on the road leading to Stalham Poultry. If you weren't driving it, could it have been your husband?'

The solicitor twitched again but Fiona spoke over him with a definite 'No'.

'If you don't share a bedroom, Mrs Collier, how can you be so sure your husband didn't take the car out?'

'Because the garage door isn't far from my bedroom window. It makes a clatter and whine. That I would have heard. I always sleep with my window open.'

Chris looked at her for a long moment. She glanced at Greg Geldard but he showed no signs of wishing to intervene.

'Thank you, Mrs Collier. That will be all for now, but we may need to speak to you again. Could you please wait a little while?'

Outside the interview room she said to Greg, 'She would make a convincing witness in the box.'

'She would,' he agreed. 'Let's see what we get from her husband and then have another word with her.'

As they walked down the corridor to the next interview room, Jill Hayes came round the corner waving a sheet of paper.

'Can I have a word, boss?' she asked. 'There's something I think you should see before you talk to Collier.'

The solicitor emerged from Interview Room One and gave them a supercilious stare as he moved along to Room Two.

'Come in here, Jill,' said Greg, and they moved into the informal suite, used for interviews with children, and closed the door behind them.

'I've been looking at the papers you got from HR at Poultry Enterprises,' she explained. 'I've noticed something. All the labour at all the sites that were part of the original business were supplied by bona fide gangmasters operating under licence from the GLAA. The only sites covered by the special contract set up by Austen Collier are those that were taken over when Poultry Enterprises bought Stalham Poultry.'

'Yet Mr Collier worked for PE before the takeover,' remarked Greg.

'Yes. He was already a director of PE back in…' She looked down at the papers in her hand. '…back in 2012 at least. But I can't find anything that suggests dodgy dealing with gangmasters until early 2016 and it only affects the Stalham Poultry sites.'

'So, what was different about those sites that meant Mr Collier felt free to use illegal employment contracts there but nowhere else?'

'And why did he suddenly embark on that venture, when he hadn't in the past?'

Greg looked at Chris. 'Unless the initiative came from someone at Stalham rather than from Mr C himself?'

'It makes sense,' replied Chris. 'As far as we can see he stayed on the straight and narrow until after the takeover, and the affected sites are only those that were part of Stalham Poultry. At the very least, management on those sites had to be turning a blind eye. Perhaps they were more active than that. Perhaps there was already illegal gangmaster activity underway, and Mr C just cashed in.'

'Ok, let's see what he has to say for himself.'

As it transpired, he had very little to say other than 'no comment', and he said that indefatigably. After an hour in which the only time his tune had varied was when he agreed his name and address, Greg leaned back and closed the folder in front of him. The solicitor jumped in immediately.

'If you have nothing further to ask my client then I assume he and his wife can leave now.'

'Not quite yet.' Greg paused and thought a while, looking Austen Collier straight in the eye.

Collier shifted a little in his seat, then looked away. Greg let the silence drag still longer, then when another unhelpful intervention from the solicitor seemed likely, he said, 'Let me sum up. We have documentary evidence and supporting statements that show the teams working on all the old Stalham Poultry sites were employed on illegal contracts that were arranged by you, Mr Collier. You have so far declined to offer any explanation of these contracts. Are you aware that operating as a gangmaster without a licence is a criminal offence which carries a maximum penalty of ten years in prison and/or a fine? It is also illegal to enter into arrangements with an unlicensed gangmaster. That carries a maximum sentence of six months in prison and/or a fine.

'At the very least you have entered into arrangements with an unlicensed gangmaster. At worst you have operated as an illegal gangmaster. So, Mr Collier, you are heading for court either way. And as long as you persist in this policy of silence, the more you claim power and responsibility, the more I am forced to conclude that you have indeed been operating as a gangmaster and are looking at a substantial prison sentence.' He paused again.

Austen Collier persisted in looking at the table.

'And that brings us to the murder on the night of 3 April and the fact that your wife's car was caught on CCTV near the site late that evening. She states she was home in bed. I ask you again, where were you, Mr Collier?'

Collier looked at his solicitor, who intervened with 'My client has repeatedly said he has no comment to make.'

'Then we will take a break, and I suggest you use it to explain to your client that unless he can tell us why one of his cars was near Stalham Poultry on that night, and whose bright idea it was to exploit Lithuanian workers through illegal gangmaster activity, I will be arresting him for operating as an unlicensed gangmaster and possibly for murder. Interview suspended.' And he left the room.

Back in the office, Greg and Chris filled mugs with thick black coffee and sat down at his desk.

'I still don't think he's the brains,' said Chris. 'I think there's someone else involved among the Stalham management.'

'So who do you fancy? Metcalfe, Innes or Willis? Or all three?'

'Not Innes. There's no evidence he travelled to Hungary or anywhere else and he doesn't seem to me to have the clout. I can't see Collier listening to him. Unless he's a great actor and we're not seeing the real man.'

'Always possible, but I've never yet come across a master thespian, have you? Mostly criminals are fairly dim and obvious. Let's go with the obvious for now.'

'In that case, if I'm going to stick my neck out, my money is on Metcalfe. Willis is just keen to avoid trouble from his bosses. Anything for a quiet life. Metcalfe is the one who couldn't care less about the welfare of the staff. He pays lip service to health and safety, but in reality he couldn't give a hoot. He must have known where and how the men were living, but that didn't bother him either. He has travelled for the company.'

'That's all true of Willis too.'

'Yes, I know, but Willis doesn't feel,' she hesitated, 'ruthless enough. Nor decisive enough. Whatever the precise reason for the murder, someone acted swiftly and ruthlessly.'

Greg let a silence fall as he strung paper clips together into a long chain. 'I think you're right,' he said slowly. 'But we have no evidence, and if we go looking for some we risk focusing on what fits the theory and overlooking what does not. I think we need to go back to square one at Stalham and review everything we think we know and all the alibis we've turned up so far.'

'And Mr *no comment* Collier?'

'I'm going to arrest him for acting as an unlicensed gangmaster and remand him in custody. Maybe a night in the cells will make him rethink.'

It was Steve who took a furious Mrs Collier back to her home, although whether she was more angry with the police or with her husband he found it difficult to decide. He was under instruction to check over all the cars belonging to the Collier establishment, and after some muttering about warrants and a very cold look, Mrs Collier unlocked the up and over garage door and pushed it up. Steve noted that, as she had said, it made a clatter as she did so. He checked around both cars. The sporty Mercedes E class with the number plate A1 COL, and the dark blue BMW Z4 with the number plate F1 COL.

'Any other cars?' he asked.

'No just these two. I don't know about you, but I find it difficult to drive more than one car at a time.'

He ignored the sarcasm and went over to the Z4 again. 'Had this long? It's a nice car.'

'Not long. About a year I think. And yes, it is a nice car, but it's also a cold day and I'm freezing. Have you finished?'

'Yes thank you,' he said politely. 'For now. What was your old car?'

'Another BMW, although what business it is of yours I really don't know. Now, if you've finished, I'm going into the house and I'm going to get my husband a decent solicitor, or at least a better one than that useless wet rag he's so keen on. Goodbye.' She closed the garage and slammed into the house with a decisive bang of the front door.

*

Back in his car, Steve rang Greg.

'Problem, boss,' he said. 'That car caught on CCTV at Stalham. Am I right in thinking it was a pale-coloured saloon?'

'Yes, I think so. Hang on.' Greg went over to the white-board and found the photo. 'Yes, silver or white I'd say. Possibly a BMW but the picture is a bit blurred.'

'Well Mrs Collier's current car is a dark blue Z4. Nothing like.'

Greg was silent a moment. 'So her number plate was cloned.'

'Or it was her old car with the old number plates on it.'

'Surely you take the personalised plates off when you sell a car?'

'Yes. But some folk aren't very careful with them. They leave them lying around or they end up in a skip at a garage after the new plates are put on.'

'Are you still in Neatishead?'

'Yes. Sitting outside the house.'

'Ok, go back and ask her where her old car was sold. Which garage. Then ring me back.'

There was a pause, long enough for Greg to explain to Chris that the CCTV evidence was less useful than it had appeared, then Steve was back.

'Right, boss. Mrs C says it was a private sale to one of her husband's mates. She thinks he was called Metcalfe.'

20

Different threads

The investigation of Ted Jackson's dilapidated cottage did not take long. There was little in the two-up two-down other than battered brown wood furniture, a sofa and armchair leaking stuffing, an unmade bed and ferret cages, which themselves lent a certain unique and pungent note to the atmosphere. The only incongruous item was a large and expensive flat-screen TV on the wall in front of the sofa.

A reinforced metal gun cabinet was fixed to the bedroom wall and was found to contain the shotgun for which he had a licence and some ammunition which was rather more dubious. They also found a building society savings book at the bottom under the ammo boxes, and the total balance made them whistle.

'He was doing well out of something,' remarked Tony Nicholls, as he handed the book to Jim Henning.

'And all within the past year,' noted Jim. 'I wonder if that dates the start of an enterprise, or just when he abandoned an "under the mattress" approach and started using banks. Have we checked under the mattress?' he asked suddenly.

'Yes,' replied Tony with a grin. 'Nothing there and nothing under the bed either except examples of his dodgy taste in photographic literature.'

Jim dropped the account book into an evidence bag. 'We'd better do a check on other local branches to see if he had any other accounts. Have we found a next of kin yet?'

'No. We've asked around locally and only the old folk remember his parents, long since dead. No siblings. No wife.'

'Ok. Secure the property once the SOCOs have finished.'

'What about the ferrets, boss?'

'Ah, yes, I suppose we can't just leave them. You'd better contact the RSPCA and ask if they can rehome them.'

In the Tesco car park by the main road, Dragan was watching as the police cars and scenes of crime van went by. He picked up his phone.

'All gone now,' he reported, then listened. 'Do you want me to clear up?' And after a pause, 'Ok.'

Back at Wymondham, Jim went to the Ops room to update Greg on the morning's findings. He found him in energetic conversation with Sarah, who was herself surrounded by spreadsheets.

'Hi, Jim, Sarah and I were just catching up. She's got more info on the former residents of the farm at Wayford Bridge.'

'Most accounted for now I think,' she said. 'As you know, we found the girls mainly in nail bars, eighteen in total. We've now also found twelve men working in poultry processing and a car wash, plus the original ten found in Cobham. All now interviewed, housed safely in temporary accommodation and their families notified. That just leaves our two corpses, Jonas and Tomas.'

'And on the second,' added Greg, 'I've just had a message from the diving team. They're willing to take a look in the drain and are ready to go this afternoon, weather permitting. How did you get on at Jackson's place?'

'Evidence of a recent upturn in fortunes,' replied Jim, 'both in a large, expensive TV and a building society account. Otherwise, not much else except some savage and smelly ferrets. I've left Tony Nicholls dropping them off to the RSPCA.'

'Ok. So, the latest from me is the interview and follow-up with the Colliers, Mr and Mrs. Nothing except "no comment" from Mr Collier, but Mrs Collier was more helpful. It seems she sold her last car to a colleague of her husband's by the name of Metcalfe.'

'Metcalfe? The health and safety man?'

'None other. And it seems that was the car spotted on CCTV the night that Jonas was killed in the gassing container.'

'But surely she'd have changed the personal number plate when she sold the car.'

'You'd think so wouldn't you, but she says she left all that to her husband and he isn't saying anything, so we don't know for sure. But it seems likely the old plates were left on the car for long enough for someone else to get hold of them.'

'Possibly Metcalfe himself?'

'Very possibly. We need another word with Mr Metcalfe. Chris and I will follow up there, while you liaise with the divers if that's ok, Jim?'

'Absolutely. Catch up later.'

'Before you go, there's one other thing that's been bugging me. I think we're missing something. How did the gang, if gang it is, find the locations to house the men and girls? I doubt they just landed on properties randomly. How did they arrive at the Wayford Bridge Farm and John's place in Great Yarmouth? What did those two places have in common?'

'The obvious similarity is the nature of the owner-occupier,' said Sarah straightaway. 'But on the other hand, people who are cuckooed are classically vulnerable adults.'

'Yes, I see that. But the people who pick on them, whether for County Lines set-ups or similar, are usually locals. They decide on their victim on the basis of local knowledge. But neither James Metcalfe nor Dragan Bakalov could be expected to have that sort of knowledge, especially not in both rural Norfolk and Great Yarmouth. So, how did they pick on those locations?'

'I see what you're getting at,' said Jim slowly. 'Both Tom Potter at Wayford Bridge and John in Great Yarmouth had learning disabilities. They would have been known to and supported by the authorities, at least when they were younger.'

'And both had been discharged from that support as they got older. So, who would have known where they lived, how they lived, and the nature of their vulnerability?'

'Those authorities themselves,' hazarded Jim.

'Right. At least, that's a reasonable place to start. Can we do a check on the records? Who and what organisations were involved with Tom and John? Are there any common links, particularly of caseworkers or other people who have access to the files? And have any of them got criminal links or been displaying any odd spending patterns? That's our next task. Find that link.'

To his surprise, the rendezvous point given to Jim was not the old lairage yard in Ferry Lane but the riverbank. He found the diving team and their supervisor busy in a storage yard located above the drain outfall and a rigid inflatable moored in the river just below it. The area around all the activity was taped off from inquisitive warehouse workers and he had to identify himself a couple of times before he got access to the main site.

'Jim Henning,' he introduced himself to the man in the high-vis jacket labelled '*Coordinator*'.

'Jack Mann,' he replied.

'I don't know why, but I assumed you'd be starting at the landward end of the drain,' remarked Jim.

'We considered it, but taking account of the images from the robot camera, and the fact that the drain is wider and more robust at this end, it made sense to start a diver off here – both because the images that suggested there might be something worth looking at in the drain were closer to this end, and so that the diver can call a halt if they think the risks are too great.'

'Makes sense,' said Jim, peering over the edge of the river wall to the boat below. 'Has anyone gone into the drain yet?'

'Just about to.'

He joined Jim at the wall and waved to the three figures in the RIB below. One waved back and the radio in Jack's hand crackled.

'All ready, over,' it said.

'Received. Go ahead, over,' replied Jack.

One of the dark shapes in the boat reached up to the drain exit and, with a boost from the others in the boat, wriggled in. There was silence for a while, then a series of short messages indicating slow progress. Jim leaned on the wall and checked his watch, then his memory of the tide tables he had consulted earlier in the day.

'How long do we have before the tide rises too high?' he asked Jack.

'About two hours, longer if we were prepared to take greater risks, but I won't sanction that unless there's a very good reason.'

The radio crackles continued to report nothing of interest, and time was running out when Jim was struck by a change in tone. The man in the boat reporting progress sounded excited.

'Boat to Coordinator. Mandy reports object in the drain ahead of her. Going to collect and return, over.'

'Coordinator to Boat, pass on "well done". But say she's to return promptly, over.'

'Boat, understood and confirmed, over.'

'The boat has a cable connection to the diver in the drain,' explained Jack. 'Otherwise reception is too poor. It seems she's found something.'

It was a tense wait for the diver to return, and the tide was lapping only a few inches below the drain when an arm holding an evidence bag and then a head emerged. She scrambled into the boat and appeared to be showing the bag and its contents to her colleagues as the RIB moved along the riverbank to where a ladder gave access to the yard. Jack and the rest of the team waited in silence.

Mandy scrambled swiftly up the ladder and handed the bag to Jack, then stripped off her goggles and helmet.

'This is Mandy,' introduced Jack, 'and Mandy, this is DI Jim Henning.'

Jim saw a thin-faced woman with a hawk nose and close-cropped hair.

'I'm always picked on for the tight jobs,' she said cheerfully. 'There's some advantage to being small.'

Jack was holding up the bag and peering at its contents, then held it out to Jim. 'I think Mandy's found a murder weapon,' he said, 'but not the one I think you were expecting.'

Inside was a crossbow, in camouflage colours and complete with scope.

'Looks like a hunting crossbow,' said Jack. 'Not a child's toy anyway. An expert may be able to identify it further, but it looks like it'd deliver a significant punch.'

'It was caught in gravel about thirty metres from the river entrance,' said Mandy. 'As soon as I get back to base I'll mark it on a map and provide you with a statement.'

'Thanks,' said Jim, taking the crossbow and bag from Jack. 'This is really helpful. I'll get it to the SOCOs ASAP. Thanks for your help.'

Greg looked round his team in the Ops room that evening and felt that, despite small breakthroughs, the atmosphere was tired and a little despondent. He tried to rally the atmosphere with a little good news, but it felt heavy going.

'To sum up,' he started in a cheerful tone, pointing to relevant photos on the board behind him as he spoke.

'One, working with the GLAA we now know where all the men and women are who were held at the Wayford Bridge Farm. All are now safe.

'Two, we have evidence that the illegal contract under which the men were working at Stalham Poultry was agreed by Mr Austen Collier.

'Three, thanks to the diving team, we have what is very probably the crossbow used to kill Ted Jackson. Although why it was dumped at the old lairage unit in Ferry Lane when they had the whole of Norfolk to choose from, heaven knows. Anyway, it's now with forensics to see what they can find.

'We know that Mr Jackson, poacher of his parish, suddenly started earning a lot of money last year. We have evidence that he had been catching glass eels, and we have a link between glass eels and Stalham Poultry where Jonas died on the night of 3 April. The outbreak of bird flu at Riverside Hens, unlucky neighbours of Mr Jackson, argues a link between Stalham Poultry and Mr Jackson.

'We have found where we are pretty sure Mr Jackson was killed and went into the River Ant on the night of 7 April, although we can't prove it as yet.

'We know that a car with the number plate F1 COL was spotted on CCTV near Stalham the night that Jonas died. It appears it was not Mrs Collier's current car, but rather her old one, sold to James Metcalfe last year.'

'Or perhaps a similar car using her number plates, boss?'

Greg paused. 'I suppose that's theoretically possible, Chris,' he conceded. 'But the images were pretty good after the specialists had finished enhancing them. It's definitely the same colour and model, so with the number plate as well, I think we can take it as a working hypothesis it was the old Collier car.

'In short, we have good evidence of links between the three deaths: Jonas, Tomas and Ted Jackson. Two of them worked at Stalham Poultry and Jackson's links are via glass eels.'

'And how the bird flu spread?' added Jim.

'Quite.

'We have the weapon/means for two of the deaths. We have movements of a car now owned by Metcalfe linked with the first.'

'What we don't have,' said Sarah, 'is hard evidence of the reason for any of the deaths. And anything tying Metcalfe to any of them.'

A silence fell.

'The thing to remember,' said Greg, 'is that it's been only a week, and in that time we have freed thirty young men and women from what was no more nor less slavery. We've nailed one of the guilty parties for that, and I propose to charge him formally tomorrow. Mr Austen Collier at the least will be behind bars for a while.

'Meanwhile, go home, get a good night's sleep, and tomorrow we should have some results from the forensics on the knife and Mr Metcalfe safely in our custody suite with questions to answer.'

Sarah stopped him on his way out the door, with a hand on his elbow. 'I don't want to hold you up, Greg,' she said.

'You look as tired as anyone. But I think we are overlooking one aspect. How were the men and women brought into the country? None of them has admitted to knowing any of the names of the men who arranged their travel, and I think they're afraid. All any of them will say was that they were brought in an old jeep or similar. No details at all. Do you mind if I follow up that angle? It might provide us with some of our missing links.'

'Yes, thank you, Sarah, you're right. I'm ok with that.' He smiled tiredly and waved as he went to his car.

By the time he got home, Isabelle was already in bed. There was a note on the kitchen table.

'Pie and beer in the fridge. I have an early start tomorrow so I'm sleeping in the spare room to avoid disturbing you. Sleep well. I.'

He looked at the pie – M&S steak and kidney – but couldn't be bothered to go through the process of reheating it. He made himself a cheese sandwich and ate it standing up, by the window overlooking the garden, drank the beer, and went to bed.

21

10 April, a bad start

Greg had meant to get up early enough to catch Isabelle before she left, but a night disturbed by nightmares in which giant eels chased him down a muddy drain as the tide rose, meant that he overslept. By the time he made it downstairs, unshaven and bleary-eyed, Isabelle had gone. He spotted an envelope on the hall table by his car keys, and smiled as he recognised her handwriting. He'd save that until he was dressed and ready for off.

A quick shower and shave and even quicker breakfast later – the milk was off and so even cereal was out of the question – he paused by the door to pick up keys and note, then went to his car. Tearing open the envelope he read the note inside, then read it again, feeling his anticipatory smile stiffen on his face. He read it a third time, then fumbled for his phone and rang Isabelle's number. There was no answer. There was a long moment while he sat there, both hands on the steering wheel and staring blankly through the windscreen. Then he put the car into gear and drove off towards the A47 and Wymondham. Beside him on the passenger seat, the note in Isabelle's clearly graphic handwriting lay face up. After three readings, the words rang loudly in his head.

'Dear Greg, I never thought to write these words, but I find I have to. I am leaving for a while. I'm sure you will have noticed that I haven't been happy for some time, that I feel we have grown apart. I will be staying with a friend. I will let you know when I have decided what I want to do next. Please take care of yourself. I'm sorry. I.'

The news, the unexpected and brusque communication, had shocked him and he shook uncontrollably all the way to Wymondham. After, he had no recollection whatsoever of the drive, and was endlessly grateful that his autopilot apparently functioned well enough for him to arrive without hurting anyone else. As he walked into the station he felt suddenly weakened and diverting sharply into the toilets he threw up his morning juice and coffee, then sat for a while in the little private booth. Once he left it he knew there would be no more privacy for the rest of the day, and no time for personal tragedy. One last huge sigh, and he emerged to face the mirror, straighten his tie, and note with a minimum of satisfaction that at least he hadn't wept. The black hole where his heart used to be was apparent only to himself. He walked firmly, and only a little stiffly, into the Ops room.

Phil and a civilian assistant Greg hadn't met were already at work with the outputs of multiple CCTV cameras. Ned was in a corner tapping busily at his laptop.

'Give us some good news, Ned,' said Greg.

'Not much from me I'm afraid,' he replied.

'Anything on the crossbow?'

'The good news is that, amazingly, considering where it's been and how it was found, we have managed to isolate some partial fingerprints. No DNA though.'

'And the bad news?'

'We haven't yet matched the fingerprints to any on our database.'

Greg forced a smile, and said, 'Thanks Ned,' before moving on. Just before he reached those labouring over the CCTV tapes, his phone rang. The momentary thought that it might be Isabelle faded as fast as it arrived.

'Constable Nicholls for you,' said the voice.

'Hi Tony,' said Greg. 'What?' then stopped.

'Ok. What are the fire brigade saying? Ok. Secure the scene. I'll get you some help.'

He looked round the room, just as Jim came in.

'Jim, Tony Nicholls has just rung in. Ted Jackson's cottage burnt down this morning. The fire brigade think it's arson. Can you get over there and see what's what? I'm hoping to interview our friend Metcalfe this morning.'

The cottage was a bleak waste of blackened timbers and cracked brick. The roof was gone and only the old chimney still reached up to the sky. The overriding smell was of wet char and smoke. Jim joined Tony at the line still marked by incident tape.

'What are they saying?' he asked, nodding to the fire officers still busy round the remains.

'Evidence of an accelerant,' replied Tony. 'They think a lot of petrol was splashed around the stairs and ground floor, then a match thrown in. Nothing sophisticated. As you can see,' he turned around to survey the scene, 'there are no near neighbours and the fire wasn't discovered until a chap coming off night shift noticed the flames. It had a good hold by then.'

'When was that?'

'Around 5 this morning. His shift finished at 0430 and he was driving past on the road over there when he spotted the flames leaping from the upstairs windows. He called it in and the fire brigade responded in less than twenty minutes, but there was nothing they could do except stop it spreading. They're still damping down as you can see.'

A large man wearing an Incident Commander tabard came over to Jim.

'You'll be wanting a report,' he introduced himself. 'Clayman, Incident Commander. It's definitely arson. There's an empty petrol can in the hedge over there. We haven't touched it. I'm pretty certain it was petrol used to set the fire, and quite a lot of it up the stairs and round the downstairs rooms. I'll let you have an official report as soon as I'm back in the office.' He pulled the tabard over his head and waved to another fireman by the trucks. 'I'm handing over command now, as it's just a question of damping down. No casualties that we can see.'

'The house was empty, or should have been,' replied Jim. 'Thank God we'd moved the ferrets!

'I'm told the fire was reported at 0505 this morning and was visible across the fields by that point,' went on Jim. 'Any idea how long before that the fire would have been set?'

'Not long. A matter of minutes I would think. Once the petrol was lit the fire would spread very fast.'

'Thank you. Tony, where's our witness from this morning?'

'Gone home for some sleep. I'll take you over.'

The shift worker was still up and drinking tea with his wife when they arrived at his terraced cottage a few miles away.

'Should be in bed,' he said by way of introduction. 'And I'm definitely going to regret this later, but it's a bit difficult to settle after all that.'

'Well I'm grateful for the chance to talk to you Mr?'

'Jewson,' supplied Tony.

'Mr Jewson. I gather you spotted the fire from the main road.'

'That's right. It wasn't that easy to see with the sun rising behind it, but something about the glow attracted my attention and when I looked again I realised I could see flames leaping, not just the sun.'

'So the fire had already reached the upper floor?'

'That's right,' said the man again. 'I pulled over to ring 999 on my mobile, then I turned off the main road to see if there was anyone needed my help. It took no more than a glance to see there was nothing I could do about the fire, so after sort of hanging around a bit, I got back in my car to wait for the fire brigade to arrive.'

'Did you see anyone else? Anyone else near the burning cottage?'

'No. The place seemed deserted.'

'Any vehicles?'

'Not by the cottage. I didn't see anything after I turned off the main road.'

'And before that?'

'A Land Rover went past me while I was making the call.'

'I don't suppose you got the number?'

'No.'

'Or noticed where it came from?'

'Not really. It wasn't going very fast so it might have come out of the side road, or I suppose he may have been rubbernecking.'

'He? Did you see the driver?'

'I suppose I must have? I hadn't thought about it. But now you ask, yes, I saw one person in the car, the driver, and it looked like a man.'

'Any other details? What did he look like?'

'No idea, sorry.'

'And what about the Land Rover?'

'Well. I think it was an old one, sort of green, you know, the way they all used to be. Sorry, I don't remember anything else.'

'You've been very helpful, Mr Jewson, thank you. We'll get that written up into a statement and then we'd like you to sign it. Thank you for your help.'

Jim looked at Tony as they walked back to the car. 'May be nothing, but may be worth following up. We'll have to see what we can get off CCTV.'

'Not much round here I'm afraid.'

'No. I didn't think so. Can you do a door to door with all the neighbours in a couple of mile radius. It's not so very many. Ask when they became aware of the fire and what they saw, but also about any visitors to Jackson's place that they may have noticed, especially any with an old Land Rover.'

'Will do.'

In Wymondham, Greg's day wasn't getting any better. Bill Street, detailed to bring in Mr James Metcalfe, had telephoned to say he couldn't find him at Stalham Poultry.

'What do you mean, you can't find him?'

'According to Mrs Pritchard he was due in today, and she thought she heard him in the outer office earlier, but by the time we got here, no sign of hide nor hair.'

'Have you tried his home?'

'Mrs P tried ringing him, both his mobile and at home, but no answer on either. She's tried head office too and he's not there. We're just off to see if he's home.'

'Ok let me know when you have him. I want to see him today. No excuses. Arrest him if you have to.'

Bill drew a blank at the Metcalfe home on the edge of Norwich too. The small detached house was one of a group of seven in a small, gated estate. After fruitless knocking on front and back doors he tried the neighbours. The ones to the right with a smart BMW in the drive denied any knowledge of their neighbour.

'Hardly see him,' they said. 'Keeps himself to himself and seems to travel a lot. The folk at The Pines might know more.'

The Pines had a Mercedes C class in the drive and a Mini in the open garage. More banging on doors and a smart lady answered.

'Can you keep it down please,' she requested politely. 'My husband's on an international call.'

She did invite them in as far as the kitchen. 'I don't know much about the Metcalfes,' she said. 'Mrs M left around a year ago and we haven't seen much of Mr M since. I did see him this morning as he left for work. I'm Jen by the way.'

She was interrupted as a tall, lean man came through from one of the back rooms. 'Sorry,' he apologised, 'but it's taken me two weeks to set up that call and I didn't want to cut it short. I'm Carl Howick. How can we help?'

'He's asking after Mr M,' explained his wife. 'Coffee?' She waved a cafetière.

'Thank you. I'm trying to find Mr Metcalfe. We expected him to be at his office in Stalham but he's not there.'

'I said I saw him leave this morning,' explained Jen, 'but not since.'

'Oh, I have,' replied her husband. 'My office faces the side,' he explained, 'and I saw him drive up a little while ago, then come out of the house with a couple of bags and drive off.'

'D'you know what time that was?' asked Bill.

'Well, I hadn't started my call. I was just putting some papers together and preparing myself, you know, so I'd say about an hour ago.'

'That would be, around 1015?'

'Yes, that sounds right.'

'And that's when I was in the gym,' remarked Jen, 'so that's why I didn't see him.'

'You mentioned a couple of bags. What sort of bags were they? Briefcases perhaps?' asked Bill, making notes.

'No, more like a biggish suitcase and a smaller one.'

Bill looked up. 'Thank you, that's helpful. And thank you for the coffee.' He handed over a card. 'Perhaps you would ring me if he comes back.'

'Sure. Ok.'

'I don't suppose you have a phone number for Mrs Metcalfe?'

'I shouldn't think so,' said Carl, but Jen had gone to the cluttered pinboard on the wall.

'It's just possible,' she said, then 'Yes.' She turned round holding a Post-it note skewered by a drawing pin. 'She gave me her mobile number when they were having some work done, just in case I needed to contact her about the workmen, and it's been pinned here ever since.'

'I keep saying you should sort that board out,' remarked Carl.

And Jen replied, 'It's just as well I didn't,' as she handed the note to Bill.

Back in the car Bill rang Chris. 'Bird's flown,' he said succinctly. 'At least, he seems to have made it away on his toes and his office weren't expecting him to be travelling, so that's a reasonable assumption. We do have a phone number for his departed wife. Shall I give her a ring?'

'Yes. See if she knows where he might have gone or whether she's had any contact with him recently. Thanks Bill. I'll let the boss know.'

Informed of the further bad news Greg grimaced, ran his hands through his hair and said, 'I think we'll have another word with Austen Collier. See if he knows anything. Come on, Chris.'

*

Back in the interview room, Austen Collier was belligerent and nervous by turns.

'Mr Collier,' began Greg, 'you have been arrested and charged with operating as a gangmaster without a licence, which carries a maximum penalty of ten years in prison. You'll appear in court later today for your bail hearing.'

'It's utter nonsense,' interrupted Collier. 'Nonsense. I just employed the men provided to me.'

'That's not what you said yesterday,' said Greg. 'Yesterday you claimed that the employment arrangements for those men were entirely down to you, and the HR team at your office confirmed it was something for which you personally took responsibility. Yesterday you said, and I quote,' – he looked down at his notes – '"the men were seeking work and opportunities in England" which you gave them. You housed them and provided them with transport and support. You implied that the conditions under which they were living were, in your view, entirely acceptable and the deductions made from their pay for the dubious pleasure of living in squalor were entirely reasonable.'

'It was no less than they were used to,' huffed Collier. 'I was assured the arrangements were normal, usual.'

'Who assured you?'

The solicitor at Collier's side opened his mouth, then shut it again as Collier said, belatedly, 'No comment.'

'I don't think you understand your position, Mr Collier,' said Greg, leaning back in his chair. 'So let me explain it to you again.

'You are currently charged with operating as an

unlicensed gangmaster. That's bad enough. But there are no less than three suspicious deaths associated with the use of illegal labour at Stalham Poultry, and if your involvement is as serious as you are leading us to believe, we can only conclude that you are involved there too. In that case you will be facing charges of murder, or at the very least, conspiracy to murder.

'On the other hand if someone else, in reality, arranged the recruitment and supply of the men living at Wayford Bridge and working at Stalham Poultry, then you are guilty only of entering into an agreement with an unlicensed gangmaster. Not only is the penalty for this crime considerably less, at a maximum penalty of six months in prison and/or a fine, but the motive for three murders to cover up your involvement is also significantly less.'

He paused. Collier looked at his solicitor, who shook his head, then looked down at the table.

'Perhaps I should leave you to think about it,' Greg said, and stood up to leave the room.

'Wait,' said Collier suddenly. 'What three murders? I have only heard of one.'

Greg looked at him and sat down again. 'The death of Jonas Balciunas at Stalham Poultry on the night of 3 April, the death of Tomas Simonis in Great Yarmouth sometime between 3 and 5 of April, and the death of Ted Jackson on the banks of the Ant on the night of 7 April.'

'But I had nothing to do with any of that,' exclaimed Collier over the protestations of his solicitor.

'I think I should have a discussion with my client,' said the solicitor, rising, but he was overridden again.

'No. Not murder. I had nothing to do with anything

like that. I didn't even know about two of them. I didn't know the men were illegal. I didn't know any of this.'

'The men weren't illegal,' said Greg softly. 'They had a perfect right to work in the UK as EU citizens. It was your treatment of them that was illegal.'

'No. It wasn't my idea. I just…' He hesitated.

The solicitor tried to interrupt again, but again was overridden.

'James Metcalfe set it up,' he said. 'He arranged it all. Everything was already in place when Poultry Enterprises bought Stalham Poultry. He brought the whole scheme to me. He said we could get good workers for a fraction of the cost. He said that we could charge them for living expenses, and the company would pay us well for the contract. He set it all up. He never told me he wasn't licensed. It was his set-up. His responsibility. Just ask him.'

'We would love to do so, Mr Collier. In fact I have a lot of questions to ask James Metcalfe, but he isn't around to answer them. He's not at work or at home. In fact he seems to have made himself scarce and left you to carry the can. Do you know where he might have gone?'

'No. What do you mean, he's not at work? He should be.'

'He's not,' answered Greg. 'Oh, and by the way, Mr Collier, your claim that you didn't know he wasn't licensed to provide labour will not wash. It was your responsibility to check. I'm sure you've heard of due diligence.' And he left the room.

22

A trap has two ends (old saying)

Dragan was driving down the main road congratulating himself on a good piece of work, when he got the call. Ignoring the hands-free rules he answered his mobile with a gruff 'Yes?' Then, 'Done it. All sorted. Nothing left for anyone to see. Nothing left.' And he laughed.

The voice on the other end seemed agitated.

'I said, nothing to see. Nothing to find,' he repeated. 'All gone. All burnt.'

There was another rant from the phone and he pulled over to a lay-by.

'You want me to sort him too?' he asked.

More squawking, then he said, 'Ok but you need to set up. Needs English voice to make the call. Or whatever. Otherwise, no go.'

*

Sitting by the side of a quiet road near Horsey, James Metcalfe swore, banged his fist on his steering wheel, then realising his phone was in the same hand and somewhat at risk of damage, threw it violently to the passenger seat. He looked over his shoulder but there was no one near and no one had observed him. Gripping the steering wheel so tightly it hurt, he leaned his head on his fists. How the hell had it all gone so badly tits up? And so fast. One minute he was coining it nicely, with that pompous twat Austen all set up to take any flack, next that greedy interfering bastard Jonas is poking around things that don't concern him and a bird flu outbreak wrecks all his arrangements. Now what to do?

How the hell was he to deal with that interfering, meddling first responder? Bad enough that he kept turning up at Stalham Poultry, but now he was palling up with that blasted Lukas, and Lukas knew too much, whether he realised it or not. It couldn't be another coincidence. Not meeting him in the evening. Obviously that bastard was doing some investigating of his own, and he was getting too close. Much too close.

He put the car in gear, still thinking hard.

Later in the day he pulled up by the turning to a small camp of holiday villas. He waited there for some time, watching the traffic pass by without apparent interest, then as dusk fell he started the engine, turned in at the entrance and ignoring the welcome signs pointing to the now unmanned reception, drove round to a small, drab villa at the back of the park. It was the work of but moments to take his two cases in. He drew all the curtains before turning on one dim light, and sniffing damp hurried to switch on the heating. Then he sat down at the table with his phone and a road map of Norfolk.

'Dragan.'

'Yes.'

'That job I have for you.'

'Yes.'

'I'll try to send him to you early tomorrow morning or failing that, later in the day or the day after. But it may take two or three tries.'

'Why?'

'Because I can't guarantee he'll be the one sent in response to my emergency call. I'm going to give you map references for three locations. When I tell you, you will go to location A first. If the wrong man turns up you will do nothing. You will then go to B. Same thing. And again at C if necessary, and if that fails we try again another day.'

'Not good. Not tidy,' said Dragan.

'I can't help that. Have you got a better idea?'

There was a pause while Dragan thought, then he said, 'Just leave? Not worth the risk?'

'You know why we can't do that.'

'Ok. Give me locations.'

After they were passed along and Dragan repeated them back, Metcalfe added, 'No mistakes this time. If it's the wrong man, no action. None. If it's the right one, I don't want to see him again.'

'Ok.'

The holiday chalet was definitely damp with disuse. He tried to remember how long it had been since anyone had used it, and thought it must have been more than a year. The bedding, folded and put away in the airing cupboard so long ago, was unappealing and he spread it out over the back of a chair near the fire to air, then settled down to the sandwich and can of beer he had bought in a hurry from a garage en route. He hoped, with some fervency, that his stay need not be prolonged, and checked through the paperwork in his carry-on bag. The quick flick through the wallet he kept specifically for travelling became an urgent search and then a frantic tunnelling through the whole bag. When he sat back in the chair and picked up his half-empty can of beer, the realisation was unavoidable. His second passport was not there.

For the first time since his hurried departure from the Stalham unit via the back gate as he spotted the police car come in through the front, he started to panic. His rudimentary plan had been to mop up the one loose end, then leave the country for a while until the hue and cry died down. He had faced the fact that he might not be able to come back, but with a healthy balance in a Channel Island account and a useful stash of euros in his bag, he was well equipped to skip to the continent and start a new life elsewhere. He had even begun to look forward to the change and a new challenge. With capital and ideas, he had no fears for the future. Or at least, just the one.

His partners had been blunt about the risks of exposure. They had approved the summary resolution of the problems posed first by Jonas and then Tomas. They had suggested, in a manner that made the suggestion irresistible, that the trail which led to Ted Jackson should also be terminated.

Dragan, reporting to them as well as to him, had raised fears that the meddling emergency responder was conducting his own investigation and, unlike the police, had connected the deaths of the poultry workers with the death of the poacher. So now, he had orders to deal with him too. This time there was no doubt it was an order, not a suggestion.

Metcalfe went to the window and lifting a corner of the curtain looked out across the deserted chalet park. There were no other lights that he could see, other than those near the entrance. He pondered a swift departure from the UK and the possibility of disappearing abroad. Perhaps the Caribbean? First he'd need his spare passport, sitting securely and irritatingly in the safe at home, rather than ready for use in his wallet. Then a quick dash to a major airport, perhaps Manchester. Much better than hanging around to mess with the emergency responder. He sat down again to drain the dregs from his can, knowing that he was fantasising. Whatever the attractions of a quick exit, he knew he dare not ignore his instructions. He wanted, desperately, to escape from the current mess. But not to spend the rest of his life looking over his shoulder. He crumpled the can in his hand, pulled on his coat and got back in his car. Either way, he still needed that passport.

It was Metcalfe's bad luck that his neighbour Carl was on a follow-up call to his US counterpart at the unsocial hour of 1am. Several exchanges during the evening (UK time) and afternoon (US time) had culminated in near agreement. So near, that both men had committed to consulting colleagues and getting back to each other before the US evening was out.

Carl had reflected ruefully that while his opposite number was working into the evening, he on the other hand was going to be up until the early hours of the morning. When he eventually put the phone down on a successful deal for both parties he had been facing out of his office window at just the right time to see his neighbour pull up to the garage door and go into the house. He hesitated, then nipped downstairs to pass on the message from the police, but by the time he got there the car was driving away again.

Back in the house, he pulled the card the policeman had given him from the pinboard and rang the number. He got a duty officer who made a note of the message, then, yawning, Carl at last went to bed.

Back at the chalet, Metcalfe put the passport (name William Hardy; occupation salesman) in the travel wallet and retired for an uncomfortable and short night. Barely four hours later, he booted up the burner phone from his travel case and made the 999 call.

'Ambulance, is the patient breathing?' asked the call centre.

'Yes. No. I don't know. He's gasping.'

'Can you tell me what's happened?'

'I think he's fallen off the cliffs. I found him lying at the bottom.'

'How far has he fallen?'

'Maybe twenty feet.'

'Has he any obvious injuries?'

'His leg's twisted under him. His neck looks odd.'

'Ok caller. I'll get someone to you as quickly as I can.'

'Hurry. He keeps gasping.'

The call centre operator caught the eye of the supervisor. 'The nearest ambulance is some way off. I think we need the first responder.'

'Ok.'

'Can you stay on the line, caller? We have someone coming to you.'

'Ok but my phone is nearly out of battery.'

'The caller's gone,' said the operator, as the first responder on shift and the nearest ambulance were despatched to the location below the cliffs at Scratby.

Dragan, waiting in his vehicle behind the public toilets on the clifftop, saw the emergency response vehicle arrive. He watched the burly man with the heavy bag jog down the steps to the beach, then drove off.

'Wrong one,' he said into his phone.

'Damn. Try again this evening. Be ready at 1830 in location B.'

The emergency responder and the ambulance crew used a similar word, as it became plain they had been the victims of a hoax call.

For the rest of that day, Metcalfe ventured out only once to pay a quick visit to Tesco and stock up on ready meals. He bought a bottle of whisky while he was at it, then spent the rest of the day lurking behind closed curtains, playing games on his iPad and obsessively watching news programmes for any announcements relating to himself. As dusk fell, he removed the SIM card from his burner phone, replaced it with another from his modest collection, then made another call.

'Ambulance. Is the patient breathing?'

'No. I found her face down in the sand.'

'Ok. We'll get someone to you as quickly as possible. In the meantime, I'll talk you through how to do CPR.'

Following the operator's instructions, Metcalfe thumped the sofa next to him in time with the count, then rang off.

In the control room, the operator looked up at his supervisor. 'They were following my instructions, then the phone went dead,' he reported.

'Ok. The emergency responder is on their way, and an ambulance. You can't do any more for the moment. Take a break.'

On his way to the location given, Ben rang the control room back. 'Have you alerted Caister Lifeboat?' he asked. 'I realise this isn't a seagoing emergency but they are all first aid trained and they could give me a hand while we wait for the ambulance. And they're on the spot.'

'Will do,' said the coordinator.

The couple of floodlights in the car park made the darkness on the dunes almost visible. There was a clear demarcation between yellow light fuzzy with evening mist resting on battered tarmac and scarcely penetrable blackness flowing around hillocks of marram grass.

For the second time in one day, Dragan watched an emergency responder leap out of a brightly marked car and set off with a heavy bag, this time across the dunes. Quietly he climbed out of the old Land Rover parked by the new lifeboat station, and after a pause took the alternative route to the designated location via the beach. He slipped the big army knife from the cuff on his arm to his hand.

The location picked out by Metcalfe was a good one. Possibly better for Dragan's purpose than the one by the cliffs. His target was just sliding down the face of the dune as Dragan cautiously stuck his head over the ridge by the beach. He saw the man look round for the casualty, running his torch beam over the sides of the hollow in the marram grass, then he put his bag down and got out his phone.

'Can I just check the location?' he said. 'I can't see anyone at the coordinates supplied.'

'God, I hope it's not another hoax call,' said the control centre. 'We had one this morning. The location I have is what3words...'

Under cover of the conversation, Dragan launched himself from the top of the sand ridge and onto his target. Ben's phone went flying as the knife rose and fell, but the knife hit a second bag on the responder's back and the blow, which should have ended the fight there and then, inflicted only a glancing wound and for a crucial moment stuck in the webbing. Ben shouted both with shock and pain as he went down and then rolled as quickly as he could to his feet. He was aware of blood trickling down his back, and his right arm didn't seem to be working properly. But he still had the torch.

His assailant got up swearing and spitting sand, but he didn't seem inclined to give up. There was still a large blade in his hand.

In the hopes the phone was still functioning Ben shouted, 'I've been attacked. It was a trap. Man with a knife,' and he shone the torch beam into the man's eyes in the hope of dazzling him.

The man came towards him, knife held low, and Ben made an attempt to knock it out of his hand with the torch. It didn't work and the man laughed as he came on.

Ben realised this was a fight he might not win, and eyes firmly on the knife he shouted again, 'I'm being attacked. Knife.'

Before he could say more there was an answering shout from the beach behind him and flashes of more powerful torches. The assailant looked up, just as two powerful figures in high-vis jackets came over the top of the ridge.

'Watch out,' warned Ben. 'He has a knife.'

For a split second, it looked as though the knife man would stand and make a fight of it. Then he turned to run.

One of the high-vis jackets ran swiftly down the face of the dune, then leapt. Dragan, unused to much running on soft sand, went down hard, his knife under him and his face in the sand. The lifeboat crewman sat on his back, while his colleague pushed Dragan's head firmly into the sand until suffocation appeared imminent. Ben sank down onto his bag.

'Ok, mate?' asked the lifeboatman as police sirens wailed in the lifeboat car park and blue flashing lights could be seen in the distance.

'Not entirely,' said Ben. 'He got me with the knife. But it could've been a lot worse. Thank you.'

'So what happened?' asked the one at Dragan's head,

and then added, 'Stop struggling, mate, or I'll push your head in the sand again.' And to Ben, 'You really seem to have peed off this casualty.'

'I think it was a trap,' said Ben. 'There never was a casualty. I got here, found nothing, then this chap jumped me. How did you get here so quickly?'

'We were asked to help by your control room, and were already on our way when we heard you shouting. Here come the reinforcements,' as police and paramedics came over the dunes.

The reinforcements quickly divided into two. The paramedics, attracted by the shouts from the lifeboat team, headed straight for Ben. The police took over the restraint of the far-from-subdued Dragan, heaving and struggling face down in the marram grass.

'Where are you hurt, Ben?' asked the first paramedic, kneeling by Ben's side.

'Back,' he said, as waves of sickness threatened to overcome him. 'Sorry,' and he leaned sideways to throw up on the sand. 'Bit of shock now too,' he added with a twisted grin. 'Jake isn't it?'

'That's right. Better out than in, mate,' replied Jake as he cut away Ben's jacket and applied pressure to the wound. 'Nasty cut, Ben, but I don't think he hit anything vital. Your shoulder blade did a good job of stopping the blow.'

'Just glad the backpack did a better one.'

'Absolutely.'

A few feet away, the police had succeeded in yanking Dragan to his feet, not at all gently. As they did so, there was a shout from the lifeboatman who had been sitting on his head, and he pointed his torch at the knife now visible where Dragan had been lying. One of the police stepped forward and picked it up cautiously in a gloved hand. The torchlight glinted off the dark blade as he put it carefully into an evidence bag.

'Well spotted. I think this is going to be of considerable interest.'

'Hang on,' Ben shouted suddenly, as he caught a glimpse of his assailant through the crowd of police, paramedics and lifeboat crew. 'I know him.'

The police turned sharply.

'His name's Dragan. Dragan Bakalov I think. He works at Stalham Poultry.'

'Well now,' said a policeman who had joined the crowd just in time to hear Ben's identification. 'That's very interesting, Ben. Are you sure?'

'Certain.'

Jim Henning turned to Dragan. 'Dragan Bakalov, I'm arresting you on suspicion of grievous bodily harm, attempted murder and carrying an offensive weapon in a public place. You do not have to say anything. But it may harm your defence if you do not mention when questioned something which you later rely on in court. Anything you do say may be given in evidence. That should do for now,' he said with some satisfaction.

Dragan stared blankly and said nothing.

'He speaks English,' added Ben. 'Not perfect but enough to understand the caution,' and then gasped as Jake increased pressure on his wound.

'We need to get you to hospital,' said Jake. 'At the very least you need stitches. The rest can wait.'

'Quite right,' replied Jim. 'Where are you taking him?'

'The James Paget.'

'Fine, we'll catch up with you there. Ben, we'll let Paula know that you've been hurt but are going to be ok, and we'll make sure she gets to you at the hospital.'

'Thanks,' said Ben, as he was taken away by the paramedics to the ambulance.

A few yards away Dragan, still silent, was being hustled into a police car, handcuffed and under restraint.

Back at the chalet park, Metcalfe waited for the call that didn't come, and realised that something else had gone wrong.

23

Manhunt

Jim rang Greg with the news immediately as he reached his car.

'I think they've made a mistake,' he said with some satisfaction. 'One of the Stalham Poultry toughs has just made an assault on Ben Asheton. God knows why, but it's definitely that dodgy Dragan from Stalham and he's been arrested in possession of what, unless I'm very much mistaken, is a knife matching the wounds found on Tomas.

'Ben was lucky. He was stabbed in the back but the knife was partially deflected by his backpack and a couple of crew from the lifeboat came to his rescue. It could have been very nasty, but he's going to be fine. I'm on my way now to pick up his wife Paula and take her to the James Paget to see him. If he's fit enough I'll take his statement at the same time.

'I arrested Dragan and he's on his way in to you at Wymondham. So is the knife and his mobile phone.'

'Well done, Jim. How did you come to be there?'

‘Heard the call-out on my car radio and as I happened to be on my way home, I diverted to the lifeboat station. I arrived just as the local team were restraining Dragan. Ben identified him and I recognised him too, although I wouldn’t have been able to put a name to him.’

‘Is Ben going to be ok?’

‘So the paramedics said, but obviously I’ll check when I get to the hospital. I’m about to pick Paula up. I didn’t think you’d mind as he’s one of our own.’

‘Of course not. Let me know what else you find out. Chris and I will interview Dragan when he gets here.’

‘One other thing,’ said Jim. ‘A message from Ben. He says Lukas told him that Dragan was a graduate of a Romanian orphanage, with all that implies. He’d guessed that Dragan would give us the silent treatment and thought the orphanage might help explain both his loyalty to those who rescued him from it, and his complete failure of any empathy with anyone else. I’m passing it on, in case it helps when interviewing.’

‘Chris,’ Greg bellowed. ‘Developments!’

The Ops room quietened as Greg sent as many staff as he could home for a break. Strong black coffee, cola and bought-in pizza revitalised the remaining team as they prepped for Dragan’s arrival.

Chris and Jenny mulled over the evidence relating to Stalham Poultry staff while they waited. Sarah took a slice of American Hot One and incautiously waved it at Greg, scattering half-cooked jalapeños over his desk.

‘Oops, sorry,’ she said. ‘I’ve been thinking about traffic?’

'Traffic? In what sense?'

'We've been working on the assumption that the folk at Wayford Bridge were brought in from Eastern Europe to work at Stalham, and that someone also took out glass eels in the opposite direction. But we haven't identified how or in what. As the movement was from other EU countries and of EU nationals, there was no need to smuggle them in. But it does seem likely that the transport was pretty rough and ready. They didn't waste money on anything else after all.

'The glass eels, however – they would have needed to be smuggled out under cover. So, are we looking at a single transport route, carrying men in one direction and glass eels in the other, or are they totally separate? And if there is a link to Stalham Poultry, what is it?

'The Defra vets looked pretty hard at the company's links with poultry plants in Eastern Hungary. They found regular movements but no evidence that explained the movement of disease. The timing didn't fit. I'm coming to the conclusion that the movement of Stalham Poultry transport is a red herring. On the other hand, there was a possible link between movement of a director, Austen Collier, and movement of disease. So, my theory now is that there is a transport route which brings men in and glass eels out, and it was mediated or organised by Collier or someone else at Stalham. Find that route, and we may find what precipitated the spate of murders. What was that first death of Jonas intended to cover up?'

'Except Collier says it was all organised by James Metcalfe.'

A head came round the door and nodded to Greg.

'Ok, Dragan's here. Let's see what we have on him, then, I think, home for everyone. We'll pick up from here tomorrow morning.'

Rather as expected, the interview with Dragan delivered absolutely nothing. He refused to speak in any language and refused to engage with his solicitor.

Greg regarded Dragan in frustration, mindful of the information he had been passed from Ben. He opened his mouth several times to say something, and several times thought the better of what he planned to say. He thought it unlikely that an inexpert approach to untangling Dragan's primitive loyalties was likely to succeed, but he had to try.

'I understand you feel a strong loyalty to your bosses in Lithuania,' he said eventually, using the interpreter to ensure understanding. 'But I think you need to take a long hard look at how they are treating you now. They've taken all the profits, but they're leaving you to take all the penalties. Does that seem fair?'

Still silence.

'I gather they rescued you from a very bad place,' he tried again. 'But they've used you for years and now they're leaving you in another bad place. Don't you think you've more than repaid their early help?'

There was no sign that Dragan was even listening. Greg persisted for over an hour, but got nowhere. At the end of that time he leaned back and exchanged glances with Chris, then looked again at Dragan. His sallow face was impassive, his hands relaxed, the arms with the multiple tattoos lay loose on the table before him; barbed wire embraced both wrists and five stars ran up his right arm, while a dagger decorated his left. Greg exchanged glances with Chris and tried to remember what he had learnt about gang tattoos. If he was right, the barbed wire denoted prison sentences served and the stars sometimes signalled murders. He looked at the dagger inked on skin and then again into the blank eyes opposite. Whether with new understanding, or because he was projecting assumptions, Greg felt that the man in front of him was little more than a shell: a violent husk that was capable of extreme action at short notice, but incapable of feeling any emotions other than rage and greed. He shuffled his papers together and stood up.

'We'll make no progress here,' he remarked to the empty air, and the two police left the room.

A further frustrating hour later, Greg went for a final word with the forensic team before heading home. A couple of them were working late with Ned. Dragan's clothes from the evening were laid out on the table and Ned looked up as Greg entered the room.

'We've got him for the stabbing of Ben,' he said. 'Blood on his clothes and blood on his hands too when he was brought in. I don't think there'll be any difficulty matching it up with Ben Asheton. The knife is going to pathology to match up with the data from the body found on the beach, but I don't think there's much doubt it will be a match there too. Of more interest is the phone. I've handed it over to the experts but early indications are that there have been a number of calls to and from the same location.'

'Same number?'

'No. Two different numbers but they both pinged the same phone masts. They're still working on it. Should have a report in the morning. Also, he had car keys in his possession. According to uniform they matched an elderly Land Rover at the far end of the lifeboat station car park. We're bringing it in for a proper look.'

'Ok. Thanks Ned. I'll catch up with you tomorrow.'

One last word with Sarah, and Greg headed for his car and the homeward drive. The events of the day fading into the background, his mind returned to the events of the morning. Keeping busy had successfully kept him distracted for most of the day. Now he had no choice but to focus on what he would find at home. As he drew up outside he was disappointed but not surprised to find the house in darkness. The hall and kitchen were exactly as he had left them that morning, even to the post still lying behind the front door. Isabelle hadn't been in the house since she left that morning. There was only one message on the answerphone which, for a brief moment, lifted his hopes. But it was a reminder that he had a dental appointment the following day.

One he needed to cancel, he thought.

He went to bed with a glass and a bottle of Springbank single malt. When he put the light out the bottle was half gone, but still sleep did not come to ease the burden of thought.

The morning brought with it a vile taste in his mouth, a thumping headache and a determination not to seek that route to oblivion again. A stinging hot shower followed by a sudden turn of the temperature gauge to minimum brought some level of alertness and Greg set off, back to Wymondham, with the profound hope he was not stopped and breathalysed as the chances of failure were, he estimated, high to certain. The only person he saw on his way in was Jim, who took one look at him, then diverted via the kitchen for a very strong mug of coffee which he slapped on the desk in front of Greg.

'Get yourself around that, sir,' he commanded, then turned to close the door to the main room behind him. 'Greg, you look awful. What's happened?'

Greg reached across the desk and buried his face in the mug. It was too hot to drink, so he put it down again, noticing with faint horror that his hand was shaking. Not raising his eyes from the desk he replied, 'Isabelle's gone. She left yesterday. I've had no message or contact since.'

Jim sat down opposite. 'Shit,' he said. Then again, 'Shit. Were you expecting it? No sorry, obviously you weren't. I thought she adored you. She'll be back surely.'

'No idea,' said Greg. 'I've no idea why she's gone, unless it's this job. Or she's met someone else. Or both.'

'You need to take some time off. Get this sorted, for both your sakes.'

'No. Absolutely not. The work's all that's keeping me together. Don't say anything, Jim. To anyone. Just give me a moment to drink this coffee, for which thanks by the way,' he smiled crookedly, 'and I'll be back on the job.'

'Are you sure you're ok to work?' asked Jim. 'To put it bluntly, you smell like you hung one on last night.'

'Bugger. Yes I did a bit, but I'll be ok I promise. And

that's the last time. If you think I'm falling down on the job, by all means come and tell me, but I'll be ok once I get going. Better be coffee and mints then.'

'And open the window!'

'Ok yes.'

'And while you're doing that, I'll get someone to fetch you a bacon butty from the canteen.' Jim stuck his head round the door and hollered.

When he turned back, the window was open, fresh cold air was blowing through the room, and the coffee was half drunk.

'So,' said Greg with a return to briskness, 'tell me about your discussions with Ben last night. And update me on how he is.'

Jim sat down again, shivering slightly in the chilly air. 'Ok. Well the good news is that Ben is expected to be discharged this morning. It seems the cut, though it bled a lot, wasn't much more than a flesh wound. He'll be off work for a while and he'll need physio but no long-term effects.

'He says he got a shout to a casualty in the dunes near the Caister lifeboat station yesterday and Dragan, as it appears, jumped him from behind with a knife. He was lucky the dispatcher heard the row over the phone, and even luckier that a couple of lifeboat crew arrived over the ridge like the US cavalry. One of them tackled Dragan and sat on his head until we arrived, while the other went to Ben.

'Ben recognised Dragan as soon as he was dragged to his feet, but has no idea why he was targeted. He's responded to three calls connected with Stalham Poultry: the first the death in the gassing container, the second the body of Ted Jackson when it was fished out of the Ant, and an accident involving Dragan himself. But as he said, that's because they all happened on his patch. He couldn't think of any reason why that made him a target. However, when I spoke to him on the phone this morning he remembered something else. When he and Paula had a night out last week, they bumped into Lukas and his wife and spent the evening with them. He's wondering now if someone saw them together and jumped to some conclusions.'

There was a bang on the door and Ned stuck his head round. 'God, it's cold in here,' he remarked. 'Are you on a fitness kick? I thought you might like the results so far from the mobile. As I said last night, there were several calls to the phone from different numbers but all from the same or a very similar location. Dragan also made calls back to two of the numbers. Other calls seem to have been to Norwich, and a few to an overseas number believed to have been in Lithuania. But get this – one, a couple of weeks ago, was to Ted Jackson's number.'

'Another link with Stalham Poultry,' said Greg slowly. 'Well done Ned. What about the car?'

'Nothing much so far except the remnants of a lot of takeaway meals. But I've got the team checking CCTV for the registration.'

As Ned left the room Jim asked, 'Have we found James Metcalfe yet?'

'No. Chris is speaking to his wife or ex-wife – not sure which it is – and that's another number we've been checking for on the CCTV, but we haven't laid hands on him yet.'

'I think we should check the area around that phone mast, just in case it was Metcalfe ringing Dragan.'

Greg went over to the map on the wall. 'The area pinpointed was here,' he said, pointing at a stretch of coastline between Yarmouth and Scratby.

'That's holiday park territory,' said Jim immediately. 'I'll tell Chris to ask if the Metcalfes ever had a holiday home round there, or any links to one. The chaps looking at the CCTV could concentrate on these roads,' he pointed, 'and perhaps a couple of unmarked cars wouldn't hurt.'

James Metcalfe had not had a good night and he was not having a good morning. Silence from Dragan he could only assume was bad news. He ran several more optimistic scenarios through his head, but reluctantly had to acknowledge they were no more than wishful thinking. There was no explanation of Dragan's non-communication more realistic than the failure of his mission and his arrest.

He threw the three SIM cards he had used into the bathroom basin and ran the tap until they disappeared, picked up his bags and drove away before anyone on the holiday park was moving. The car, even with his replacement number plates, was now a liability. It had to be changed. Thank God for Plan B.

The problem was the next few hours and the next few miles. He was much too close to the focus of police attention. As he headed for Acle and the A47 he tuned the radio to the local channel and the local news. The report of an attack on an emergency worker in Caister confirmed his assumptions about Dragan's likely fate, and he congratulated himself on getting out without loss of time. By 0600 he was on the A11 and heading south. By 0730 he was in the beginnings of the Cambridge morning rush hour and shortly after, left the A14 for the village of Madingley. Stopping at a locked farm gate he held his breath, but the code on the padlock had not changed and he was able to access the drive unobserved. For a moment he pondered locking it behind him; but just in case he should be in a hurry to leave, he hung the lock back on the chain without securing it and followed the winding drive down the hill to the small farmyard at the bottom.

There was no farmhouse, just farm buildings, and as far as he could see there was no activity. He followed the drive to the right, and parked by an old barn with big shuttered doors. The code on that padlock had not changed either. Dragging the doors open with some difficulty as they sagged on their hinges and scraped the concrete, he looked over his shoulder again, then went inside. Somewhat to his surprise, most of the space was taken up by a huge CLAAS combine and its header. Behind the header was what he had come for – a neat white Elldis campervan, all fuelled up and ready for the next part of his getaway, except for one small fact. The combine header was between the campervan and the door.

Just for a moment he flushed with anger and frustration – to be so near escape, and then to be stopped by careless parking. His rage overtook him and he punched the side of the combine hard. That gave him bruised knuckles to go with his bad temper, and he shook his hand, trying to think of a solution. He scrambled round to the van and unlocked it. Everything was in place and the dust would soon blow off, or could be washed off. But there was no route out of the barn other than the big doors at the front. He climbed out again and rambled round the barn, seeking inspiration and a way out. He got the former when he spotted a tow rope, neatly coiled and hanging on the wall of the barn. Unhooking it, he carried it round to the barn doors, examining carefully the header and the trailer it stood on, presumably for transport when the combine was making its way to its field of operations. After some thought he attached the tow rope to one end of the header, and reversed his car up to the open doors. Looping the rope over the towing bracket took but a moment, and after another careful look round he got in his car and revved the engine.

Ten minutes later, the header was sufficiently askew that he could get the campervan out of the barn. He transferred his bags to the van and drove the car into its place in the barn, then went to close the barn doors. Heave as he might, the end of the header was now in the way and the doors wouldn't close fully. There was no room to try the towing manoeuvre again, and no time either. He gave up and left the doors chained as closed as he could manage, then drove the campervan back up the twisty drive. This time he did lock the gate behind him and headed for Madingley, the A11 and Stansted, now in a vehicle that would not attract attention from the ANPR cameras.

In Wymondham, the camera team were on a roll. Alerted by Jim to focus attention on the Yarmouth to Caister coastal area, a sharp-eyed civilian had noticed a familiar car with an unfamiliar number plate.

'It could be coincidence,' she commented, drawing attention to an unusually good view of a silver BMW on the road to Caister, 'but it does look very like the one we spotted near Stalham Poultry on the evening the first death occurred. I think he might have changed his number plates.'

'Well, we do know the ones used that night belonged to the previous owner, so it's possible. Have you run a check on these?' pointing at the screen.

'Yes. And they belong to a maroon Ford.'

'Well done. What time was this taken?'

'0540 this morning.'

'Ok, let's see if we can find out where it went. Spread the net wider. If it's the man we think it is, he may have been doing a runner after Dragan's little job failed.'

In the Ops room studying the whiteboard, Greg suddenly had the feeling that the pieces were starting to come together. Chris, returning from her call with Mrs Metcalfe, reinforced the sensation.

'One possible lead from the soon-to-be ex-wife,' she reported. 'She didn't know anything about a holiday home. She quite reasonably asked why they'd need one since they live here. But she did say they had a campervan. It's stored on a farm near Ormesby St Michael. I've got someone going round to check now.'

'Did she know the registration?'

'No. Unfortunately not. She said that numbers aren't the sort of thing she remembers. She had a vague feeling it might have a Y in it, but that was all. She's looking to see if she has any paperwork, but thinks it's unlikely.'

'Hang on, this might be the chap I sent,' and she answered her mobile, then, 'No further forward I'm afraid.

Yes, the farm does store campervans from time to time, but the Metcalfe one was collected over six months ago. And no, they didn't know the registration either. They didn't keep any records. It seems it was a pretty casual arrangement. Metcalfe paid cash for some space in a lean-to barn and that was that.'

'Any description of the van?'

'White, and three berth. That's all.'

'Not very helpful. Ok. Let's see what ANPR shows up.'

Ruth, the sharp-eyed civilian, was fired up by her earlier triumph. Concentrated scrutiny of fuzzy camera action left her with sore eyes, a headache, but a powerful sense of success. She had successfully tracked the silver BMW with the maroon Ford number plates to the M11, the A11 and the A14. Then lost it.

'I've got it on ANPR as far as the A14 near Cambridge, then nothing,' she said to Greg. 'I imagine it left the dual carriageway for side roads where there's no cameras. Sorry, that's as far as I can track it.'

'Very well done Ruth, and especially for spotting it was the same car even though the number plate had changed.'

'Well it wasn't so difficult once we were told to focus on that area near Caister,' she said. 'There's not much moving at that time in the morning.'

'Still, very well done. I think a call to our colleagues in Cambridge is in order. You did check the roads further south I assume?'

'Yes, boss. But nothing. I even tried looking at similar cars in case he'd changed the number plates again, but nothing that didn't check out with DVLA.'

'No, I think it's a reasonable guess that he's changed to another vehicle, maybe the campervan. But until we get the registration we won't make much progress.'

Greg made the call to Cambridge himself, as he was asking for a favour. The surprise was that they rang back within half an hour.

'That car you were looking for. I think it's turned up. We've had a call from a farmer in Coton. He has another farm near Madingley and he rents space in his farm buildings for storage. He went down to do some work on a tractor today and noticed that the door to one of his buildings had been tampered with. He's had trouble before with travellers, so he's pretty hot on security. Anyway when he checked, a campervan that had been stored there had gone and been replaced by a silver BMW with the registration number you gave us. He's pretty cross actually because in extracting the campervan, whoever took it has damaged what he called his "combine header".'

'I don't suppose he has the registration of the van and knows who left it there?'

'Yes, he has. He's a very switched-on chap and he keeps a database of everything stored on his property. The campervan is an Elldis 115, white, registration AH54 WLS. A Mr James Metcalfe rented the space in the barn for twelve months and paid cash in advance.'

'Great. Got him. Thank you very much.'

'Let me know when you lay hands on him won't you. My farmer wants to sue for the damage to his combine.'

'He may have to wait in line. We want him for three murders, unlicensed gangmastering and possible modern slavery.'

'I'll let him know.'

*

'I need a word with Ruth,' said Greg to Chris and Jim, who had just come in. 'Is she still around?'

'I think so. Taking a break from cameras.'

Greg ran Ruth to earth in the canteen, resting her eyes over a hot chocolate.

'I've got some news for you,' he said, dropping into the seat opposite.

'You've got the campervan?' she asked.

'Almost. You were right. He did the swop at a farm near Madingley, just off the A14.

We have the registration now and I've put out an APB on it.'

She drank her remaining chocolate so fast she almost choked, and wiped the brown moustache off inelegantly with the back of her hand.

'Let me at it,' she said, and scurried back to her computer.

With Cambridge and surrounding forces focused on the campervan, Greg went back to Sarah.

'I've been thinking about what you said, about the travel to and from Eastern Europe.'

'Me too,' she said, pushing her hair back from her face. 'I've been revisiting the paperwork we got from Stalham Poultry after that first death.' She gestured to piles of paper on her desk. 'These are copies of what the vets turned up. As they said at the time, there's nothing that suggests the bird flu came in with movement of meat products. The dates don't fit. The only thing that looks possible are the travel claims for mileage and ferries by Austen Collier. He seems to have made a habit of going back and forth between Harwich and the Hook of Holland. There's nothing more recent than early March, but if he kept up the same pattern of travel, he'd have gone again in early April.'

She shuffled though the pile of photocopies and produced the paper she was looking for. It was a claim for multiple journeys by car ferry and associated substantial mileages going back over several months, countersigned by Austen Collier. Greg was about to put it down again, when he paused. His eyes narrowed.

'Hang on a minute,' he said, and putting his head outside her office door he shouted, 'Chris, have we got a copy handy of Collier's statement?'

'Mr or Mrs?' she asked.

'Mr.'

'Yes, here.'

She brought it over and Greg put the two papers side by side.

'I don't think it's the same signature,' he breathed.

The two women studied it in silence.

'It's not,' said Sarah finally. 'The A and the C look similar but the rest of each word are quite different.'

'We'd need an expert to be sure.'

'We can get an opinion,' said Chris, 'but why don't we ask Mrs Pritchard first? She'd be familiar with his signature.'

'Good idea. Give her a ring and ask a few pertinent questions. Depending on her answer, we may need to bring her in.'

*

Chris gave some careful thought to the questions before she rang Mrs P. She didn't want to lead the witness.

'Sorry to bother you,' she said, 'but I've got a few questions about how overseas travel is organised in your company. I believe you do a lot of it?'

'Yes, for the directors,' she replied. 'As I explained before, it was a job I brought with me when I transferred from HQ to the role at Stalham.'

'Can you go through the process for me?'

'Pretty simple really. They tell me when and where they want to go. I book the travel and the hotels.'

'And how are the costs covered?'

'I make the payments from here on anything I book, using a company credit card. Any additional expenses they incur, they fill in a form and bring it back signed with their receipts. I put them through to accounts for payment.'

'Do you keep copies?' asked Chris.

'Well of course I do. Filed for each month.' She was clearly irritated at the imputation of lack of efficiency.

'Great. Can you go back to March for me and look up some travel claims?'

There was a pause as Mrs P got the file out of the cabinet, then she spoke again.

'Ok I've got you on speaker,' she said, her voice echoing slightly. 'What was it you wanted to know?'

'Go back to the first half of the month if you would. Is there a claim for multiple ferry trips to the Hook of Holland?'

There was the sound of pages flipping and then Mrs P said, 'Yes, paid to Mr Collier.' There was a pause. 'That's odd,' she said slowly. 'Can you hang on while I check my diary?'

Chris held on patiently, and after another pause Mrs P came back on the line.

'It's odd,' she said. 'The form is signed by Mr Collier but he was on leave that week. I remember because I took my holiday the week after. I arranged temporary cover while I was away and the girl must have put this one through. I don't remember seeing it before. Perhaps he put the wrong date on and she didn't notice.'

'But it is signed by Mr Collier? Perhaps he posted the claim form in while he was away on holiday?'

'Yes,' said Mrs P, 'although…'

Chris waited.

'He couldn't claim on personal travel. The company's very strict on that. And the signature looks a bit funny. Not his usual one. Perhaps he was in a rush.'

'Perhaps he was,' said Chris, and went back to Greg.

'Definitely worth checking with the experts,' she said, as she reported back. 'And I suggest we compare the writing with that from Mr Metcalfe.'

'But what was the point?' asked Greg. 'Why not make the claim normally? And if not a kosher claim, why do it at all? Why forge a signature?'

'Greed,' said Sarah and Chris unanimously.

And Chris added, 'Without Mrs P's eagle eye around, he spotted a chance to defray his costs. So he did, just because he could. I bet if we check, the money was never paid to Austen Collier. I'll check his bank account.'

24

Closing in

Sleeping uneasily under the Stansted flight path, James Metcalfe tossed and turned in his slightly damp sleeping bag. The drive from Madingley to Bishop's Stortford services on the M11 had gone smoothly. It was only as he rejoined the motorway that he realised he had been driving with his shoulders hunched, as though someone was watching over his shoulder. The relief of being in an unknown vehicle, free at last of police awareness, was immense. Tucked away in his unknown and unnoticed campervan at the back of the car park, he'd enjoyed his takeaway burger and retired to bed. It was only in the early hours of the morning that the background noise woke him and destroyed any remaining chance of further slumber. Giving up the effort, he sat up and used one of his phones to search morning flights from Stansted to Europe. He didn't much care where he went, so long as it was out of the UK, but he was particularly pleased to book a seat on a mid-morning flight to Amsterdam. From Schiphol he could fly anywhere, he knew. Just a few more hours, and he would be out of England, out of reach.

By 0700 he had freshened up in the services loos, as much as was possible anyway, and breakfasted on a Starbucks coffee and croissant. By 0730 he was in the queue for the long-stay car park, experiencing a momentary qualm as he approached the barrier about the eligibility of his van and whether it would get under the barrier. Much to his relief, the van was just under the maximum height limit and he passed through to park at the back of area Q. He thought it unlikely he would be able to retrieve the van and hesitated over dumping the keys in a waste bin. At the last minute he put them back in his pocket, balanced his carry-on bag on his suitcase and headed for the shuttle bus.

To his disappointment, the check-in desk for his easyJet flight was not yet open. With a return of the hunched shoulders, he perched uncomfortably on a ledge by the windows and waited. There did seem to be a lot of police and security around. He reassured himself that there was always a lot of security around an airport, and no one seemed to be paying him any attention. He wished he'd thought about a hat or something just to change his appearance a little, then realised that was an easy problem to solve and popped into the nearest concourse shop. Newly equipped with a grey baseball cap, he pulled it on and headed for the opened check-in desk. Now, of course, there was a lengthy queue.

It seemed to take forever to get to the front, and he irritably ignored several attempts at conversations from fellow queuers. Once at the desk, however, he showed his alternative passport, checked in one bag and went through to the security line with his carry-on bag. One hurdle surmounted.

The line for security checks seemed even slower than usual and he congratulated himself on having paid for the fast track. He pulled the cap down over his face as he approached the head of the line and placed his bag, phone and iPad in the tray provided. He assumed there were cameras around, and kept his face turned down as he inched along the conveyor belt to the scanner. He didn't notice the extra man behind the X-ray machine, nor his earpiece, nor the photo he was checking on the phone in his hand. Nor did he notice the nod he gave to his colleague on the scanner, but he did see his bag diverted to the hand checking area and he sighed heavily. What had they spotted now? An umbrella that looked like a rifle? An undeclared but clearly lethal hairdryer? He reminded himself to be chilled and low key, and stepped forward when asked.

'Is this your bag?'

'Yes.'

The man with the phone in his hand stepped forward. 'Would you be so kind as to come this way please?'

'What? Why?'

'This way please, sir, if you don't mind.'

Metcalfe started to back up, but bumped into another security guard suddenly standing behind him. Still protesting innocence and bewilderment, he was ushered into a side room. The big security guard behind him followed him in and stood by the wall, his arms folded. The door was locked behind him.

'Why am I here? What's the problem?'

He got no answer and no response. Out on the concourse the guard in charge of the fast-track checking process was on his radio.

'Got him, sir,' he reported. 'Yes. Pretty certain. I'm sending you a photo from my phone.'

A pause and his radio squawked again.

'Yes. Understood. We'll keep him in custody until they arrive.'

'Boss, boss!'

At the whiteboard in the Ops room, Greg suddenly realised that Jenny was trying to get his attention.

'We've had a call from that smallholding in Ormesby. You know, the one that used to house James Metcalfe's campervan. They're asking, are we interested in the long wheelbase Land Rover he left there?'

'Are we what? Why on earth didn't they mention it when we were there?'

'No idea, boss. It seems it's only just occurred to someone that it might be of interest.' She rolled her eyes.

'Get someone round there ASAP to take a look.'

'I'll go myself if that's ok with you? I could take Meg with me to give it the once over.'

'Good idea.'

Jenny was met at the farm by the farmer's daughter, Caroline.

'I'm so sorry,' she apologised. 'We should've shown you

the Land Rover when you were here before, but the silly old sod never thought about it. I've been telling him for years he should keep proper records, but he's allergic to paperwork and he never even mentioned it belonged to the same man until last night.'

'Well, never mind that now,' replied Jenny. 'Let's have a look at it and then I'll get my dog to give it the once over. Where is it?'

'Round here, in the old barn at the back.'

Jenny surveyed the old grey, long-wheelbase Land Rover parked in the rickety barn.

'Do you have a key?' she asked.

'No, but you'll find the windows are easy to open if you want to get access. Just push and slide and they'll open. These old models aren't exactly secure.'

'How long has it been stored here?'

'I don't know for sure. A few years in total, but it comes and goes.'

'Does it indeed. When was it last off site?'

'Oh, quite recently. Around the end of March I think.'

'And who drives it?'

'According to my Dad, occasionally it's Mr Metcalfe. But the only person I've seen driving it's a big man with tattoos. That's why I didn't realise it was Metcalfe's. I don't know his name, the big chap that is, and he doesn't talk much. I don't think he speaks much English.'

'I see.' Jenny was looking at the number plates. 'These aren't British are they?' she muttered. The plate read AVR 359 and bore a small flag. She photographed the plate with her phone and mailed the picture to the Ops room, then fetched Meg from her car.

Meg was delighted to be working and ran round the vehicle busily, but without apparently finding anything. Boosted in through the side door, the inside was a different matter. Without giving a definitive signal for money, explosives or drugs, she was very interested in the bench seating in the back. Calling her back and beckoning her out, Jenny got on her phone to DCI Geldard.

'I think we need the SOCOs out here, and we'll probably need to bring this vehicle in. Meg's not signalling drugs or anything else she's trained on, but she's very interested in the back of the vehicle. I think it warrants a close look. And it seems it's been driven by both Metcalfe and a man who sounds like Dragan Bakalov. If someone could send me a photo, I can try that on the family here. Oh, and I think the number plate is East European. I've sent a pic in.'

'Good. Thank you, Jenny. Can you stick around until the SOCOs arrive and I'll get that photo to you?'

Greg went back into the Ops room and added to the data on the whiteboard. Sarah came in just as he was drawing a line between the photos of James Metcalfe and Dragan Bakalov.

'We've another link,' he said. 'They've both been driving the same long-wheelbase Land Rover and it was out of storage just before the murder at Stalham. We need to find out what's interesting the dog in the back of the car, and see what forensics can find. But it's another link, I'm certain.'

'I've got some news from the Lithuanian police too,' said Sarah. 'Dragan is known to them. He's never been convicted of anything in Lithuania but they say he had a record in Romania. Their main concerns were his links with organised crime in Vilnius. They say they've never been able to prove anything, but they think he was a fixer for one of their nastier crime dynasties. Unfortunately every time they got close, a witness would disappear or change their story. Then he disappeared off the scene himself, and they haven't seen much of him for the past few years. They think he's reappeared from time to time, but only for short visits.'

'What intelligence do they have about the workers?'

'Not much. None of them have any records, except perhaps the odd traffic offence. As far as they've been able to establish, talking to family and friends, all were genuinely economic migrants, keen to earn enough to send money home, or to save enough to go home and set up a business. As far as the families knew, they accepted a deal which included transport to the UK and a job on arrival. Many of them had been worried about lack of contact over recent months, but when they made enquiries locally, either the contact had disappeared, or they were threatened with repercussions if they made a nuisance of themselves. For most, that was the first hint they had that anything was amiss. Some of them had been worrying themselves sick.'

'When is Metcalfe arriving here from Stansted?'

'Should be here any time.'

'Then I think we should see what this Land Rover can tell us first. Let him stew for a bit.'

25

Loose Threads

By the time Greg got down to the garage, the forensic team had gutted the old Land Rover.

'This is what we wanted to show you,' said Ned.

Peering in the back door, Greg saw that the bench seats on either side of the rear compartment had been removed.

'They were made to come off easily,' said Ned. 'Some of the original versions of this model had the seats on hinges so they could be folded out of the way when the vehicle was needed for bulk transport. In this one, the space beneath had been filled with these.' He pulled an insulated box out and showed Greg what he meant. 'The sides and lid have been insulated and there are air holes at the top. I think these were designed to carry something living.'

'Glass eels?' asked Greg.

'Yes, I think that's possible. The boxes we found at Stalham and in the Ant would fit. But I don't think it's the whole story. They've been smarter than that. You know we speculated this might have been a two-way trade – eels out, drugs and men in? Well I think that's right, but it wasn't drugs coming in. Look.'

He showed Greg the interior of a couple more boxes. They contained traces of sawdust and had a distinct smell.

'It seems they didn't have time to clean these out properly,' said Ned with some satisfaction, 'and this also explains why Meg got so excited.'

'Am I right?' asked Greg. 'It smells like dogs to me.'

'And clearly it did to Meg too. This has been a very sophisticated and cost-effective operation. I think they were moving eels out, puppies in, and the transport of the workers both added to the profits and provided cover for the other livestock. But it also means they needed a sophisticated handling system at both ends too. Someone has been receiving the eels in Lithuania, and someone else has been selling puppies here in the UK.'

'I wonder if the gangmastering was always part of the scheme, or an add-on?' mused Greg.

'I'd guess it was an add-on, because it was the transport of men and the involvement of Stalham Poultry that caused the whole thing to unravel. A bright idea that someone had for some extra profits that, from their point of view, went horribly wrong. Before that, it seems probable that the movement of eels and puppies had gone on under the radar and very successfully.'

'So, now we need to find links to an outlet for puppies. God, this gets more complicated by the minute.'

'Look on the bright side, boss,' said Ned. 'The

complications are what gives them away. The more people in the know, the more links in the chains, and something has to give. We just need to pull on the right loose thread and it'll all unravel.'

Fired by that thought, Greg went back to his office and a strategic discussion with Jim, Sarah and Chris.

Repeating Ned's words he said, 'I thought, and I think, that's an incredibly helpful way to look at it. So, suggestions team, on which threads we pull? Which are the leads that will give us this case on a plate?'

There was a pause as they all thought, then Sarah spoke up.

'I haven't had chance to report back, but there are some promising lines of enquiry in social services. So my priority loose thread would be, who pointed them towards Tom Potter and John Hyde? When we have the social services link, we can find out who their contact was at Stalham.'

'I'll go after the puppy end,' said Chris. 'If the last lot came in at the end of March, they must have taken them somewhere to keep until they were sold on. And the selling is normally online for that sort of puppy, so we can look for adverts. Typically those puppies have major health problems too, so we can also look for aggrieved new owners and the vets who had to deal with the sick dogs. I'll keep on top of the team looking at bank accounts too.'

'That leaves you and me, Jim, interviewing James Metcalfe and reinterviewing Dragan Bakalov, given the new information we have to hand. I think we should also get back to the workers who were transported in that Land Rover and ask them if they had any inkling what they were sitting on. I know they were reluctant to talk before, but *now* we have a better idea what to ask. I've a good feeling about this. I'd better brief the Chief Super first, then let's get to it.'

Back in the team office, Chris looked up from her desk as Sarah passed through the room.

'Now we've got the additional names from the passport, we need a new production order from the court to get the information from the bank accounts. It needs a DI to authorise the request. Are you ok to do that?'

'Yes of course. What have you asked for?'

'Well, detail on the bank accounts obvs,' replied Chris shortly.

Sarah sighed rather noticeably. 'I need to know precisely what you have asked for if I am to authorise it.'

'It's on the form,' Chris smacked it down on the desk, 'but if you need me to spell it out, I've added these new names to the request we made earlier with regard to James Metcalfe. So essentially I'm asking for details from the identity documents used to open the accounts, bank statements, any deposits and withdrawals but also any safety deposit boxes and credit and charge card statements. With the information from the forged passport and the latest on James Metcalfe and his attempt to run, I don't think we'll have a problem getting the order.'

'Sounds fine. Hand me the paperwork and I'll countersign.'

'Thanks. Let's hope they get a move on.'

*

Greg and Jim regarded James Metcalfe and his solicitor for a long, silent moment. Metcalfe was leaning back in his chair, arms folded and a belligerent expression on his face. His solicitor, the grey silent man provided previously by Poultry Enterprises, shuffled in his seat. He didn't look as though his private discussions with his client had gone well. In reality they hadn't gone at all in any meaningful sense, as Metcalfe had declined to speak even to him.

Greg leaned over and clicked the button to start the tape, then he and Jim introduced themselves.

'For the benefit of the tape, would you please introduce yourself, Mr Metcalfe?'

Metcalfe said nothing.

The solicitor cleared his throat, shuffled some more, then introduced himself.

Metcalfe continued to say nothing.

'Let the record show,' said Greg, 'that also present is Mr James Metcalfe. Mr Metcalfe, I am going to caution you before this interview proceeds any further.

'James Metcalfe, I am arresting you on suspicion of acting as an unlicensed gangmaster, of conspiracy to commit the murders of Jonas Balciunas at Stalham Poultry on the night of 2-3 April, Tomas Simonis on or around the night of 4 April at the Bridges storage yard in Ferry Lane, Great Yarmouth, and Ted Jackson on the night of 7 April on the banks of the River Ant. I am also charging you with conspiracy to commit the attempted murder of Ben Asheton and with the illegal smuggling of glass eels out of the UK and of puppies in. You are not obliged to say anything. But, it may harm your defence if you do not mention when questioned something which you later rely on in court. Anything you do say may be given in evidence.'

The solicitor had scribbled furiously as the long list of charges was read out, and Metcalfe, despite his belligerence, had turned a sickly shade of grey.

'I assume you have some evidence on which to base this absurdly long list of offences,' attempted the solicitor.

'Oh yes,' said Greg with some satisfaction. 'Perhaps you'd like to cover the key headings, DI Henning.'

'Ok,' said Jim. 'Let's start with the gangmaster license. We have documentary evidence that the men at Stalham Poultry were employed under a contract which exacted unreasonable and excessive deductions from their wages, purporting to pay for substandard and indeed downright illegal accommodation, transport to and from work, and foodstuffs. We have evidence to show that the men were brought to England in small batches of eight or so at a time, in a Land Rover, registered in Lithuania, owned by you and usually driven by Dragan Bakalov. The contract for supply of this labour to Stalham Poultry was agreed between you and Austen Collier, making you guilty of operating as an unlicensed gangmaster. Any comment, Mr Metcalfe? No? Shall we go on then?

'Jumping to the smuggling charges, we have forensic evidence that shows the same Land Rover has been used for the transport of both eels and puppies. The unlicensed export of glass eels from this country, as I am sure you are aware, Mr Metcalfe, renders you guilty of the offences both of failure to notify movement of animals, and evasion of a prohibition on the export of goods. We have been able to track certain movements of that Land Rover from the UK to Lithuania and we have reason to believe the glass eels were offloaded at the same time that workers were collected for their trip to England. The police in Lithuania are following up the movement of the eels from there. It would appear you have some very unpleasant associates in Lithuania, Mr Metcalfe. I hope, for your sake, you haven't upset them.

'With regard to the evidence that containers hidden under the Land Rover seating had also been used to transport puppies, it's likely that further charges will follow relating to the illegal import of puppies too young to travel, together with yet more charges associated with trading standards and animal welfare violations.'

'Even if it were true that the car had transported puppies, you can't possibly know how old they were,' sneered Metcalfe.

'On the contrary,' said Jim, shuffling though the files in front of him, 'we've already found four instances of puppies bought within the last week having to be taken to local veterinary surgeries because they were sick. All of them were less than seven weeks old. All of them were suffering from infectious disease and two have already died. I doubt those are the only cases we will find.'

'And what's that to do with me?'

'All of the purchasers had responded to an internet advert by ringing a mobile phone number. The SIM card for that number was retrieved from the drainage system at your chalet near Caister. Putting the card down the washbasin was a bit of an error wasn't it, Mr Metcalfe? And not your only one either.

'All of those puppy purchasers would very much like a chat with you, Mr Metcalfe, but I told them they would have to wait their turn. Which brings me to the serious charges of conspiracy to commit murder and attempted murder. I assume you are aware we already have your co-conspirator in custody. Dragan Bakalov?'

Metcalfe opened his mouth, then shut it again with a glance at his solicitor.

'Something you wished to say, Mr Metcalfe,' asked Greg. 'No? Let me pick up the story then. As you know, we have three murders and one attempted murder under active investigation. We have evidence that links both you and Dragan Bakalov to every case. The only issues we need to resolve now are, which of the attacks were carried out by you, which by Dragan Bakalov, and to what extent he was acting on your orders.

'Let's take the attempted murder of Ben Asheton. In this case we have Dragan Bakalov arrested in the attempt, multiple phone calls between him and you leading up to the assault, and your attempt to flee the country immediately after. Anything to say yet, Mr Metcalfe? No?

'Let's carry on then. Working our way back in time, the next case is the death by crossbow of Ted Jackson, poacher and supplier of glass eels. We have your car in the vicinity of Mr Jackson's riverside shack, and we have partial fingerprints on the crossbow we believe was used to deliver the fatal bolt: the crossbow we recovered from the drain connecting the Ferry Lane storage site to the River Yare. Those fingerprints were not on our database until this morning, but as you know, Mr Metcalfe, your prints were taken when you were detained at Stansted. They're definitely a match. Why, I wonder, are your fingerprints on a crossbow in a drain by the river, Mr Metcalfe? And who was stupid enough to dump it into a drain already implicated in another death? I must admit that seems more like Dragan than you.

'Still no comment? I'll carry on shall I? The death of Tomas Simonis was by a stab wound to the chest. As I've said, we've evidence that his body was dumped in the same drain as the crossbow. Unluckily for you, the day he was killed, there was a severe storm and a high tide. It seems the sudden flood of rainwater was sufficient to wash the body into the river, from where the tide and current took it to the beach at Caister. Even more unluckily for you, there was no such storm after the crossbow was dumped, and it caught on a pile of gravel, making it very easy for us to retrieve.

'There's forensic evidence that the knife which killed Tomas was identical to, or was the same knife as, that used on Ben Asheton by Dragan Bakalov on the evening of 10 April. In this case therefore, we don't think yours was the hand that actually delivered the blow, but we do think yours was the guiding mind. Tomas Simonis was found to be in possession of a large sum in euros. Had he been blackmailing you, Mr Metcalfe? Had he threatened to go to the authorities with stories about slavery and smuggling?'

Greg paused again, but there were no signs anyone else wished to contribute to the conversation.

'So finally, the death that brought us onto the scene in the first place. The death of Jonas Balciunas in the temporary gassing chamber at Stalham Poultry. We have your car leaving the vicinity of the poultry unit several hours after you signed out at the gate and around the time forensics say Jonas died. We have blood and other body fluids on overalls that belonged to you which have been DNA matched to Jonas. The stains are consistent with the person wearing the overalls having delivered the blow that stunned Jonas prior to him being placed in the gassing chamber. Why not just complete the job there and then, Mr Metcalfe? Another blow would probably have finished him off and avoided the hassle of placing him in the gassing chamber. Was that to give you chance to get clear of the site before the body was found? Or was it, perhaps, that this was your first foray into murder and it was a bit of a shock to your system? A blow to the head is a bit upfront and personal isn't it, Mr Metcalfe? Is that why all the later attempts were either at some distance, like the crossbow, or delivered at one remove by Dragan Bakalov? I think you've found it easier to give orders than to take action.'

Metcalfe and his solicitor looked at each other, then the latter spoke up.

'So far we've not heard anything other than small snippets of circumstantial evidence, none of which are sufficient to tie my client to any of these crimes, so if you've nothing else we'll be off.'

'Oh but we do have something else. Quite a lot of something else, so with all due respect, Mr Metcalfe, I'm afraid you'll be benefiting from our hospitality for some time yet. Interview suspended.'

And Greg and Jim left the room.

*

Back in his office Greg sighed.

'We have a lot more details we can hit him with, and we need to take him through item by item, but that solicitor is right on one thing. It is all circumstantial. Unless we can get one of them to talk, I'm not sure we can get either of them on the main charges.'

Poking her head round the door, Chris announced, 'Mrs P is here.'

'Ok, we'll have a chat with her next. Jim, let's review what we have and what's missing with the DC later this afternoon.'

'Mrs Pritchard, thank you very much for coming to see us. There're just a couple of points where we find ourselves a little confused. A couple of areas we think you can help us clear up.'

'Do I have anything to worry about?' asked Mrs P, patting her immaculate French pleat a little nervously. 'Because if so...'

'No I don't think so,' replied Greg with as much reassurance as he could muster. 'It's just that we've some questions about how things were done at Stalham Poultry and we think you're the best person to ask.

'For example, when we spoke to you in the beginning, you said that when you were short-handed it was your job to contact the gangmaster and arrange for a replacement to be sent. We assumed, wrongly, that you rang head office. Who did you contact?'

'Oh, that sort of question,' she said with some relief. 'That's straightforward. I had a phone number I rang and left a voice message. Then I'd get a text message back saying who would be sent and by when. It was usually pretty quick, so it worked ok.'

'Did you ever speak to the gangmaster?'

'No, I don't think I ever did. I did comment on that once to Mr Willis but he just said "if it ain't broke don't fix it", so I didn't say anything again.'

'What was the number you rang?'

'Oh I don't think I could remember it just like that. It was a mobile number. But I've got it on my desk. I could let you have it when I get back to the office.'

'Thank you, that would be very helpful. Now, you also explained how travel was arranged, who booked what, who paid what and how it was authorised. Essentially, you did most of the bookings, and paid for flights and hotels on the company credit card.'

'Yes, that's right. And all the credit card returns were checked at head office to be sure I didn't charge anything to the card that I shouldn't.'

'Yes, we understood that. Very sensible system. You also explained that when directors and other staff made claims for other expenses you would check the receipts, then pass the claim to head office for payment.'

'Yes, that's right too.'

'So, the bit we need to be clear on – and sorry to keep coming back to this – is what happened with the claim for ferry trips to the continent and associated mileage. This doesn't seem to have been checked by you and no one seems to have made sure this was genuine company business.'

Mrs P flushed at what she clearly interpreted as criticism.

'I told them before,' she replied, 'that it happened while I was on holiday. The temp who covered for me put the claim through and head office paid it without questioning why it didn't have my countersignature on it.'

Greg produced the document.

'Yes I see it doesn't have your signature,' he said. 'Just some rather scribbled initials in the box. So this went to head office without you seeing it. Have you ever handled any similar claims?'

'Yes, I didn't see it. I'm certain of that. I'd never have put it through without asking some questions. And no, I never handled any similar claims. I don't like to make accusations, but it looks very much as though someone has cheated on their travel claim, and that's a sacking offence.'

'It appears to be signed by Mr Collier but you also said you didn't think it looked like his signature,' remarked Greg in a neutral tone.

'Absolutely. And,' she pronounced triumphantly, 'it's not his usual bank details either. I've seen them so often I could just about quote them from memory. These are different.'

Outside the interview room Greg looked at Chris. 'Did you get anywhere with the bank account listed on the form?'

'Just a name and an address. The address doesn't check out. It belonged to a block of flats in Norwich that's been demolished.'

26

Hard Decisions

Margaret looked at her hard-working team with some sympathy. Greg, Jim, Sarah and Chris were all showing signs of wear and tear, although she noticed with concern that Greg looked the worst, his eyes shadowed and his mouth, in repose, settled into a hard line. They squeezed round her small round conference table, piles of paper in front of each.

'Coffee and doughnuts,' she said with a flourish and smacked both into the middle of the table. 'I always think a sugar boost is in order at this stage of an investigation.'

They all smiled, but she noted that Greg's did not reach his eyes. Had this all been a bit much for a newly promoted, newly transferred DCI? She mentally chastised herself for not keeping a closer eye on him and made a note to have a private chat after the meeting.

'So, where are we at? I've kept up to date with your

briefings, but a summary of the cases we have and what can or cannot go to CPS would be good.'

Greg looked up from his papers. 'Ok, let's start with the easiest one. I think we've got Austen Collier cold on the charge of using an unlicensed gangmaster. We have documentary evidence that he signed off the contract which supplied the workers to Stalham Poultry. We have statements supporting the documentation from the HR team at Poultry Enterprises and other supporting information from Mrs Pritchard at Stalham Poultry. I'm pretty confident on that one, but I don't think we can tie him to any of the murders, and indeed I don't think he was involved.

'Next, we've got Dragan Bakalov, caught red-handed in an attempt to kill Ben Asheton. At the very least we can prove GBH and associated offences. We might succeed with attempted murder. At the moment Bakalov is saying nothing.

'As for James Metcalfe, this is the tricky one. Before we go to the murders, I'd like to summarise where we are on the smuggling enterprises, because I think these are key to what happened. You others, please chip in with detail if I miss any.

'We have evidence that glass eels had been stored at Stalham Poultry. We found a box there that had traces of eel blood in it and prints on it that have since been matched to Metcalfe. We can demonstrate that Ted Jackson was poaching glass eels and that he had been paid significant sums over recent months. We've not yet traced where the money came from, but now we have the forged passport belonging to James Metcalfe we have a new name and other details to aid the search. A court order has gone to the banks and we're waiting for their response. We've found traces of glass eels in a vehicle belonging to James Metcalfe and also traces of puppies, and we have evidence that the vehicle undertook a number of trips by ferry from Harwich to the Hook of Holland in the early part of this year. Mr Metcalfe somewhat foolishly submitted a claim for the ferry costs through his business, and a writing expert is willing to state that the forged signature of Austen Collier and other writing on the form matches that of James Metcalfe. We expect the ferry company's records to confirm the crossings.

'We have traces, of some at least, of a consignment of puppies that was sold in late March and the contact mobile phone number used for these sales belonged to a SIM card found at the address where Metcalfe hid himself prior to making a run for it to Stansted. If we can trace the money movements, I think we have met the criteria for a prosecution relating to the smuggling of glass eels and puppies.'

'One additional point on that, boss,' interrupted Chris. 'I have an update on banks. The bank account listed on that form – the name matches that in the forged passport found on Metcalfe when he was detained at Stansted. They're going to send over details of transactions.'

'Good. Chris, keep on to them to check if there are any other bank accounts associated with that name.'

Margaret leaned over and topped up the coffee mugs. 'So your thinking is, the murders were precipitated by threatened exposure of what must have been a very lucrative two-way smuggling operation.'

'That's right.'

'Plus,' added Sarah, 'the complication that the Lithuanian end of the smuggling and labour supply businesses seems to have been run by an organised crime syndicate. The English end may have been getting instructions on how to deal with any little problems, and the Lithuanian means of dealing with problems seems to be pretty final. I've had some very helpful background from colleagues in Lithuania. They're very keen to assist in the hope that what we turn up will enable them to nail a crime syndicate they've been after for some time.'

Greg picked up the threads again. 'Ok, turning to the murders then and starting with the first. As far as the murder of Jonas Balciunas is concerned, we have Metcalfe signing out and his car leaving Stalham Poultry at around 2230, then reappearing in the vicinity of the rear fence on CCTV around midnight, but at this point wearing the plates that belonged to the car when it was Mrs Collier's.'

'Ned checked the poultry unit's own security cameras,' chipped in Chris, 'but they'd been overwritten by the time we got them.'

'We have traces of Balciunas' blood and other body fluids on Metcalfe's overalls, consistent with his having delivered the blow that stunned Balciunas prior to the body being placed in the gassing chamber. We have traces of Metcalfe's DNA on the body. But, defence will argue the car footage is open to other interpretations, that blood on his overalls doesn't prove he was wearing them at the time, and that of course his DNA is on Balciunas because he assisted with the resuscitation attempt. We do also have Lukas Jankauskas' evidence that Jonas claimed he had a plan or a means of getting away from the Stalham Poultry set-up.

‘The evidence around the murder of Tomas Simonis is even looser. We have evidence of where he was killed. We know it was a knife like that wielded by Bakalov on Ben Asheton, but no conclusive evidence it was the same knife. We found cash on Simonis’ body, but have not yet been able to trace its source. My belief is that he and Balciunas were blackmailing Metcalfe about the smuggling enterprise, but as yet we have no proof.’

‘And Ted Jackson?’ asked Margaret as Greg paused to gulp some coffee.

‘That’s another tricky one,’ he admitted. ‘Again, we have Metcalfe’s car in the vicinity on the evening he was killed. We have some evidence that ties him to the supply of glass eels to Metcalfe and we have a partial print that matches Metcalfe’s on the crossbow we recovered from the drain in Southtown. What we don’t have is any proof that was the crossbow used to deliver the fatal bolt. It’s the right type, but not the only type that can fire the sort of bolt recovered from the body.

‘On the other hand, we have some evidence tying Bakalov to the arson attack on Jackson’s cottage. His Land Rover was seen near the cottage by the man who rang emergency services about the fire. The number plate and general appearance match the photo on his dashcam and it still had a petrol container in the back when we took it from the car park at Caister lifeboat station after the attempt on Ben Asheton.

‘Then there’s all the data we picked up when Metcalfe went into hiding and made his dash for the continent. The SIM cards found at the chalet near the coast were used for calls to Bakalov on and around the night he attacked Ben

Asheton and prior to the fire at Jackson's place. They also tie him to sales of puppies and there are some calls from Lithuania. The false passport is also highly suspicious and ties him to bank accounts we're still exploring.'

There was a pause. They all drank more coffee and Jim surreptitiously wiped a sugar moustache from his lip.

'Wow,' said Margaret as the pause seemed to be lengthening. 'I've attended several of your briefings, but it's only when it rolls over you in one huge heap that the sheer scale of what was going on hits you. How on earth did Metcalfe keep all those balls in the air? He seems to have been a very busy chap.'

'It's my guess,' said Sarah, 'that although the original idea for cheap labour and possibly the glass eels was probably his initiative, quite a lot of the complexity was added later by his contacts in Lithuania. And a lot of the legwork has probably been done by their contacts too. For example, although he seems to have been the first point of contact for puppy sales, there's no evidence he got directly involved in handling the dogs once they arrived in Norfolk. The purchasers we've managed to trace describe at least two different men handing over the dogs, one of which may be Bakalov. I think Metcalfe ended up as the front man, and then found himself dancing to their tune. Bakalov seems to have been working partly for Metcalfe and partly for his old bosses in Lithuania.'

Margaret stirred impatiently in her seat. 'There's too much "seems" and "guesses",' she said. 'Apart from the unlicensed gangmaster charges I don't think the CPS will be willing to run with what we've got so far. We need to track the movements of money. Barring good luck, I think that's the only way we'll be able to tie either of our two suspects to the murders and the arson. Incidentally, you haven't mentioned the issue of modern slavery.'

'The GLAA don't think they can make that stick,' replied Sarah. 'Their best chance was with the girls in the nail bars, but none of them are willing to give evidence or even talk much. Same with the men. So I think they've decided to settle for shutting this enterprise down and nailing Collier and Metcalfe respectively for use of and acting as an unlicensed gangmaster.'

'The other breakthrough will be if we can get either Metcalfe or Bakalov to dob in the other,' added Greg. 'I don't think it'll be Bakalov. I think he's too well trained by his Lithuanian bosses. And too tough. But I haven't given up on Metcalfe yet. His dash for the continent proves his nerve isn't unlimited.'

'Ok. Thank you, team. This has been a really useful discussion from my point of view. Come back when you've got the banking data or a breakthrough with Metcalfe and I'll back an approach to the CPS. Greg, could you stay behind for a moment?'

The rest filed out, and Greg looked at his boss a little nervously, wondering if he was in for a bollocking.

As the door closed behind them Margaret asked, 'How are you, Greg? This has been an incredibly challenging case for your first in Norfolk and you've had a lot to deal with, one way and another.'

Greg looked at her sharply, wondering if Jim had been talking, but she met his eyes blandly.

'One thing I do want to make clear,' she went on, 'is

that I'm pleased with how you've taken up the reins. You've got both Jim and Sarah onside, I've watched you delegate effectively and you've kept on top of a very complex case. You do need to follow up the banking data as a matter of urgency, but I don't think there've been any major delays. The only thing that's worrying me is how much it's affecting you. Moving to a new area and a new job on promotion are hard enough, without having to tackle this sort of case at the same time. How are you and…Isabelle isn't it? How are you settling in?'

Greg opened his mouth to say fine, then closed it again on the reflection that if Margaret found out later what was going on she might not be pleased at his lack of candour.

'Not great to be honest,' he found himself saying. 'Only Jim knows at the moment, but Isabelle has moved out.'

Margaret regarded him silently for a moment. 'I'm really sorry to hear that, Greg. House and job moves are always a very stressful time and it can be hard on partners when officers are working at the level called for by a major enquiry. Do you want some time off to spend with Isabelle?'

'No. Absolutely not,' he replied forcefully. 'I don't think it would help at this point. And to be honest, work is what's keeping me focused.' He looked at her anxiously and found that she was looking at him with a very similar expression.

'I won't pretend that's not a relief,' she said. 'I know we say no one's irreplaceable but I have to say it would be pretty damn difficult to replace you at this point in the investigation. But please do come to me, Greg, if there's anything you want to talk over. And I'm glad Jim knows. You'll find he'll have your back if or when it's needed.'

'I already have,' Greg assured her. 'Now, if you'll excuse me, I need to chase up the banks.'

When Greg got back into the Ops room, Chris and two civilian assistants were already hard at work on the phones. Chris turned as he entered, pulling her headset aside.

'I think I'm getting somewhere,' she said. 'I've got the manager at the bank in Norwich on the line, and he's confirmed he's got clearance from his boss to send us what we asked for. It should be through shortly by email with password-protected attachments. From what he's said on the phone, the activity on the account has been fairly limited, with regular large payments going in and the payments out also usually involving substantial sums but being relatively few in number. Some at least have been transfers to a bank in the Channel Islands.'

'And the other bank? The one in Cambridge?'

'Nothing yet, but we're chasing that one too. I'm going to stick around until we get those emails in from Norwich. I'll let you know if there's anything immediately exciting, but I doubt it's worth you hanging around now, boss. Why don't you get yourself off home for once? You look like pondweed.'

'Well thank you, Chris,' replied Greg. 'That's made my day. I'll take you at your word though. Just be sure to contact me if anything comes up.'

'Will do,' she said, already turning back to her screen and sliding the headset back in place.

Arriving back at the rented house by the cathedral, Greg was surprised to see Isabelle's car in the drive. Mouth dry with anticipation, he slid his key in the lock and then paused in the hall. There were two large cases at the bottom of the stairs and a box full of music. Isabelle's battered clarinet case also stuck out of the top of the box and as he looked, with a hollow space in his chest and a sudden sensation of sickness, he recognised the spiky outline of a part-folded music stand under the music. It didn't take a detective to read the runes. Unsteadily he walked into the kitchen and splashed cold water on his face, then filled a glass from the tap and drank it down. He looked at the whisky bottle, but stuck to his resolution not to seek the answer there. Then he sat at the kitchen table and waited for the movements upstairs to cease and the sound of footsteps on the stairs.

The light sound of trainers on the stairs pattered into the hall, then stopped dead. There was a pause, then Isabelle came cautiously into the kitchen and looked round.

'Greg, I didn't expect you home so soon.'

'Evidently not.'

She sat at the opposite end of the table. 'You're not going to make this difficult for me are you?'

'I doubt it. I'd like to make it not just difficult but impossible, but it seems I don't have that power.'

He looked at her. She was tracing shapes on the table with her finger, watching the movements of her own hand rather than look at him.

'You were going to leave without talking to me,' he said flatly.

'I thought it would be best. Give us both some space.'

'Best for whom? Definitely not me. So far, Isabelle,

you've had it all your own way. You've taken decisions without talking to me at all. You've decided what would suit you. I don't think I've come into it.'

'That's not fair,' she reacted indignantly. 'I've tried not to cause trouble when you're so busy with this big case of yours. And I have tried to give us a chance. But…'

'But you've met someone else.'

She went back to tracing patterns on the table. 'Yes,' she said almost inaudibly. 'I didn't plan to, I didn't intend to, but it just happened.'

'Oh don't be so wet, Isabelle.' He glared at the face he had always loved, now ugly with tears. 'These things don't just happen. There's a moment when you make a decision. When you decide, yes, I know it's wrong and I know it's breaking my vows and every promise I've made, but I'm going to sleep with this man. This other man. And you have a choice. You always have a choice.'

'You're being very hard, Greg. Life isn't always as simple as that.'

'Oh yes it is. And if you think this is me being hard, you have no idea how I'm feeling right now. This is me being civilised, when what I'd really like to do is beat the pair of you into pieces, weep and wail and drive my car off a cliff.'

She looked up at him startled, and the wandering fingers clutched the edge of the table.

He shook his head in disbelief. 'Don't you know me better than that? That's what I'd like to do. But I'm not going to do any of those things as you well know. Because I choose not to.'

She stood, gathered up her handbag and headed for the door. 'I hope it's not too cold up there on the moral high ground, Greg. Once I've put my cases in the car I'll be off. You have my mobile number and email address if you want anything, but I think it might be best if we keep our distance for a bit. I'll be in touch.'

And with that and a few moments collecting bags, she was gone.

For the longest half hour of his life, Greg sat on at the kitchen table. The light grew greyer and outside the evening chorus in the trees grew quiet. It felt like a metaphor for his future life. Irredeemably grey. Irredeemably songless. He only moved when a clutching in his belly gave warning that the physical could be ignored no longer and he had to make a dash for the loo.

'How unromantic,' he thought, as all his hopes and dreams flushed away.

27

Banks and Bother

Confident of a night spent tossing and turning, Greg was surprised to wake rather later than usual, well rested and calm. As he showered and shaved, he was forced to the conclusion that the blow having fallen, he felt rather better than he had waiting under its shadow. He realised, wryly, that certainty was better than suspicion and control was better than helplessness. Driving to Wymondham at least an hour later than intended, he started to make a mental list of things to be done, starting with getting out of the much-too-expensive rented house and finding himself something to buy.

His phone rang just as he turned into the car park entrance.

'Just arriving, Chris,' he said. 'I hope I haven't missed anything.'

'I've been going over the paperwork from the banks and I think there's something you'll like.'

'Ok. I'll be there as soon as I've picked up a coffee. Meet me in my office.'

By the time he arrived, extra-large extra-strong black coffee in hand, Chris had neat piles of paper all over his desk and a single page summary propped on his keyboard.

'I can take you through the detail later, but these are the important facts. I'm going to call these accounts Metcalfe 1, 2 and 3,' she said. 'First, there's an exact match between these sums leaving one of these accounts in cash and the same sums arriving in Ted Jackson's savings account a few days later.' She pointed at her list. 'There are more occasions when large sums have left one of these accounts and slightly smaller sums have arrived in Ted Jackson's account, presumably when he's kept some cash for immediate use.

'Second, there's one instance when cash was taken out in the form of euros. Exactly half of it matches the sum found on Simonis' body. The date of this is just one day before Balciunas died in the gassing chamber. It seems likely that Metcalfe tried to pay off both Balciunas and Simonis, but Balciunas didn't stay paid off, or there was some other dispute.'

'Is there any record of the ID numbers on the notes?'

'No, not that they've found so far anyway.'

'Damn. Sorry, Chris, this is good work, but it's still circumstantial. We don't have a hard link, like a bank transfer between Metcalfe and Jackson?'

'No. Jackson probably preferred cash. It's a miracle he put it in a savings account at all and didn't just hide it under his ferrets' cage.'

'True. What time is Metcalfe arriving?'

'We said 1000. He should've been here already. I'll find out what's holding them up.'

'Thanks. And I'll have a think about how we use this to put pressure on. We really need him to shop Bakalov if we're going to make progress.'

Heading down to the interview room half an hour later, Greg was surprised to hear running footsteps as Chris caught him up.

'Something else you need to be aware of,' she said. 'It seems Mr Metcalfe has been beaten up in the gaol. The delay was while they had him checked over by the doctor. It's lucky for him the prison officers intervened when they did. His assailant was armed with a shank made from a filed-down toothbrush. It could have got very nasty.'

'Do we know what provoked the attack?'

'No. But the assailant's been sharing a cell with Bakalov.'

'Has he indeed.'

'For the benefit of the tape…' said Greg, introducing himself and Chris, then regarding James Metcalfe for a long and silent moment. He was alone in the interview room and looking distinctly battered. One arm was in a sling, he had a black eye and a split lip, bruised knuckles and a reddened area beside his left cheekbone.

'No solicitor today?' he asked.

'I've sacked him. I wasn't happy with his performance.'

'So are we waiting for his replacement to arrive?' he looked round at Chris with a raised eyebrow.

'It appears not,' she said neutrally.

'No,' said Metcalfe. 'I don't think I need any further advice.'

'Then we'll continue, noting for the benefit of the tape that you have been offered legal representation and have refused it.

'So, Mr Metcalfe, we have been...'

'I have something I wish to say,' he interrupted again. 'First, I wish to make a formal complaint about the failure of the prison service to keep me safe. It was absolutely unacceptable what happened to me. I have been subjected to a vicious assault by a prisoner at the instigation of another prisoner. No care was taken of my safety and...'

'That's not what I heard,' said Greg. 'I'd heard that the prison officers rescued you from your assailant at considerable risk to themselves and prevented you from suffering significantly worse injuries.'

'That's as may be. But why were Bakalov and I in the same prison in the first place? You'd already charged him with one attempted murder, and then you let him get to me.'

'You think Bakalov was behind the attack on you?'

'I know it!'

'But why?' asked Chris softly. 'What would he have to gain from silencing you?'

'He's afraid I'll give evidence against him at the trial.'

'And precisely what evidence could you offer,' intervened Greg again.

'Evidence that will let you put him away for the murders of Balciunas, Simonis and Jackson.'

'Ok. Let's take those one by one. What happened with Balciunas?'

'I came upon them in the yard, arguing. Then I saw Bakalov hit Balciunas over the head with a hammer. I was too late to stop him.'

'What was the argument about?'

'About him blackmailing Bakalov over the smuggling of glass eels.'

'I see. How did the body get into the gassing container?'

'I helped Bakalov move it. That was my only involvement,' he said with a tone of self-righteous indignation. 'That's how the blood got on my overalls.'

'And Simonis?'

'I don't know for sure, but Simonis got out of the shed at the old storage unit in Yarmouth and the next thing I knew Bakalov said he'd dealt with "it".'

'Jackson?'

'Ah, I think that was under instruction from his paymasters in Lithuania. They seemed to be getting twitchy about loose ends, but I don't know exactly what happened to Jackson. I do know Bakalov set fire to his cottage, because he rang me shortly after and told me his bosses wanted me to make myself scarce.'

'Which you proceeded to do, with the assistance of the false passport. Where did you get that from exactly?'

'Also from Lithuania, again via Bakalov. I was already planning to get away, not least because I didn't like how things were going. I could see me being the next on the Lithuanian-inspired hit list.'

Greg looked down at his folder of papers, and flicked through it.

'How do you explain the frequent phone calls between

you and Bakalov in the 24 hours prior to Ben Asheton being attacked?'

'I was trying to stop him from going ahead with the attack. He'd told me what he had planned. He'd got it into his head that Ben Asheton was pursuing him, and he'd added him to the hit list.'

'So according to you, it was all Bakalov. All three murders and the attack on Ben Asheton were all down to Bakalov working under the instruction of his Lithuanian masters or off his own bat.'

'That's right.'

'But you are admitting involvement in the smuggling of glass eels and of puppies, and assisting Bakalov in concealing a body?'

Metcalfe hesitated, then said, 'Yes. But the glass eels were the Lithuanians' idea and the puppies were pretty much legal.'

'I think the RSPCA might beg to differ on that point. Judging from those we've located from the last batch, the puppies were underage and sick. Selling and transporting them in the way you did was a breach of the Balai Directive and almost certainly a breach of the Animal Welfare Act as well. As you well know.'

Metcalfe maintained a mulish silence.

'To be clear, you have accused Bakalov of the three murders and the attempted murder, but you admit to the two smuggling offences as well as the offence of operating as an unlicensed gangmaster. Will you sign a statement to that effect?'

Metcalfe hesitated, then said, 'Yes.'

'Then we'll get a statement drawn up and brought in for you to read. Thank you, Mr Metcalfe. I'll get some refreshments sent in and we'll be back with you shortly.'

Back in his office, he and Chris looked at each other, then both started to smile as he rang for Jim and Sarah to join them.

'A breakthrough,' said Chris. 'Eureka!'

'Some serious disparities with the other evidence,' Greg remarked, 'but I thought it best to get a statement agreed and signed, then we can poke holes in it, with luck with the assistance of Bakalov. Now one of them has broken ranks, we might get some assistance from the other.

Ah, here are Jim and Sarah.'

And in antiphonal chorus, Greg and Chris brought them up to date.

'How much of that do we believe?' asked Jim with scepticism showing.

'Balciunas – possible, although the evidence from bank accounts suggests it was Metcalfe paying him off, not Bakalov.

'Simonis – we have nothing tying Metcalfe to Simonis, and even on his evidence, we'd struggle to tie it down to Bakalov.

'Jackson – my guess is that it was more likely to be Metcalfe than Bakalov that killed him, on the evidence of the handprint on the crossbow, but it's not cast iron unless Bakalov will give evidence against him.

'The arson attack on the cottage – that I'm willing to believe was Bakalov, as was the attack on Ben. Have we got the recordings of the 999 call yet? We need to know if the voice on the recording is Metcalfe.'

*

The conversation with Margaret and the CPS representative, Robin Card, did not go well.

'Let me paraphrase,' said Robin, looking down his long lean nose, his shock of red hair on end. 'In summary, you have evidence on Metcalfe for acting as an unlicensed gangmaster, fraudulent use of a forged passport, the smuggling of glass eels and puppies (slightly more problematic) and possibly money laundering. Your evidence relating to the Romanian national, Bakalov, amounts to charges of the assault or attempted murder of Ben Asheton and arson of the cottage belonging to Ted Jackson. You have no conclusive proof relating to the first three murders except the unsupported statement of James Metcalfe, made in an interview where he was not provided with legal advice.

'Oh dear me, DCI Geldard. How do you think that's going to play if he retracts his accusations in court?' He leaned back in his chair so far that the legs creaked. 'I'm happy to go with the gangmaster, smuggling and associated charges with regard to Metcalfe. Likewise the assault on the first responder and possibly the arson attack with regard to Bakalov. Anything else,' he shrugged, 'I'd have to take advice but with the murder charges resting solely on Metcalfe's word,' he shrugged again, 'there are real issues both about whether he'll stick to it – and if he does, will the jury believe him?'

Reporting back to the rest of the team, Greg found his shoulders sagging as much as theirs.

'So, unless we turn up something more, we're probably stuffed on the murders.'

'Bakalov still refusing to speak?' asked Sarah.

'Yes. He's mute as a tailor's dummy. Even when faced with Metcalfe's accusations.'

'What's driving his attitude? Fear of his Lithuanian masters? Loyalty? Expectation of reward?'

'I'd guess all of the above, judging from the intelligence we have from Vilnius. He's probably gambling on the attempted murder charge being downgraded to GBH. The arson charge may or may not stick. The bosses, according to Vilnius, look after the families of one of their own who stays loyal. Bad things happen to the family of anyone who doesn't, so it's a bit of a no-brainer for Bakalov. I don't think we can expect any help from that quarter.'

'What about the risk that Bakalov ends up convicted of offences committed by Metcalfe?' asked Jim.

'I think, realistically, the bigger risk is that no one is convicted of the murders on the evidence we have at present,' replied Greg. 'What we need, and don't have, is evidence that definitively ties Metcalfe to one or more of the murders. The only possibilities that I can see are forensics that link him to one of the bodies or a murder weapon. A smoking gun.'

'Then let's look again,' said Sarah. 'Let's go over everything we have and ask more questions. And let it be someone who didn't focus on that part of the case before. Fresh eyes.'

'Good idea,' said Greg. 'Jim, you pick up the detail on Balciunas and Jackson with Sarah. Chris, you and I will go over what we have on Simonis. Ned, can you and your team help wherever you're needed? We'll regroup in,' he looked at his watch, 'in four hours. Go to it.'

*

Gathering up her papers, Sarah turned as Jenny called her name from the door.

'Sarah, someone on the phone for you from social services in Norwich.'

'At last,' she said. 'This is my loose thread about the folks who were cuckooed. Ok if I deal with this first, Greg?'

'Of course,' he waved her on and she hurried to her phone.

'It's very good of you to ring back,' she said. 'Do you have the names for me now, of the people who were responsible for the care of Tom Potter and John Hyde?'

'In the normal run of things,' replied the voice, 'there were several teams involved with both men when they were looked after by us. But only one person was directly involved with both. And I'm afraid they moved to Spain at Christmas.'

'Do you have a contact number?'

'Only a mobile.'

'What about banking details?' asked Sarah with a sudden idea. 'I assume their salary was paid by bank transfer?'

'Well yes, HR would have those details but they are of course confidential. Is there a problem I should know about?'

'At the moment we're just pursuing routine enquiries, but it would be helpful to have their name and contact details please.'

Sarah hurried into the main office. 'Chris,' she called, 'those bank details we got on the Metcalfe accounts. Am I right in thinking there were some big payments out late last year and early this? I mean other than the cash payment we think went to Jackson.'

Chris turned over a big pile of accounts. 'Yes. £5k in November and another £5k in December. Both to a V N Midgely.'

'I knew that name rang a bell,' breathed Sarah. 'That's great. Now I can have a little chat with Ms Vanessa Midgely about why she was receiving substantial payments from James Metcalfe, and what for.'

When she caught up with Jim he was driving Ned mad in the evidence store. Together they'd crawled over every bit of forensic evidence they'd turned up from all three murders.

'I can tie Metcalfe to the cuckooing,' she announced with some satisfaction. 'He's been paying an ex social services employee for information on vulnerable clients. I know it doesn't get us anywhere on the murders but it's another nail in his coffin as far as the gangmastering goes.

'If we're checking things again,' said Sarah, 'I have a question. I know the blood spatter found on Metcalfe's overalls was a match for Balciunas and he has argued that someone else borrowed his overalls that night. Have we checked the overalls for anyone else's DNA?'

'Yes,' replied Ned. 'And we found Metcalfe's as you'd expect.'

'But did you find anyone else's?'

'No.'

'And would it be possible for someone else to wear the overalls without leaving their DNA on them?'

'Hypothetically possible yes, if they were wearing coveralls under them. But under normal usage, no. You'd expect to find DNA on collar and cuffs at the very least, whether skin cells or hair.'

'So, you found nothing to suggest that anyone other than Metcalfe had worn those overalls.'

'Correct.'

'Next question. I know Metcalfe argued that the reason his DNA was on Balciunas was because he helped to put him in the gassing chamber and also subsequently helped with the resuscitation attempt. Is there any way that blood from Balciunas could have got on him during those efforts?'

Ned paused, then answered slowly, 'Again, yes its possible if he handled the head wound. But not in the form of the blood traces that we found. What we have is a clear spatter pattern, not smears. If Metcalfe had got the blood on him from manhandling the stunned body, it would have looked very different. And Balciunas was lying supine on the ground during the resus attempt. The head wound was therefore on the ground and no way could blood have transferred from there to the front of the overalls of someone using the defib. And again, it wouldn't have been a spatter pattern.'

'So, we can add that to the evidence for Balciunas,' said Sarah triumphantly. 'He has to have been present and close to Balciunas when the blow to the head was administered. Unless Bakalov was standing behind him and hit Balciunas over Metcalfe's shoulder, it has to have been him.'

The new boy in forensics had been hovering behind Ned, trying to get a word in.

'Yes?' said Ned rather irritably. 'Something to add? I thought your expertise was IT not DNA.'

The newbie, known to one and all as Tiff, pushed his specs up his nose nervously. Sarah had the feeling that if he'd had any hair at all, which he didn't, it would be flopping over his nose.

'Exactly,' he said. 'I've been reading some recent research in the States and took another look at Metcalfe's car. It's a relatively new model Merc.'

'Yes we know that,' Ned interrupted.

'But what we hadn't done was quarry its databases for all the information they hold. I spoke to the author of the recent paper. He was really helpful. Because Metcalfe linked his phone to his car, and because we now have both, the phone tells me where the car's been. Not only does it confirm he was at Stalham Poultry on the night of 3 April, but it also shows he was near Riverside Hens on the evening of 7 April.

'Better still, the car weighs the driver and any passengers for the benefit of the airbags. I have the weights here,' he flapped his iPad. 'We can weigh Metcalfe and compare the data. I think we have a pretty good chance of showing that not only was his car there, but he was driving it and he was the only person in the car.'

He looked round in mild triumph, and was not surprised to see he was surrounded by open mouths. Ned was the first to recover.

'You're serious? You can really tell all that from his phone and car?'

'Absolutely. And more, with a little more work. I can walk you through it if you like?'

'You'll need to,' remarked Sarah, also recovering the power of speech. 'And you'd better practise explaining it to a layman as the Crown Prosecution barrister is going to have to explain it to the jury.'

28

May Celebrations

Greg looked round the empty space of his new home. At present it contained one camp bed in one of the two bedrooms, and one camp chair in the sitting room before the log-burning stove. The furniture he had agreed with Isabelle he should keep was due to arrive that afternoon, but for his first night the camping arrangements had sufficed. When his mind headed down the well-trodden route of regret, he slammed the mental door. No point bewailing what he had lost. The future was what mattered now.

From the outside it was a small traditional cottage topping a low rise near the River Bure. Inside, a previous owner, with an eye on the rental market and presumably an arrangement with the local planners that wouldn't bear close scrutiny, had reduced the downstairs rooms to two large open-plan spaces plus conservatory with a view over the fields to the river. The kitchen-diner had a cosy fire and a range cooker as well as all the usual kitchen cupboards and a Butler sink. The living space had shelves, a wood floor and the aforementioned wood burner. Upstairs was the bedroom where he had spent a surprisingly peaceful night – except for the tawny owls in the wood behind – one other room and a surprisingly palatial bathroom.

Wandering round with his mug of coffee, he leaned on the wall of the small conservatory, enjoying the river and the waterfowl. From the Ouse to the Bure had been a big step and in some ways a painful road. But he had a strong sense of homecoming. A chime from his phone interrupted the peace and he dashed out to his car, leaving the forgotten mug on the window shelf en route. Today was the day that Bakalov and Metcalfe were due in court for their bail hearings; so today was a big day.

As arranged, he met Chris in the car park by the combined Norwich courts.

'All ok?' he asked.

'Ok,' said Chris. 'In theory we're on at 1000, but you know what the courts are like.'

'Well, this is my first experience in Norwich, but I don't suppose they're any different than York. Endless delays and unexpected adjournments.'

'Yup. But at least this should be a priority, as we're already close to the twenty-eight days.'

'They're still seeking bail I assume?'

'No change as far as I know.'

Greg emptied his pockets for the security check and handed over his open briefcase.

'Do we know who's on the bench for our case?' he asked as he passed through the security arch.

Chris was picking up her bag and coat from the security guard.

'It'll be on the board up there,' she nodded at the screens ahead of them.

'Court Three,' noted Greg. 'Ok let's go on up.'

It was 1020 when Greg was called in and asked to present his evidence relevant to the bail application. He sat in the public seats as Chris was asked additional questions. The judge wasted no time dismissing the application for bail on the part of Bakalov, on the grounds of the seriousness of the offences with which he was charged and, in light of the prison attack on Metcalfe, the risk of witness tampering.

The CPS barrister took to his feet, concluding the case for refusing bail for Metcalfe.

'In summary, Your Honour, James Metcalfe is not only accused of a number of serious offences including the murders of Jonas Balciunas and Ted Jackson, but he has also already made one attempt to escape justice by leaving the country using a false passport. We have no reason to believe that he would not make a repeated attempt if granted bail.'

His Honour was swift to make his decision. Bail refused.

By the time Greg got back to River Cottage it was after 2pm and the removal van was already there. As instructed, the men had commenced unloading and placing the furniture in the various rooms on the basis of labels tied to legs and handles: blue for the sitting room, red for the kitchen-diner, brown for the conservatory, yellow for the main bedroom and orange for the spare. All that had worked well, but a huge mound of boxes had accumulated in the kitchen and sitting room.

Greg went to the box labelled 'open first' in huge letters and removed the kettle, teapot, mugs and tea. There was milk in the car and he'd just made himself his first proper cup of tea in his new home when he was surprised by the sound of vehicles coming up the farm track to his door. There were three cars.

'Surprise,' said Chris getting out of the first one, as Jim emerged from the second and Ben Asheton with his wife from the third. 'We thought you might need a hand, or rather several hands.'

Paula looked round. 'And we were right,' she said. 'The furniture is always the easy bit, assuming it will go in through the doors. The boxes are the worst.'

'She'll never let me forget the dresser that spent three months in an outhouse because we couldn't get it round the corner to our kitchen,' remarked Ben. 'We're here to help. You just tell us what goes where, and we'll put things on shelves or in cupboards, whatever you want.'

'Sarah's coming on later,' added Jim, 'bringing a few pizzas with her, so supper's sorted too.'

As the women set to, Jim took the opportunity for a quiet word.

'Good result this morning,' he said, then looking sideways at Greg, 'Are you ok with this? Everyone was keen to help, but if you need your space, just say so. We won't be offended.'

Greg looked back and smiled. 'I'm grateful,' he said, and didn't need to say more.

By the time Sarah did arrive with six boxes of pizza, salad, and garlic bread, curtains were hung, pots and pans were on hooks, cupboards filled with china, and after a brisk discussion about ordering books by size, colour, or alphabetically by author which Greg won on the grounds that they were his books, books were on shelves. Many hands helped with the pizza and they were all settling down around the unlit wood burner when Greg intercepted a series of nods, winks and grimaces between Paula, Chris and Sarah.

'I'll get it from the car shall I?' said Chris, and dashed off before anyone could stop her.

When she came back she was carrying a large box and a plastic carrier bag.

'This is a house-warming present from all of us,' she said. 'If you don't like it or it doesn't suit, then I will return it, so please do be honest.'

Greg looked round at them all, then opened the box. Inside was a tortoiseshell kitten, complete with bed and blanket. He looked up to see them all watching him nervously.

'I always feel a home needs a cat or a dog,' said Paula.

And Jim joined in. 'You said you'd be getting a kitten when you had a proper home, but if we've got it wrong then just say, because we wouldn't want the kitten to be anywhere it isn't wanted. We agreed with the breeder that if you had the faintest hesitation about it, we'd return her immediately. In fact, we had to promise faithfully we'd do that. She only let us bring her away because she knows Ben and Paula well.'

Greg lifted the kitten out of the box and held her under his chin, where she snuggled close.

'Of course I want her,' he said, and had to turn away to hide wet eyes. 'What shall I call her? Any suggestions?'

'There's been a difference of opinion on that,' said Chris. 'Some of us think she should be Felonious,' she looked pointedly at Sarah, 'and some of us think Bobby, which can after all be male or female.'

Greg caught a glance from Jim. 'Both brilliant suggestions, but I think I'll find it easier to shout "Bobby" down the garden than "Felonious". So Bobby it is.' He sat down still cradling Bobby.

'Come on, let's eat the pizza before it gets cold,' said Chris with some satisfaction.

And amid laughter, they did just that.

Main Characters

Defra Officials and contractors

Emma Knight	Regional Operations Director (emergencies)
Bill McKnee	Chief Regional Vet
Jim Mackie and Monica Irwin	Senior Vets
Joe Simkins	gassing unit supervisor

Norfolk Police

Chief Superintendent Margaret Tayler	
Detective Chief Inspector (DCI) Greg Geldard	
Detective Inspectors Jim Henning and Sarah Laurence	
Detective Sergeant Chris Mathews	
Sergeant Phil Peters	drone handler
Constables Davidson and Nicholls	on duty at Stalham Poultry

Ned George	crime scene coordinator
Constables Bill Street Jill Hayes Steve Hall Phil Coleman	investigation team
Constable Jenny Warren (dog handler)	chauffeur to Meg, Springer Spaniel

At Stalham Poultry

Austen Ralph Collier	company director, married to
Fiona Louise Collier	
Pete Willis	site manager
Stan Innes	biosecurity
James Metcalfe	health and safety
Mrs Pritchard	site secretary
Lukas Jankauskas	employee, married to
Esther Jankauskas	
Jonas Balciunas Matis Zukas Tomas Simonis Dragan Bakalov	contracted workers

Others

Ben Asheton	First Responder, married to
Paula Asheton	
Ted Jackson	poacher
Tina and Nick Williams	proprietors, Riverside Hens

Rob and Anne Bailey	owners of Broads cruiser, 'Farmer's Lady'
Ian Rhodes	a manager, Bridges Agriculture
Henrik and Big Dave	watchkeepers, Caister Coastwatch

+ miscellaneous walk-on parts

Glossary

Defra	Department for the Environment, Food and Rural Affairs
what3words	App that divides the globe into 3m squares, each identified by a unique three-word reference
Shipfinder	Marine traffic tracking app

Among other topics, this book explores the issues of illegal exploitation of labour and modern slavery. If you are affected by these issues, or have concerns about people around you, please contact one of the following:

Gangmasters and Labour Abuse Authority:
0800 432 0804 to report problems www.gla.gov.uk

Citizens Advice
03444 111 444 www.citizensadvice.org.uk

Lightning Source UK Ltd.
Milton Keynes UK
UKHW010624230721
387608UK00003B/206

9 781800 420854